Dear Reader,

There is nothing so joyful as the sight of a newborn baby.
Its perfect hands, tiny feet and sweet, trusting face will
melt even the hardest heart! Babies are symbols of all
that is best in the world. Their futures are filled with
possibility and hope. And by having a baby, a man and a
woman will find that their lives are eternally
intertwined.

In *Wanted: Mother,* Annette Broadrick, Ginna Gray and
Raye Morgan have created tender, wonderful love stories
about the marvelous and unexpected changes three
couples find when a baby comes into their home. Here,
parenthood is just the beginning of a lifelong journey and
celebration of love. Love of the child…and the love our
heroes and heroines feel for each other.

So come share the surprises, the rewards and—above
all—the joyous love to be found when a man and woman
take on life's greatest challenge of all: parenthood! We
hope you enjoy every minute of it!

Sincerely,

The Editors
Silhouette Books

D0834906

ANNETTE BROADRICK
GINNA GRAY
RAYE MORGAN

WANTED:
MOTHER

Silhouette Books

Published by Silhouette Books

America's Publisher of Contemporary Romance

SILHOUETTE BOOKS

WANTED: MOTHER

Copyright © 1996 by Harlequin Books S.A.

ISBN 0-373-48318-X

WHAT'S A DAD TO DO?
Copyright © 1996 by Annette Broadrick
SOUL MATES
Copyright © 1996 by Virginia Gray
THE BABY INVASION
Copyright © 1996 by Helen Conrad

Printed in U.S.A.

CONTENTS

WHAT'S A DAD TO DO?

Annette Broadrick

Chapter One

The persistent sound of the doorbell eventually seeped into Tess's sleep-drugged mind. She fought her way to bleary-eyed consciousness, managing to open her eyes wide enough to focus on the digital clock beside her bed.

It was barely six o'clock.

In the morning.

A Saturday morning.

A no-work, chance-to-sleep-in kind of morning.

Whoever was at her door must have decided to make a career out of pressing the button—continuing to lean on it with unremitting, relentless enthusiasm despite the fact that no one was responding.

Tess wasn't sure she could respond, even if she really cared to find out what kind of idiot would be so rude. Her body refused to cooperate with any of the signals her sluggish mind was attempting to send.

The faithful caller downstairs didn't appear to feel the slightest bit of remorse for Tess's physical or mental condition. The doorbell continued to echo throughout her Pasadena, California, condominium with an irritating persistence.

"All right, already," she finally muttered, pushing herself into a sitting position with trembling arms.

She'd spent the greater part of the night in the bath-room exhibiting the rather disgusting symptoms of some kind of stomach virus. She hadn't stopped throwing up until sometime after four o'clock, when her stomach had finally seemed to notice that she had absolutely nothing more to offer to the process and mercifully eased its cramping pains.

The muscles just below her ribs were still sore. At the moment she felt weaker than a newborn tiger. And three times as mean.

The doorbell continued to ring.

She fumbled around the foot of the bed for her knee-length robe. Whoever was there was certainly going to receive a piece of her mind! Of that she was sure. At the moment, however, she wasn't too cer-tain she had a piece to spare. Her mind seemed to have taken some sort of vacation, no doubt under the reasonable impression that her body could be safely counted on to remain horizontal for a few more hours.

Not a bad assumption, considering the night she'd just spent. Too bad the idiot at the door didn't seem to understand that a doorbell not answered should be treated with some respect and left alone after a proper interval of nonresponse.

These dark thoughts accompanied a barefoot Tess as she made her way down the stairs, across the hall and to the front door. By the time she jerked open the door—the safety chain still in place—several methods of exquisite torture had already popped into her head, all of which she would take delight in performing on whomever stood on the other side of the threshold.

"Can't you have a little mercy at this time of morning, for God's sake..."

Her voice trailed off as she stared at her early-morning caller, her mouth slightly open in stunned disbelief.

The man comfortably leaning against the stair railing, his finger still pressed firmly against her doorbell, looked as disreputable as any of the homeless people that seemed to congregate along some of the off ramps of the Ventura freeway...with the exception of the obviously expensive cameras and equipment draped around his neck.

His blond hair was overdue for a trim and his lean cheeks were covered with at least two days worth of beard. His silver-gray eyes looked tired and a little bloodshot.

And his clothes? The least said, the better. Not only did the faded jeans, jersey, battered denim jacket and hiking boots show how hard they'd been used, but they also didn't look particularly clean.

But his grin was as spectacular as a tropical sunrise.

Tess closed her eyes and swallowed, hoping against hope that she was hallucinating, or even better, just having one of those awful nightmares that sometimes accompanied a virus.

Unfortunately for her peace of mind and uncertain stomach, he was still standing there when she opened them once more. At least he'd had the decency to remove his finger from the doorbell before she'd been tempted to sever the damn thing to gain some blessed silence.

He slowly straightened to his full height, a good five inches over her own not inconsiderable five-foot-seven-inch frame. He eyed her warily—as well he should!—keeping that damn grin of his firmly in place, knowing exactly how lethal a weapon it was against any angry attack she might make.

"What are you doing here?" she finally asked, disgusted at herself to once again discover that she could never stay angry at the man in front of her when he looked at her in that way, no matter how just her cause might be. "You were going to Tibet for two years," she managed to say with the last remnants of her irritation. "Can't you read a calendar, Jamison? You've barely been gone two months. Come back in another twenty-two months, all right? But *not* at six o'clock in the morning!"

She hated herself for noticing that even his memorably lopsided grin looked a little beat. That wasn't her problem, was it? The L.A. area was full of hotels and motels, a great many out by the international airport. He certainly hadn't needed to come all the way to Pasadena to—

"Is that any way to greet your best pal in the whole wide world, Tess?" His eyes took on a sparkle, damn him anyway, as he took a step closer to the door.

She eyed him morosely. "You might have been my best pal in the third grade, Craig, but I've had reason to revise that opinion more than once in the twenty-five years since then."

They both knew she didn't mean a word of it, that they had always been there for each other through the years, and he was kind enough to let her muttered remark pass without comment.

After all, he knew her well enough to know how sacred she considered her sleep time, and yet here he was on her doorstep at six o'clock on a Saturday morning—a severe test for the most enduring friendship.

He lifted his arms high above his head, stretching and twisting with a groan. "I know it's early for you. I didn't plan it this way, believe me. I feel like I've been flying for days to get here. We've got to talk, Tess. Aren't you going to invite me in?"

She gave his suggestion a great deal of thought before murmuring, "Do I have a choice?"—a rhetorical question if she'd ever heard one, because she already knew the answer.

Tess closed the door in order to unhook the chain, then threw it open and turned away, saying, "Come on in, but don't expect me to talk to you anytime soon. I'm going back to bed where I intend to sleep through the next several hours." She paused at the top of the stairs and added with a little more cordiality, "Make yourself at home. I'll see you later."

The closing of her bedroom door echoed throughout the place.

Craig had already scooped up his duffel bag and stepped inside by that time so that he was able to watch her progress up the stairs. She was still muttering something to herself when she closed the door—no doubt something uncomplimentary about him and all of his ancestors. He was glad he couldn't make out what she said.

He winced when her bedroom door slammed shut.

The numbing sense of dull fatigue he'd accumulated by crossing a series of time zones settled around him like a familiar cloak.

He was here now, that was the important thing. She hadn't slammed the door in his face, which was a good sign. She'd actually spoken to him. Another good sign.

Of course he'd known she wouldn't be thrilled to see him at six o'clock in the morning. He smiled, thinking about the years he'd known her and what a grump she was until she finally woke up. She would have faced the president of the United States with a similar attitude at six o'clock in the morning, and she had actively campaigned for the man.

She'd come around eventually. When she did, he intended to talk to her about the revelations he'd had during the past two months. About her. About him. About the two of them.

He'd never been so nervous concerning the outcome of anything in his entire life than he was about her reaction to what he intended to tell her.

He still stood in the foyer, aware of the silence around him. The refrigerator hummed in the kitchen. There was a clock ticking in the living room. Otherwise, he could hear nothing but the sound of his own breathing.

Now that he was here he wasn't certain what to do next. He ran his hand through his hair. A hot shower sounded good . . . that, and a fresh cup of coffee. He was sick of old, reheated coffee and stale rolls.

Craig wandered into the kitchen and searched through her cupboards until he found what he needed, then went through the familiar routine of making coffee. While he was waiting for it to brew, he carried his battered duffel bag into the den. One wall, almost entirely made of glass, looked out on her backyard, which was surrounded by a high stone fence.

He dumped the contents of his bag into a heap on the floor and pawed his way through the pile, looking for the cleanest of his dirty clothes, before heading for the shower downstairs.

While he scrubbed his face and shoulders with some kind of feminine-smelling soap, Craig worked on emptying his mind of anything but thoughts of the present moment. He refused to rehearse what he wanted to say. That sort of thing never worked out for him, anyway. It was better to just take life moment by moment as it occurred.

After rinsing away the remaining lather from his hips and thighs, Craig remained under the hot, stinging spray, allowing the water to soothe his battered body. As much as he enjoyed traveling around the world, capturing the wild beauty of some of the earth's most primitive areas with the lenses of his cameras, there were times when he yearned for such sybaritic pleasures as hot running water and strong water pressure, not to mention the precious gift of electricity and all the attendant appliances that modern civilization had come up with to make life a little easier. The more he traveled, the more he appreciated all the comforts of his homeland.

Eventually he turned off the water, found Tess's extra supply of disposable razors and shaved.

By the time he'd gotten dressed and thrown his first batch of clothes into her washing machine off the kitchen, Craig was more than ready for some coffee. He poured himself a cup, then returned to the den where he settled back on the comfortable sofa and propped his bare feet up on the coffee table.

He felt a little strange, being here at Tess's place. She'd bought it a couple of years ago while he was on one of his trips. His visit two months before was the first time he'd been there.

In the past he'd stayed with his folks whenever he happened to be in town. His family had lived in Pasadena since long before he was born, but after that last earthquake, his mom had announced that she'd had enough. So they'd ended up moving to Scottsdale, Arizona.

He wasn't sure if he was going to visit them this trip or not. He really wasn't sure what he was going to do about a lot of things, just yet. So much depended on Tess.

God, he'd been such a fool the last time he'd been here. He still couldn't believe it. He'd flown in to L.A. from Arizona the day before he was to leave for Asia, figuring he'd look up Tess, since he hadn't seen her in a few years.

He'd gotten a room at one of the hotels near the airport, then called her. That's when he'd heard all that she'd had to face since they'd last talked on the phone.

Years ago they'd lived next door to each other, but their lives couldn't have been more different. She'd grown up never knowing her father. He'd left before she was born. She'd lived with her mother who seemed to be at work all the time, leaving her grandmother to look after her.

Her mother had died a few years ago, but at least she'd gone quickly. Not like her grandmother who had slowly succumbed to cancer over a long period of time.

Tess had taken a leave of absence from work to stay with her grandmother those last months, acceding to the older woman's wishes that she not be placed in a hospital to die.

Craig discovered during their telephone conversation that Tess's grandmother had passed away a few weeks before. He'd taken Tess to dinner that night and they had talked, really talked, in a way they'd never done before. He'd seen a side of Tess he would never have suspected existed. She'd always seemed so self-sufficient in all the years he'd known her. Never had she seemed so vulnerable.

It had done something to him, seeing her so uncertain about picking up the threads of her life once again, having no one left in her small family to love and look after.

He'd continued with his travel plans, of course. That had been his first mistake. He should never have left her the way he did. Once gone, he couldn't get her out of his mind.

He recalled how amused his mother had been when they were children that Craig and his other buddies had been willing to let the tomboyish Tess hang out with them—go on hiking trips, take part in the neighborhood sports, even become an honorary member of their secret club.

In high school, Tess had still been a part of the same group. She'd even dated one or two of his friends, as he recalled. He'd never dated her, of course. It would have been like going out with his sister.

Or so he'd thought back then.

So when had his feelings changed?

He didn't know. He might not ever know. And did it really matter all that much, now?

All he knew was that after that last visit with her, nothing would be the same again for him where Tess was concerned. He just didn't know what he was going to do about it.

It was up to Tess.

The seductive scent of frying bacon and freshly brewed coffee eventually roused Tess a second time that morning. Without opening her eyes, she inhaled deeply, smiling to herself.

Granny was up, she thought dreamily, and was going to surprise her with—

Her eyelids flashed open and she sat up in bed. Granny had died three months ago, and even before then, she'd been too ill to get out of bed. So who—?

Memories of her early-morning caller flooded through her and she groaned, falling back onto her pillow.

What was Craig Jamison doing back in her life?
What impish force of fate had drawn him to return to
Pasadena now when he was supposed to be gone for
years? How could she ever successfully deal with the
feelings he evoked in her if he kept popping up in her
life this way?

A slight sound from the doorway drew her attention. Think of the devil and there he appeared. Craig
peered around the door, meeting her disgruntled gaze
with another one of his smiles before continuing
through the doorway.

"Your coffee, Ms. Cassidy. Just the way you like
it."

He looked a little better than he had earlier. He'd
obviously showered, shaved and found jeans and a
shirt in slightly better condition. They were wrinkled, which wasn't surprising considering the way he
packed, but they looked clean.

"What time is it?" she asked, scooting up in bed
and greedily reaching for the cup without actually
making eye contact. She was never her best in the
morning, but particularly not after the night she'd
had. Her hair hung limply around her shoulders and
she was wearing her rattiest nightshirt.

"Sometime after eleven. I'm really sorry about
getting you out of bed this morning. I was actually
due to arrive last night, but there were all kinds of
delays with my flights. I suppose I could have gone to
a hotel—"

She waved her hand as she blissfully inhaled the aroma from the cup she held in her other one. "You don't owe me an apology, Craig, you just caught me at an awkward time." She rubbed her stomach ruefully. "I spent most of the night battling some kind of stomach bug and had only been asleep a couple of hours when you got here. Sorry about the reception you received."

He dismissed her apology, eyeing her warily. "You're sick? I wondered why you were so pale. Did you call a doctor?"

So much for trying to prefend. Craig, bless his heart, could be brutally honest at times. It was one of his endearing qualities . . . and one of the most irritating.

"In the middle of the night? Of course not! Besides, I don't even know a doctor to call. I'm generally as healthy as a horse, thank goodness."

Craig studied her for a long time, feeling unsure of himself. He didn't want to hurt her feelings by commenting on the fact that she looked wan and tired and much too thin. She'd taken her grandmother's death hard, he knew, but shouldn't she be recovering a little by now?

"If you have any more symptoms like that, maybe you should have a friend recommend someone. You could be anemic or something."

"Naw. I probably ate something last night that disagreed with me. A couple of friends and I went to a movie after work and ended up having dinner afterward. It was probably a combination of too much rich food too late at night. As a matter of fact, I'm much better now." Feeling that she had successfully countered any and all of his concerns, she asked, "So, what are you doing here? Did the powers that be decide to run you out of the country? I understand that the political situation there isn't the—"

"Tess?"

She blinked at the sudden interruption and the serious expression on his face and tone in his voice. Oh, dear, what could be wrong?

"What is it?" she asked, straightening a little more.

He looked around the room, then perched on the end of her bed. He looked down at his cup, which he held in both hands.

"Is it possible you could be—" He stopped and cleared his throat, lifting his gaze to meet hers. "I was just wondering if you're all right, otherwise."

She knew that she must be looking at him as blankly as she felt. "What are you talking about?"

"Come on, Tess. We can't just ignore what happened that night as though it never occurred."

Of all the subjects she might have thought about discussing with Craig, their last night together wasn't one of them. Good heavens. She'd never discussed it with anyone and never intended to. It had happened. What was there to say, after all?

"Oh...that," she muttered, knowing her face must be flashing like a neon sign. She took another drink of her coffee, not knowing what to say to him. Blast him, anyway, for bringing it up!

"Is everything okay in that regard?"

He watched her blush with something like astonishment. Tess Cassidy blush? He would never have dreamed it could happen. When she didn't immediately answer him, he had a sudden sinking feeling in his stomach.

"Well?" He prodded her a little impatiently.

"It's too soon," she finally blurted out, looking everywhere in the room rather than at him.

"C'mon, Tess, don't be embarrassed, of all things. What did you think, that I wouldn't wonder about it, worry a little? Now talk to me. It's been two months. Surely you'd know whether or not—"

She interrupted him, rushing her words. "I've never been very regular and since my grandmother died I haven't paid much attention to things like that. It happens when it happens, that's all."

"All I'm asking is, has it happened since I was here two months ago?"

She shook her head, not looking at him.

Craig could feel himself reacting to this news. This wasn't why he'd come back. Well, of course it was, in part. But he really hadn't expected that— "Don't they have those tests you can take at home to find out?" he finally asked.

She glared at him. "I suppose they do, but that doesn't mean that I should— That you should think that I'm— Anyway, it doesn't really matter. If I am, I am. I'll deal with it, okay?"

That sounded more like the Tess he remembered. She tried to be so tough. Nothing would ever get her down, no sirree. She might be going down for the count, but she'd go out slugging. Only this time, her eyes were giving her away. She couldn't hide the fact that until he'd brought up the subject, she'd never considered the fact that she might very well be pregnant. He could see the fear lurking in the back of her eyes.

He moved closer to her, within touching distance, and removed her cup from her clenched hands. Placing it on her bedside table, he took both of her hands in his. They were chilled, much too chilled for the temperature in the room.

"Tess, honey, listen to me. We need to know, all right? Maybe it was too rich food. Maybe it was too late to be eating. Or, it could be your body trying to tell you something."

Her wide, dark chocolate-colored eyes seemed to grow larger in her face.

"Why don't you let me make us an omelet for breakfast?" he continued. "Then, if you're feeling all right we can go to the store and—"

"No. I don't want to go to the store. I'm not about to—"

"Then give me your car keys and I'll go to the drugstore for you. I don't mind. The thing is, we really have to know. Okay?"

"You're serious about this, aren't you?"

"Yes, I am. I realized after I left that if anything had happened, if you needed to get in touch with me, you wouldn't know where to find me. I wasn't thinking clearly that night, or I would never have let things go so far without having some sort of protection. We both know we didn't plan any of it to happen. But it did. I couldn't forget it. I found myself thinking about you all the time, wondering if I'd ruined our friendship, wondering if you'd ever forgive me. I wasn't able to concentrate on what I was doing. So I decided to come back."

Her hands were getting a little warmer. He took that to be an encouraging sign, even though her expression was as wary as ever.

"Wouldn't a phone call have been sufficient?" she asked with a hint of belligerence.

"No. I missed you and I wanted to see you again."

"Huh. You probably didn't believe I'd tell you the truth."

"Would you have?"

She was the first to drop her eyes. "Supposing...just supposing mind you, that I *am* pregnant. What difference could it make to you?" Her chin was tilted defiantly.

He put his arms around her, ignoring the stiffness in her body. "If you are, then I need to be here."

"No, you don't. My mother took care of herself just fine. She didn't need any help from my father. If I'm pregnant, I'll deal with it."

She said all of that while she was pressed against his chest. He wondered if she knew he could feel her trembling. This whole situation was going to be much trickier than he'd first guessed.

Damn, he hoped she wasn't pregnant. Not now. Not yet. He'd wanted to tell her what he'd discovered about his feelings first. He'd wanted to find out how she felt about him, if there was a chance for the two of them. Oh, he wanted her to have several of his babies eventually, after they'd had time to plan a wedding, invited all their friends, planned their life together.

Holding her made him more aware of how fragile she was, despite her tough demeanor. *Oh, Tess, don't push me away. Let me past all your barriers, as you did that one night two months ago.*

"I'm not your father, Tess," he finally replied. "I don't know why he wasn't there for your mother and for you. But I intend to be here for you. You couldn't get rid of me if you tried, honey."

She pulled away from him and looked him squarely in the eye. "I'm not pregnant," she stated flatly.

He almost smiled. "You know that for sure, do you?"

"I just told you. I'm not all that regular so—"

"So we'll take a test and find out, okay?"

"We?"

"A figure of speech. I'll buy it. You take it."

She gave an exaggerated sigh that didn't fool him at all. "Oh, all right. I'll do it just so you'll quit nagging. You can be the most persistent pest in the world when your mind's made up about something."

He got up, feeling that he'd won a very crucial round between them, even though he was very aware that there were several bouts ahead of them both.

"I'll go make our omelet. I'll see you downstairs." It was a good time to retreat and give her a chance to deal with the recent shifts in their relationship.

Chapter Two

Tess watched Craig walk out of her bedroom and hoped that she would wake up any minute now, having dreamed all of this. If so, she would make a promise to herself never to eat rich food after eight o'clock again.

What was she going to do?

It had never once—not once—occurred to her that she might be pregnant. How could she have been so naive? She had tried to block any memory of Craig's visit because too much had happened that she wasn't ready to face yet.

Such as the fact that she'd ignored everything she'd ever been taught about men because it was Craig, her childhood friend, whom she trusted with her life. Even now, she cringed at how eagerly she had gone into his arms, how she'd practically begged him to make love to her. Just thinking about it made her squirm with embarrassment.

She definitely wasn't ready for this.

She could only pray that the test would be negative. Then they could chalk the whole thing up to experience and put it all behind them. Craig could get on with his life while she got on with hers. She would then do her best to forget that for one evening Craig

Jamison had shown her a side of herself she'd never known existed . . . a side that could never be encouraged again.

Well, sitting here in bed wasn't going to get her anywhere. She tossed back the covers and got out of bed. At least her stomach remained docile, for which she was devoutly grateful. As a matter of fact, she was hungry. Wasn't that a good sign?

She walked into the bathroom off her bedroom and flipped on the light. Oh, blast. She stared into the bathroom mirror at the purple circles under her eyes—the only color in her face. She actually looked worse than she felt.

Oh, happy day.

The cowardly part of her yearned to crawl back into bed and pull the covers over her head until Craig forgot about her and went back to wherever he came from...Tibet, Taiwan, Timbuktu, she didn't care, as long as he was gone.

She knew Craig too well. There was no getting around him when he had his mind made up about something. The sooner she took the blasted test, the sooner he would leave.

She hoped.

With a sigh she turned on the water in the shower and stood under the spray, consciously blanking out her mind to everything but the feel of the water sluicing over her body.

By the time she returned to her room to decide on something to wear, Tess had become a little more reconciled. Not much, but some. Craig had always been a responsible kind of guy. Why should he be any different now?

Craig's stomach was already rumbling at the delicious scent of the food he was placing on a plate. When Tess walked into the kitchen, he didn't bother to glance up as he said, "I poured you some juice. Hope that's okay."

"Thanks."

By the time he turned around she was seated at the bar across from him. He smiled when he handed her a plate of toast. She'd pulled her dark hair into a ponytail that reminded him of the little girl he used to know. He filled her coffee cup before sitting down beside her.

"Hope you're hungry," he said. "I got a little carried away. I kept finding more things to put in it."

She took a sip of her juice before she answered him. "I suppose I should be. It all smells good." She made a show of taking a bite of the omelet.

She was nervous, something he could definitely understand. "I can't remember the last time I ate," he said after a few minutes. "I think my stomach's convinced I gave up food."

Tess smiled at the way Craig attacked his breakfast with unabashed enthusiasm. She'd always liked that in him. In fact, he had many traits that she admired.

However, his need to explore the world wasn't one of them. When she married—actually it was more like *if* she ever married—she wanted a man who would be willing to settle down and make a home with her. She wasn't absolutely certain that such a man existed, though. She'd certainly never run into one in her circle of friends and acquaintances.

Like Craig, they were all eager to rush out and embrace the world rather than settle down with a nine-to-five occupation.

She'd always known and accepted that Craig was a free spirit. Never at any time in the years she'd known him had she ever looked at Craig as marriage material. Of course none of that had ever mattered. It was enough that he was her best friend in all the world.

And he cared about her. She knew that. Why else was he here?

Who would have believed that the simple ringing of the telephone last April would have been a signal that her carefully planned out life might be reduced to shambles?

"I'm coming, I'm coming," she muttered, shoving the door between the garage and the kitchen open with her elbow. Her arms were filled with bags of groceries. "Whoever you are, don't you dare hang up now!'' She slid one of the bags onto the counter and grabbed for the wall phone. ''I'm here, I'm here. Hello?''

There was no sound on the phone, not even a dial tone. Then a deep male voice said hesitantly, ''Is this Tess Cassidy's residence?''

''Craig? Is that you? Craig! Where are you! *Omigod.* I haven't heard from you in ages!''

He began to laugh. ''Yep. It's Tess, all right. How've you been?''

''Oh, Craig! It's so good to hear your voice. I'm fine. Where are you?''

''I just checked in at the Airport Inn. I've been visiting my folks. You remember they moved to Scottsdale.''

''I remember. I've really missed your mom since they moved. How are they? I think I owe her a letter or something. You know me. The world's worst correspondent.''

''Both of them are looking great and acting like kids again. I told Mom I planned to call you when I got here. She said to be sure to give you her love...Dad's, too, of course.''

Tess blinked back unexpected tears. She'd been so weepy lately. But the Jamisons were the closest people to family she had and she hadn't spoken to Craig in so long.

''The last I heard you were exploring the Hebrides Islands. When did you get back to the States?''

"A couple of weeks ago. I take it you got my post-cards."

She smiled to herself. "Yes. I'm keeping them in a scrapbook and marking the postmarks on my globe. Receiving your cards is the only chance I'll probably ever get to see some of these places."

"I know this is short notice, but I'm flying out of here early tomorrow morning. I was wondering if I could take you to dinner?"

She looked around at all the groceries and laughed. "I'd love it, Craig. I can't wait to see you. Gosh, it's been years!"

"Yeah, I know. But we'll make up for it by talking nonstop for the next several hours. Look, I'll get a cab and come on over now, if that's okay."

"More than okay. You don't know how much I've missed you and your family lately."

"Mom told me the news about your grandmother. I was really sorry to hear it."

The blasted tears welled up again, just at the mention of her grandmother. "She was ready to go. She was tired of dealing with the pain. But I still miss her. So much."

"Of course you do," he replied gruffly. Craig cleared his throat. In a much lighter tone, he said, "I'll be there in about an hour."

"Good. See you in a little while."

She hung up, only then realizing she was still clutching one of the grocery bags. Hastily she placed it on the countertop, then began putting everything away, mentally reviewing her clothes hanging in her closet.

She wished she had something new to wear. Not that it would matter. Craig hadn't seen much of anything she owned. Even if he had, he wouldn't remember it. She smiled at the thought.

After racing upstairs, she hopped into the shower, making sure to keep her hair dry, quickly soaped and rinsed herself, then hurriedly dried off and went in search of something appropriate to wear to dinner.

In the end, she settled for her basic black sheath. She grabbed the black stole her grandmother had made for her, the one with silver glitter woven through it, freshened her makeup and was on her way downstairs when the doorbell rang.

She raced to the door, made sure it was Craig, then flung it open.

It just wasn't fair. How could one man look so good? He was dressed in khakis and a blazer, his shirt collar open. "You've grown," he said with a grin.

She grabbed his hand and pulled him inside. "Nonsense. It's just the shoes."

"Ahh. Maybe that's it. I've never seen you in high heels before."

"Well, they aren't exactly what you wear to go hiking or to play neighborhood ball."

They stood there in the hall, holding hands and grinning at each other.

"I'd forgotten how beautiful you are," he finally said, causing her cheeks to heat up uncomfortably.

"And you've finally learned how to compliment a person rather than insult them."

"Me? Insult you? Never."

She just shook her head. "Would you like a drink before dinner?"

"I have a cab waiting. I made reservations here in Pasadena before I left the hotel so I guess we'd better get going."

"Oh, Craig, we don't need a cab. Send him on his way and we can go in my car."

"You sure?"

"Of course. Don't be silly."

"I'll be right back."

She watched him hurry down the steps and pay the driver. She was glad to be able to catch her breath. She couldn't get over how wonderful he looked. It had been almost three years since she'd last seen him. Those years had been good to him. There were a few more lines around his eyes and mouth, but that was all. He seemed at peace with himself.

Some of his photography was already being sold for substantial amounts. It was amusing, really, to ponder the contradiction that made up the person. Craig looked like a professional football lineman, but he had the soul of a poet.

Not that he'd ever admit to such a thing. But his photographs gave him away, revealing his sensitivity to nature and to all living things. From the grandeur of the mountains in Alaska to the mysterious Everglades of Florida, from the Isle of Skye to the Australian Outback, Craig's artistic eye managed to capture the beauty of the planet.

Most of his treks were arduous, and only an experienced, athletic, and very determined person could have kept up with the grueling schedule he kept.

She was proud to be his friend.

He bounded back up the steps, wearing that fabulous smile of his. "Shall we go?" he asked.

"Sure. This way." She led him through the kitchen and out into the garage, handing him her car keys.

On the ride to the restaurant, she asked, "Where are you headed this time?"

"Tibet. I met a guy on the plane coming back from Scotland who'd been there. From his descriptions, I knew I'd have to see it for myself."

"You didn't stay here in the States long."

"I know. My folks have already given me the lecture on that one. But you know me," he said, grinning, "I get restless if I stay too long in one place."

"Do you miss coming back to Pasadena when you return to the States?"

"Yes, I do. I mean, I'm glad the folks found a place where they can relax and enjoy Dad's retirement, but it's not home to me—you know, the home where I grew up. The place is small, but they're pleased with it. Said the upkeep is not as time-consuming. Gives Dad a chance to play more golf.''

Dinner seemed to go by like a dream. Later Tess couldn't remember much about what they'd talked about. Craig asked about mutual friends of theirs, and she told him what she knew about their activities.

By the time they returned to the condominium, she was feeling relaxed and very mellow. ''Would you like another glass of wine before you leave?'' she asked, once they'd gone inside.

He stretched and sighed. ''Sure. I can always catch up on my sleep during the flight tomorrow.'' While she filled their glasses in the kitchen he wandered through her place, until he reached the den. ''Wow. When did you do this?''

She knew what he had found and couldn't help blushing, wondering what he must think. She hadn't intended for him to ever find out that she had painstakingly gathered copies of the photographs he'd taken through the years and had them arranged on an entire wall in her den.

She walked in to find him standing with his hands in his back pockets, staring at the arrangement. She noticed he'd discarded his jacket and shoes. ''Different places. Some of them you'd sent me, some I found in a gallery and others your mother was kind enough to add to my collection.''

"This must have taken quite a lot of effort to put together." He stepped closer to one of them. "I'd forgotten about this one." He tapped it. "This was the first photo I ever sold."

"Sunset at Malibu," she said. "I was with you that day, remember? I wasn't surprised that the picture turned out so well. That whole day seemed like magic. One of those perfect days that southern Californians never get tired of."

He turned around, taking one of the glasses. "You're right. I'd forgotten. Those were some carefree days, weren't they?" He touched his glass to hers. "Here's to the days of our youth. May the future be filled with as much inspiration as the past."

They sipped their wine. "It's a little chilly in here tonight. How about a fire?" she asked, looking away from his expressive gaze. She reminded herself that Craig saw her as the sister he'd never had. She couldn't allow herself to be caught up in the headiness of his undivided attention.

"Sounds good." He went over to the fireplace and began to arrange the wood while Tess kicked off her shoes and sat down on the sofa.

When thinking about it later, she remembered that he had sat in a nearby chair at first. She wasn't sure how the subject returned to her grandmother, but eventually she found herself telling him what those last few months had been like for her. She'd tried not to break down as she described how tough it was to pick up the pieces of her life once her grandmother was gone. She'd stayed with her grandmother around the clock those last few weeks, so that her days and nights had been filled with activity.

Once her grandmother was gone, she'd felt lost, even though she'd had her job to go back to and her life to resume.

She wasn't certain when Craig moved to her side, or when he put his arms around her. She only knew that she needed him at that moment in a way she'd never needed or wanted another man.

"Ah, Tess," he whispered, running his finger along her jaw. "I'm so sorry you had to go through all of that alone. I wish I'd been here for you."

"There wasn't anything you could have done."

"I could have let you know I cared."

"I knew that."

"You did?"

"Mmm-hmm."

He smiled. "I'm glad." He brushed his lips against hers and she felt as though a bolt of electricity ran through her. When his mouth lingered, hovering over hers, she eased closer to him and kissed him back.

His kiss was everything she had dreamed it would be. She could feel his heart racing beneath her palm, and when he pulled her into his lap she could tell that he was aroused.

She didn't care about anything else at that moment except to continue feeling what he was making her feel. She gave herself up to all the sensations that Craig's kiss was arousing in her, eagerly following his lead, silently encouraging him to continue what he had so innocently started.

When he finally lifted his head, he looked stunned. She felt the same way. What was happening between them?

"Tess? I'm sorry. I didn't mean to..."

"It's all right." She gave a shaky laugh. "Wow. That was pretty potent."

They were reclining on the couch, their arms around each other. She was fascinated by the feel of his body pressed so closely to her. She'd never allowed herself this freedom with a man before. It was heady stuff.

She slipped her hand beneath his shirt, and felt his ripple of reaction to her. A new sense of power and purpose took over. Imagine, being able to provoke such a strong response in him.

Feeling an unfamiliar sense of daring, she unbuttoned his shirt, then placed a kiss on his chest. His groan made her smile with a sense of accomplishment.

"Tess, I—" Whatever he was going to say remained unsaid. Instead he began to kiss her again— long, drugging kisses that set up a craving for more.

Her legs became entangled with his, his thigh high between hers, stirring her. When his hand slid beneath her skirt and moved to the juncture of her thighs she gave a tiny gasp, which was swallowed by his mouth on hers.

His touch was the spark that set her on fire. She didn't understand what was happening to her, but she wanted more. So much more. She fumbled with his belt and found his zipper. She ached to touch him as he was touching her.

Ah. At last he was free for her to touch and explore. This was Craig after all. He wouldn't mind her feverish exploration; her lack of experience was probably obvious. It didn't matter. Nothing mattered except the floating feeling that consumed her.

They were already so entwined that it took only small adjustments for him to shift where he was lying between her legs. She lifted her hips to him, afraid he was going to leave her, afraid that he would stop touching her so intimately in the exact place she needed him.

She felt the unfamiliar invasion of his body and couldn't stop herself from tensing. He paused, his mouth still pressed to hers, his tongue teasing hers. She brought her knee up, giving him more access, wordlessly encouraging him.

That first thrust brought tears to her eyes but she continued to clutch him to her, hanging on to him while he kept up a compelling pace that triggered all kinds of explosions deep within her. When he lifted his head and looked down at her, his face mirrored the wonder of what she was feeling. It was then that he threw his head back and with a cry buried himself deep within her.

He collapsed against her, rolling to the side so that his full weight wasn't on her. Unfortunately the couch was too narrow for that particular maneuver and they rolled off onto the plush carpeting of the den.

Tess landed sprawled across him, both of them still winded from the fiery conclusion of that first innocent kiss.

When she could speak, Tess said, "Why don't we go upstairs? We'll have more room there." Not wanting to have him argue, she stood and tugged at his hand until he came to his feet. Then she led the way to her bedroom.

Their second coming together had been so different from the first. They lay on the bed, touching and exploring each other, speaking in whispers. When at long last they came together once again it was as delicate as a ballet, each move leading to yet another discovery.

Eventually they had fallen asleep in each other's arms, like innocent babes who had exhausted themselves at play.

Luckily Craig had roused early enough to call a cab about four o'clock the next morning so that he didn't miss his plane. She'd walked him to the door, sleepily kissing him goodbye before tumbling back into bed to continue to dream of him....

* * *

"Tess?" His voice was so distinctive. She'd recognize it anywhere.

"Mmm?"

"Is something wrong with the omelet? You're not eating."

"The omelet?" she repeated dreamily, then remembered that she and Craig were having breakfast in her kitchen while she'd been reliving their night together! "Oh, the omelet. Oh, yes. It's delicious. Thank you for making it."

He looked at her, his expression a little concerned. "You haven't tasted it yet. Are you sure you're okay?"

He'd almost finished eating everything on his plate while she'd been dawdling over hers. She hastily dug in, not wanting to make conversation until she gained a little more control over her thoughts.

When she'd eaten every bite, she said, "That really was good. I must have been hungrier than I thought."

He smiled distractedly and gathered up their dishes. She rinsed them and put them into the dishwasher.

Craig leaned against the counter, watching her. When she was finished, he said, "Look, you go ahead with whatever your Saturday routine is and I'll run to the store."

She straightened, frowning at him. "Do you really think this is necessary, Craig? There's no rush, is there?"

"Maybe there's no rush, but it's necessary for our peace of mind. Where are your keys?"

She nodded to a wall decoration beside the garage door where a set of keys hung.

He touched her lightly on the cheek. "I'll be back in a bit." With a jaunty whistle that seemed to Tess to be out of place, considering his present mission, Craig disappeared behind the door that led to the garage.

There would never be anyone in her life to compare to Craig Jamison. But what would she do if she were actually pregnant? It was true that having his child would give her a part of him to love.

Knowing Craig, however, he would insist on their getting married. An unwanted marriage would be the worst thing she could force on him. It wasn't what she wanted, either. When she decided to marry, it would be with a man who wanted nothing more in life than to settle down with her and raise a family. Craig Jamison did not come close to that definition.

While she reluctantly reviewed what was occurring in her life, Tess stripped her bed, gathered towels from the bathrooms and started doing her weekly chores—washing and drying clothes, vacuuming and dusting, and making a list of necessary groceries for an expedition later in the day. The normalcy of her routine helped considerably to calm her.

All right. There was a possibility she was pregnant. Not much of one, really. A doctor once told her that with her erratic cycle it would be more difficult for her to become pregnant than for most women.

And what if she was? Well, she could handle it. She had a responsible position with a mortgage company, good health benefits, a great deal of accrued vacation time. She was certain she could take a leave of absence without unduly complicating her professional life.

A baby.

Tess dropped into an overstuffed chair in her living room. Could it be possible? Her heart was racing and her palms were sweating at the mere thought.

This wasn't the way she'd planned it. First, she was to meet the perfect man who would become the perfect husband. Next, she would become pregnant with the perfect baby and she and her perfect husband would become perfect parents.

Of course she'd known, realistically, that none of that was possible. What she had never fantasized about was the possibility of Craig Jamison being the father of a child of hers.

For one thing, she knew him too well and he was far from perfect. Craig would always be yearning to follow the sun, to discover what was on the other side of the mountain, to adventure down the yellow brick road.

He was an excellent photographer. That poetic soul of his was what endeared him to her. But he was far from being husband or father material, in her opinion.

Craig was a very dear friend, however the thought of being married to him shook her to her core.

Craig found her still sitting in the living room, a dust rag in her hand, the vacuum abandoned in the middle of the floor.

"Hi," he said, "I'm back."

She'd been so deep in thought, she hadn't heard him come in. His voice startled her. Glancing up, she looked at the rumpled man and shook her head. "Haven't you ever heard of an iron, Jamison?"

"Huh?" He walked over to her and touched her forehead with the back of his hand. "Are you okay?"

She pushed his hand away. "Forget it." Once again on her feet, she held out her hand. "All right, give it to me. I'll put us both out of suspense. Then maybe you can relax and get some rest. You must be out on your feet."

"Actually I've gotten my second wind. It's better to stay awake after traveling through time zones, at least until dark local time. You get through jet lag much faster that way."

"You should know," she muttered. Only then did she see that his hands were empty. "Didn't you buy the home test?"

"Yep. It's on the kitchen counter." He eyed her a little uncertainly. "Are you going to use it now?"

"Why not? It isn't going to help either one of us to sit around wondering about it."

He put his hands into his pockets and rocked from heel to toe. If she didn't know better, she'd believe he was nervous about this whole deal. Jamison nervous about anything? Hah!

Tess hurried into the kitchen. She saw the small bag innocently lying there on the counter. How could something so small and innocuous hold the key to her sense of being in control of her life and sanity?

"I don't think it works unless you take it out of the bag," Craig commented from behind her.

"Very funny."

"I thought you were in a hurry to find out."

"Not a hurry, exactly. I just think we're both over-reacting, that's all."

He dropped his hands onto her shoulders and gently kneaded them. "Don't forget that you aren't in this alone, honey. I'm here."

"For the moment, anyway." Her shoulder muscles were responding to his gentle massage by easing the tension they'd been holding and she was tempted to lean against him for continued comfort. Not a good sign at the moment. She could do this. She could do it without help.

The sudden thought of needing his help to take the test made her face heat up.

She reached for the bag holding the test and started upstairs. Glancing over her shoulder, she saw Craig watching her, his expression unreadable. Neither one of them spoke.

While she was upstairs, Craig wandered into the living room and absently turned on the vacuum. When he was through he went into the den and cleaned there as well. After recoiling the cord, he stored the machine, listening for movement upstairs.

There was none.

He didn't know too much about the tests, even after reading the instructions on every brand on display, but it seemed to him that she'd had plenty of time to get some kind of response.

Seeing her dust rag abandoned on the coffee table, he decided to dust and polish the furniture.

Once that was done, he looked around for something else to do. There was still no sound from upstairs.

Well, hell. Was he going to have to go up there and— And what? He felt so helpless in this situation. He'd had the feeling that his life was spiraling out of control from the time he boarded the plane to leave Los Angeles weeks ago.

Everything that he thought he knew about himself—his feelings toward his life's work, even the way he viewed his family and friends—all of that had changed, somehow.

Maybe he was stumbling around in some parallel universe where everything looked the same but wasn't. Or maybe he'd been reading too many science fiction novels lately.

Determined to find out what was going on, Craig took the stairs two at a time. He found Tess sitting on the side of her bed, staring at the wall.

"Well?"

Her head turned like a robot. Her eyes were just as blank. "It was positive," she said quietly.

Chapter Three

Craig walked in and sat down beside her, pulling her into his arms. "It's going to be okay. I promise you," he said. "We'll get a license on Monday. Then we'll be able to—"

She pushed out of his arms. "Craig, I am not going to marry you. Don't you see? It would never work."

"What are you talking about? Of course we're going to get married."

"There's no 'of course' about it. You're only making plans to marry me because I'm pregnant."

Craig's jaw tightened and she was reminded of just how stubborn this man could be when he set his mind to something. "Don't even think that you're going to talk me out of this one, Tess. It's really very simple. You're carrying my baby. Therefore, I'm going to marry you."

"That is exactly my point. You would never consider marrying me otherwise."

"How do you know? Maybe the very reason I came back so soon was to ask you to marry me."

She laughed, but she sounded more hysterical than amused. "You? Ask *me* to marry you? C'mon, Craig. Who do you think you're talking to? I know you too well to try to fool me. There's nothing wrong with my memory. You've always said that you never intended to marry."

"Granted I may have said that many years ago. I was still a kid. All kids spout off with remarks that don't mean anything."

"Craig, we talked about your attitude toward marriage over dinner the last time you were here. Nothing had changed since we were in high school. You made it clear that you didn't want to be tied down to anyone. You even commented how unfair it would be to expect someone to tolerate your yearning to travel."

"I was repeating my old way of looking at things out of habit. I said all of that before—" he began, then stopped. He ran his hand through his hair. "This is a ridiculous discussion, Tess. We have to look at the facts and the fact is that you're pregnant. We've confirmed it, so we look at our next step, which means that you're going to marry me."

"It means nothing of the sort. I have all kinds of choices. I can choose to raise it as a single parent, if I wish. My mother did it, and I can, too. Listen to me, Craig. You cannot force me to marry you. We are not living in the Dark Ages. Women have some rights these days. Not as many as we deserve, perhaps, but some."

Craig sighed, his frustration obvious. "Come on, Tess, don't be that way. I know this is a shock, but we're both adults. We can handle it.'' He got up and began to pace, obviously thinking about how he was going to persuade her.

Tess closed her eyes and leaned her head against the headboard of the bed. To think that her upset stomach in the early hours had actually been a high point of her day so far. Things had definitely gone downhill from the time she'd answered that blasted doorbell and found Craig standing there.

What had ever possessed him to come back so much earlier than his plans?

Obviously he'd been thinking along the same lines because he paused in his efforts to create a worn path in her rug to say, "I'm just glad I decided to come home when I did. God! It's scary to think about, isn't it? What if I'd stayed away those two years and come home to find out I was a daddy?'' He smiled at the last word, saying it again as though tasting it, becoming familiar with the new concept.

He laughed, shaking his head. She couldn't believe it. He actually laughed. This was one of the most traumatic things that had happened to her in her life and Craig was already finding something amusing about it.

There! That was another valid reason why the two of them as a couple would never work. He took everything in life too lightly. He didn't understand the seriousness of existence. Of course he had a wonderful family who loved him unconditionally, wholeheartedly accepted whatever he did without argument and encouraged him to leap off into the unknown whenever the mood struck him.

For Craig, the mood struck him often.

As for Tess, she was terrified of the unknown. She'd learned very early in life that there weren't many people in the world she could trust. She'd watched her mother struggle so that the three of them could survive, and that formed an indelible image in her mind. It was hard for Tess to believe that life was ever easy.

It was true that his enthusiasm was one of the traits that had always endeared Craig to her. She'd envied his fearlessness on many occasions, never so much as now.

He crossed his arms and planted his feet—a habitual stance of his. "You're right," he said tersely. "I can't force you to marry me. You're being pigheaded, but I'll put it down to the fact that this is all new to you, so I'm getting your typical knee-jerk, I-can-do-it-by-myself defensiveness. I don't know why it should surprise me. You've been that way all your life. But I'm telling you this and I want you to hear me, Tess. I refuse to let you go through this pregnancy alone." Before she could say anything, he was beside her in a few strides. "You aren't thinking about not having it, are you?" he asked, his horror obvious.

Why wouldn't he just leave her alone? She slid her hands through her hair, gripping it. "I haven't gotten that far in my thinking, Craig. Up until a few hours ago, the very last thing I was thinking of, much less formed any opinions about, was what I might or might not do in the event I ever became pregnant."

"I need to know, Tess. I really need to know whether you'd actually consider doing away with my baby?"

She raised her head and looked into his eyes. She'd never seen him quite this upset before. He'd gone pale beneath his tan.

"No, but look, Craig. We've only had a few minutes to think about all the ramifications of this. I don't want to make any snap judgments about anything, okay?"

"Does that mean that once you've thought things through, maybe gotten used to the idea, that you might consider marrying me?"

She eyed him balefully. "Who knows? I might take up bungee jumping, too. Just don't count on seeing it happen in this lifetime. In fact, marrying you would be quite similar to bungee jumping...all that free-fall without a guarantee that I won't hit the ground before I'm jerked around some more."

"Hey, thanks for that vote of confidence on my abilities as a husband. Look, it's not a role I've ever considered before, but I'm willing to give it a go. This is just as new to me as it is to you."

She got off the bed. "I'm going to make a cup of tea. Would you like some?"

"I'd rather have a beer."

"Sorry, I haven't gone to the store yet this week."

"Oh. Then you generally have beer on hand?"

"Nope. Just being polite."

He followed her down the stairs. "Do you need anything else? I could pick up some groceries for you." He almost ran into her when she came to an abrupt stop in the hallway.

She turned and looked at him accusingly. "You finished vacuuming, didn't you?"

He threw up his hands. "I'll confess, officer. Go ahead. Put me in handcuffs, lock me away. I dared to help you out a little."

"Oh, shut up," she said, continuing on her way to the kitchen.

"Is that any way to speak to the father of your child? Do you want him . . . or her . . . to follow your example? I would hope we could teach our child to be polite and—"

"Craig, I'm only a few weeks pregnant. I don't believe we have to worry about lessons in manners just yet."

"Maybe not, but I've heard that babies in the womb can hear things—like music and stuff. Do you want your baby to hear you saying rude things to its father?"

Tess filled the kettle, smiling to herself.

"See? I saw that. You actually managed a smile. C'mon, Tess, you don't have to take everything so blasted seriously all the time."

She set out a cup and dropped a tea bag inside. "Yes, I do, because I know you won't."

"I disagree. Life is much too important to be taken seriously. We've got to enjoy it, embrace it, celebrate it."

"Mmm-hmm." She watched the teakettle as though visually urging it to heat the water quicker.

"Marry me, Tess." He immediately went down on one knee. "Please. I'm begging you. My child is begging you. Don't torture us this way."

"Get up, you idiot, before I trip over you."

"We could have fun married. We could travel together, show the baby new sights and sounds. Think about all the places we could share with him...or her."

"That argument is guaranteed to convince me marriage with you would never work." She poured the boiling water into her cup and sat down at the kitchen bar. "I hate to burst your bubble, but somebody has to stay home and make a living."

"Aha! So that's what this is all about. Well, then, let me ease your mind, sweet-pea." He left the room, taking a great deal of life and energy with him.

Tess rested her head on the heel of her hand. Ever since she'd opened the door that morning she'd felt as though she'd been swept up in a tornado. Having

Craig around had always had that effect on her. It had been one of his most endearing qualities when they were growing up together.

Now, she wasn't so sure. How could she cope with such a high-energy person around on a daily basis?

What if your child is just like him?

Where had that thought come from? she wondered.

Craig loped back into the room. He tossed something on the counter in front of her. A rubber band held a bank passbook and a checkbook together.

"What's this?"

"Open them."

"I'm not going to go through your personal stuff like that."

He reached over and slid the band off, opening them both so that she could see them. "I can't blame you for being hesitant to marry just any guy off the street. So I'm showing you that I can take care of you."

She glanced down at the passbook, then did a double take. Had she read it wrong? She glanced at the checking account. "Craig? Where did all of this—?" She stopped, realizing that he might take her question wrong.

"From the various sales of my pictures. In addition to what you see in front of you, I have money invested in some safe securities."

She thought she had been frugal in her life, saving as much as she could each month, investing when she felt she could afford to, but she had nothing like this.

"I had no idea your photos were selling so well."

He shrugged. "I don't need much to live on, really. Just my traveling expenses and I do that as economically as I can."

She suddenly saw another aspect of this man she thought she knew so well. Looking into his eyes, she spotted the mature male lurking beneath the ebullient man. It made for an irresistible combination, there was no doubting that.

"I'll think about it," she finally said, hoping to buy herself some thinking time.

"Great! So, in the meantime, where do I sleep?"

That certainly got her attention. "At your home, perhaps?" she asked dryly.

"In Scottsdale? No, I don't think so. The commute would be too hectic."

"What commute?"

"Well, even if we don't get married right away, I need to be on hand to take care of my baby you're carrying around."

"I'm perfectly capable of looking after myself, you know. I've been doing it for most of my life."

"Of course you have, which is why you need a break. Especially now, when you have another one to look after."

She studied him for a long while. He stood across the bar from her, his stance one of sheer male obstinacy. His legs were braced apart, his arms folded, and she had a sudden flash of memory of the night they'd spent together.

She'd touched that broad chest, ran her fingers across those muscled arms and shoulders. She'd explored every inch of the man's body, making discoveries about him—and herself—that opened up a whole new world to her.

"I'm not going to win this one, am I?" she murmured, almost to herself.

That killer grin of his appeared and he seemed to relax slightly. Had he doubted his abilities to persuade her? Surely not.

"I only have the two bedrooms and I'm using the other one for an office. I suppose you can sleep in the den. The sofa folds out into a bed."

"Or... I could sleep with you."

"The bed's too narrow. I believe you were the one who pointed that out during your last visit." She could feel her cheeks burn at the memory.

"No problem. We'll buy a king-size bed. We'll go to Scottsdale and get what I've got stored with my folks and—"

"No."

"No, what?"

"I can't go to Scottsdale."

"Of course you can. Take some of your vacation time. We need to tell the folks about—"

"That's just it. I can't face your folks. Not yet, anyway. How can I? This is so new to me as it is. How can I possibly look them in the eye and admit that...that we..."

"Do you think they'll condemn us for what happened?"

"I don't know what they'll do."

"My mother, for one, will be so ecstatic over finally becoming a grandmother that we will both be embraced and forgiven for being a little impetuous."

"Impetuous, is it? I can think of other words to describe what happened."

"Not in front of the baby, if you please. We're going to have to work on your verbal utterances, I can see that. Aren't you glad I'm going to be around to help you monitor your speech?"

"Oh, brother."

He leaned on the bar so that his face was only inches away from hers. "All right, then. You win."

Seen this close, his eyes were absolutely gorgeous—so clear she could see her reflection in them. "What have I won?"

"Our discussion, debate, whatever you call it. You don't have to go to Scottsdale with me. In fact, I'll catch a flight over this evening, spend the night, rent a truck to bring my things—"

"A truck! Craig, I don't have that much room here. Just how much do you have over there?"

"My darkroom stuff, clothes, etc. I'll need transportation back anyway. It'll just be a small truck." All the time he spoke, he watched her mouth. When he paused, he leaned slightly closer, brushing her mouth with his. "Tell me you're okay with this. I really want you to be."

She closed her eyes, unable to face him at the moment. The next thing she knew he was around the bar and pulling her into his arms. He held her close to him, not saying anything, just holding her.

Pressed against him that way, she acknowledged, at least to herself, how good he felt to her—strong yet gentle, sturdy and dependable.

"The test could be wrong, you know," she finally whispered in a last-ditch effort to halt whatever was happening between them.

"I should be back by Monday. We'll go to a doctor then, have you checked over and make certain."

"Don't you think I should do that before you make definite plans to move in with me?"

He leaned back, his arms still wrapped around her waist. "You mean you're only going to live with me if you're pregnant?"

There was something odd in his tone, something she couldn't quite place. "As I understand it, the only reason you left Tibet was to find out if there were any consequences to that night we spent together. If I'm not pregnant wouldn't you go back?''

"We can decide all of that later. For now, we're going to live here together until you decide to make an honest man out of me by marrying me.''

"You've always been an honest man, Craig. And honorable. Why else would you be doing this?''

His smile was full of mischief as he said, ''Why else, indeed?'' This time his kiss was far from a gentle brushing of her lips. Instead it was much more reminiscent of a certain kiss he'd given her many weeks ago that had started all of this!

"Mom? This is Craig. I'm at the Phoenix airport. Could you pick me up?''

He'd stopped at the first bank of pay phones he found once he'd gotten off the plane from Los Angeles.

"Dear heaven! Craig! I thought you were halfway around the world! Of course I'll pick you up. Your dad's playing golf. Won't he be surprised when he gets home! I'll be right there,'' Susan Jamison said before hanging up.

Craig hung up more slowly, then leaned over to pick up the small bag he carried. He'd left most of his things at Tess's, although she'd insisted on pressing the clothes he presently wore. He smiled at the thought. She was already at work on reforming him. Who knows? He might become domesticated, yet.

He thought he'd successfully hidden his own shock at finding out that his worst fears had come true. Why else had he been unable to put that night behind him and get on with his planned trek?

He was going to be a father.

Him, a father? The idea had never been anything he'd ever considered, which was another thing. He'd never had unprotected sex with anyone and yet with Tess, he'd never given the matter any thought. It was almost as if he hadn't cared . . . as if he'd wanted her to become pregnant. Who knew where his thoughts were at that particular time?

All he remembered was the shock of discovering that she was a virgin. How could a woman as attractive as Tess Cassidy remain a virgin into her thirties? Hadn't there ever been a man she'd wanted before now?

Perhaps subconsciously he'd thought she was on the pill. He hadn't asked. Not once, even though they had spent the night getting to know so much about each other in other ways.

What if he hadn't come back? What if she'd had to go through all of this on her own? The thought chilled him. Tess had had enough heartache in her life. She didn't need any more. What if she'd tried to reach him later, to tell him that she was pregnant? Where could she have found him?

He'd blithely gone on his way the next day as though making love to his very best friend in all the world hadn't changed everything about his life and how he looked at it.

He'd learned the difference soon enough.

The truth was, he hadn't been able to get Tess out of his mind.

The truth was, he'd needed to see her again right away, not in a couple of years. He'd lost his ability to concentrate and to focus on his targeted areas to photograph. Thank God he'd followed his impulse to come back when he did.

Craig found himself at the entrance near the baggage claim of the airport, realizing that he was spacing out again, so caught up in his thoughts he was like a walking zombie.

Maybe he should have tried to sleep on the plane between L.A. and Phoenix. The truth was, he was too nervous to sleep. He couldn't remember the last time he'd stretched out on a bed for a full night's sleep. At least several days.

His mother would be along anytime now. He had to pay attention.

He wasn't exactly looking forward to telling his folks his news. Forget the fact that he was thirty-three years old and had been making his way alone in the world for over twelve years. Waiting by the curb, watching for his mother's car, Craig Jamison had to smile when he realized that he felt like a young boy again having to tell his mother he'd gotten into trouble at school.

However, the kind of situation he was now in was a sure sign he wasn't a little boy anymore!

Craig lay in one of the lounge chairs on his parents' patio, drowsing. They'd just come outside when the phone had rung, calling his mother back into the air-conditioned house.

There was a nice breeze in the shade. He could feel himself relaxing, and knew that all those time zones he'd gone through were rapidly catching up with him. If his mother didn't come back out soon, he'd be asleep. The problem was that once he fell asleep, he'd probably sleep for days. Somehow he had to hang on long enough to explain to his mother why he was there. She'd asked no questions once he'd gotten into the car, so he'd postponed telling her that he would be leaving in a couple of days, just as soon as he could rent a truck and load his belongings.

His parents had offered to have his belongings moved along with theirs when they'd left California, pointing out that there was no need for him to put his things in storage where he couldn't get to them when he was in the country.

He'd reimbursed them the cost, grateful they had room for his expensive equipment. They would understand the significance of his moving everything. He was setting up new headquarters, getting a place of his own.

It was about time. He just hadn't expected the decision to be based on his becoming a father in the near future.

He glanced around at a sound behind him in time to see his mother carrying a tray with a pitcher and glasses on it. He leaped from the chair and hurried to her. "Why didn't you tell me that's what you were doing? I could have brought that outside for you. I thought you were still on the phone."

"It just occurred to me that you might enjoy some freshly made lemonade." She glanced around—taking in the high stucco walls that enclosed the colorful backyard—with a look of affection. "Isn't it nice back here? Your dad has done a wonderful job with it. Which reminds me. That was your dad calling. He'd gotten the message I left him at the golf pro shop. He was surprised and pleased to hear you were home. However, he still has some errands to run, so it might be a little while before he gets here."

Craig set the tray down on the table between their chairs and poured them each a glass of lemonade. He handed his mother one and said, "It's just as well. There's something I want to discuss with you. Dad can hear about it later."

She settled back into her chair and gave him a level look. "I knew there was something wrong or you wouldn't be back here so soon. Did something happen in Tibet? I know the political situation there isn't stable. You know how worried I was when you first mentioned wanting to go there.''

''Actually I was quite fortunate in making some good contacts once I arrived. Although I wasn't there as long as I'd originally planned, everything went so smoothly I was able to reach some of the areas I'd hoped to get to see.'' He took a large swallow of liquid from his frosty glass before searching for an opening. Finally he said, ''This is about Tess.''

Susan straightened in surprise. ''Tess Cassidy? Has something happened? Is she all right?''

Good question. He wasn't quite ready to answer that one just yet. ''Have you heard from her lately?''

She was silent, as though mentally calculating. ''Well, now that you mention it, I guess it has been a while. You know how time can just slip away from you. I don't think I've heard from her since you were here last. You said something about dropping in to see her back then. Is something wrong? I know she took her grandmother's death hard, but I was hoping she was doing better now.''

He cleared his throat, mentally preparing to take the dive into a very deep subject. ''I believe she's adjusting to the loss of her grandmother. This is something different. She's pregnant.''

''Oh, my!'' his mother gasped. ''That doesn't sound like Tess at all. I mean, you're not saying that she's suddenly gotten married, are you? She's never given the slightest hint that she's met anyone. This would be so sudden, coming so soon after her grand-mother's—''

"She isn't married." His voice sounded hoarse in his own ears. He wondered if his mother had noticed. She seemed too shocked at his news to be aware of his behavior.

"Oh, that poor darling. She's had such a rough go of life, it seems. Her mother would be so upset to hear such a thing had happened to her daughter. That poor woman went through so much, trying to survive with next to no education. She always said that she wanted Tess to get her education so she'd be able to take care of herself no matter what. I suppose that would be some consolation for Tess to fall back on, but still..."

"I, uh, don't remember her mother very well."

"That's because she was always working. At least Tess's grandmother was there to look after Tess, but her mother was always working two or three jobs at a time. It's no wonder her heart finally gave out on her like that."

"Tess seemed happy enough when we were growing up."

"Oh, yes. She's always been one to cope with whatever came along. So dependable, so calm. I suppose that's why this latest news is such a shock. It's so out of character for her." She was quiet for a while, shaking her head. After a lengthy silence, Susan said, "Tess must have loved the man she got involved with a great deal to allow such a thing to happen."

Craig felt her remark go through him as if it were a lance, spearing him through the middle. He couldn't have spoken if his life depended on it. In some unfathomable way, he felt as though it did.

"Is there any possibility she will marry the father, do you think?" Susan went on to ask. "I think that's always the best way to care for a child if there's any hope at all that the relationship can work out."

Craig took his time draining his glass and carefully replacing it on the table between them before attempting to reply. He started to speak and found his voice was gone. After clearing his throat twice, he managed to say, "I'm the one you're talking about, Mom."

Susan stared at him blankly, as though he had spoken to her in a foreign language. "What?" She blinked, her mouth trembling slightly. When he didn't say anything more, she said, "What did you say?" There was nothing more to add, so he just sat there, waiting for the news to sink in. "Are you saying that you and Tess—?" She placed her fingers over her mouth as though to stop the flow of words and what they could mean. "I'm afraid I don't understand. I mean, how—" The news seemed to hit her with a sudden force and her voice rose. "You...got...Tess Cassidy pregnant?" she asked in a horrified voice.

Finally saying it was something of a relief... just getting it out. He nodded. "I ended up spending the night with her before I flew to Asia. It wasn't anything either of us planned. It just happened. I can't really explain it, and even if I could, what happened is really between Tess and me. But once I was gone, I realized so many things about myself, about Tess, about us growing up together, about our friendship. It was just as if all of those memories had been waiting for me to look at them from a different perspective." Craig rubbed the heels of his hands into his eyes. They felt like burning coals from so many hours without sleep. "It felt so strange to think of Tess in such a different light. I'd always considered her the sister I never had. She was just there as part of my life. I knew she was important to me. I just wasn't really aware of how important and in what ways."

His mother quietly said, "I see. You finally realized you were in love with her, didn't you?"

He dropped his hands from his eyes. "You don't sound particularly surprised."

Susan's smile was a little sad. "Well, no. Your dad and I have known for years how you felt about her. By the time you both were in high school, we found it amusing to see how you looked after her, made sure the boys she dated treated her with respect. We could tell that you didn't have a clue why you took such an interest in her," she said with a sigh, "but then boys tend to mature later than girls and we just figured that sooner or later you would discover how you really felt. Hopefully it wouldn't be too late to do something about it."

Neither one of them said anything for several moments. Craig was struck by this new perspective of his past behavior, feeling almost stupid at not understanding his own feelings sooner.

After the silence stretched out, Susan finally shook her head as though dazed. "You were so protective of her for so long, and then to hear that after all these years you were so careless as to—" She stopped, swallowed and he saw her eyes fill with moisture.

"I asked her to marry me," he offered quietly.

Her tears overflowed but she ignored them. Instead she reached for his hand and squeezed it, her smile tender. "Of course you would, and I'm glad that you didn't waste any time." She narrowed her eyes slightly, thinking back. "She must be... what?...eight or nine weeks along by now." Her smile was understanding when she added, "I know this is going to be a difficult transition for you, adjusting to having a wife and child, but at least you know you're doing the right thing. And it isn't as though you don't love her and that she doesn't—"

"She hasn't actually agreed to it. At least, not yet."

Susan blinked. "No?" she said faintly, pressing her fingers against her throat.

He looked away, focusing on the landscaping in the backyard. "I don't believe she considers me proper husband material, much less father material." He was amazed at how much that hurt him. Saying it made her attitude more real. There was a very good chance that his child might not carry his name. He wasn't certain how he was going to deal with that.

"Oh, my."

His eyes began to water, which wasn't surprising. He was going to have to get some sleep. He rubbed them once again. "Of course, I fully intend to change her mind." It was an effort to keep his voice light. "It just may take a while. But we've got some time to work things out before it arrives."

"She's sure that she's pregnant?"

"She intends to see a doctor next week, but from the indications I think it's fairly certain."

"So what do you intend to do now?"

Ah. The next hurdle. "I came over here to get all my gear. I intend to move in with her." Before his mother could respond he hurriedly continued. "I know. I know that isn't the best or most sensible solution, but the thing is, I don't want her to set up a routine that excludes me. I want to be there, right from the beginning. If she won't marry me, then I'll do it this way. I don't intend to let her out of my sight until she gives birth."

"Poor Tess. She doesn't really have a chance if you're serious about doing this."

Craig felt a heaviness in his heart. "You mean, you don't think I'm any better husband or father material than she does?"

"I didn't say that, so don't put words into my mouth. I just know how determined you can be when you set your mind to it. I also know Tess. She isn't going to be rushed into anything without thinking it through. Tess is very much her mother's daughter, you know. Her mother could have curled up and let life kick her around, but she refused to break beneath the burdens. They're survivors, both of them.'' She poured Craig another glass of lemonade.

Craig drank from his glass, then allowed his eyes to drift close.

"Of course she'll marry you," Susan said, breaking the silence. "She'll do whatever she can to give her child the stable home life she never had."

"I believe the problem is that she doesn't think I'll provide a stable home life."

Susan chuckled. "Well, not if she's looking at your past record. But I have a hunch things have changed for you, haven't they?"

"Well, yeah, once I realized she was pregnant—"

"Oh, before then, darling. The old Craig would still be in Tibet or traveling on to Afghanistan or into Russia. You wouldn't have given a thought to returning home so soon if you hadn't already been preoccupied with your feelings for Tess."

His mother knew him even better than he thought.

"So I would say that one of the ways you could convince her that you're already in the process of changing is to point out to her that you realized you loved her while you were in Tibet and no longer wanted to spend your time away from her. Isn't that the real reason you came back so soon?''

''I told her all of that . . . or at least, I think I did, something along those lines, anyway. I can't remember, exactly. I was rehearsing what I was going to tell her all the way back, but once I saw her all my planned speeches left my head.''

''Well, if you want my advice, I say that you need to get some rest before you do another thing. I wish you'd brought her with you this trip.''

''I tried, but she was shy about seeing you so soon after finding out.''

''She'll come around, eventually, give her a little time to adjust. After all, she needs you, whether she fully understands that or not. She's going to need you even more in the coming months. What you're going to have to do is to prove to her that you can be there for her, that you intend to become a part of her life and the child's life. No woman could resist knowing that. Besides, the fact that she loves you is a plus in your favor.''

''I didn't get the impression that she's feeling much love for me these days. I have a hunch that if she had a miniature doll that looked like me, she'd be busy sticking pins into it.''

''Nonsense. She's loved you most of her life. Don't worry. Once she's spent some time with you again, once she's seen that you're serious about staying here at home and caring for her, she'll come around. You just wait and see.''

"I hope so because I don't intend to walk away.''

"Why don't you go on inside and go to bed? I'll explain everything to your dad when he gets in. The two of you can visit tomorrow. There's plenty of time for all of that. This will all work out just fine, wait and see if it doesn't.''

She was smiling by the time she finished speaking. Craig got up and headed for the room they'd designated was his. As he opened the door, he heard a light, girlish laugh coming from his mother, a sound he hadn't heard in years.

"A baby!'' she said, following him into the house. "I can't wait to tell Phil he's finally going to become a grandpa!''

Chapter Four

By the time Tess got home after work on Monday, she was exhausted. There had been three accidents on the freeway, causing considerable back up in traffic and long delays. She was hot and irritable.

She was also nervous. Craig was supposed to be back sometime today. He'd called last night to tell her that he was running a little behind in loading the truck and probably wouldn't get in until late this evening.

She'd welcomed the respite. She'd spent the weekend trying to come to grips with all that had happened. The pregnancy was a shock, of course, but having Craig back in her life was an even bigger one.

How could she have agreed to let him move in with her? To sleep with her? How could she put herself in such a vulnerable position?

The earliest doctor's appointment she could get was for a week from Tuesday. What if she'd been wrong? Maybe the test was defective. What was she going to do if the doctor said she was not pregnant?

Would Craig think she had tricked him? She couldn't face the thought that he'd lose faith in her. He was too important to her. On the other hand, she cared too much for him to tie him down to life in suburbia. That's why she couldn't marry him. It would be a lifetime sentence that he'd soon regret.

She turned down the alleyway to her condominium where the garage was located, slowing as she touched the remote garage door opener. The door was not yet fully up when her back gate opened and someone stepped out into the alley.

Before she had time to wonder how someone had gotten over the high wall she recognized Craig standing there, his insouciant grin firmly in place.

He was back. So much for having a few hours to herself before she had to see him again.

She pulled into the garage, reached for her purse and unfastened her seat belt, but before she could open the door he was there, holding it open for her. "Hi. I didn't want to scare you by rapping on your back door after you got into the house, so I've been listening for you to drive up and enjoying your garden at the same time. It's really beautiful back there. You've put in a lot of work on it."

"Either you're earlier than you expected to be or I'm really late. How did you get in?"

He shrugged. "Climbed over the wall."

"Craig, that wall is seven-feet high!"

"I'm not surprised. Not a bad idea. Keeps people out."

"Obviously not everybody," she said, shaking her head in exasperation. "I hope we don't have too many athletic criminals hanging out in the neighborhood. I've always felt fairly safe, until now." She unlocked the door to the kitchen and walked inside the house.

Craig followed her. "Don't worry. I'll be here to protect you."

She was ashamed to admit to herself that she liked the sound of that.

"When did you get here?"

He glanced at his watch. "Almost two hours ago. I left as early as I could to miss the evening traffic."

"Wish I could have done that. It was horrible today, coming home. I feel badly about not giving you a key before you left. I wasn't really thinking that far ahead."

"That's okay. I'm going to have to unload the truck this evening. It's still sitting on the street, but I didn't want to miss you when you got home."

"If you'll excuse me, I think I'll get out of these clothes and into something more comfortable. I can help you unload."

"Not on your life. Until you've talked to a doctor, I don't want you to do any lifting."

"I'm sure that not everything you've brought is heavy."

"Doesn't matter. Run on upstairs while I look for something to make for supper."

"You're going to cook again? You're determined to spoil me, I can see that." She turned away, and he heard her footsteps on the stairs.

She was nervous with him. Plus she didn't ask, either during the phone call last night or just now, what his folks had said about her pregnancy.

Why hadn't he ever noticed before how carefully she covered whatever she might be feeling with that calm, competent demeanor of hers?

He was noticing so much about her, seeing her so differently now. She had never quite met his gaze just now, her eyes darting away, her hands busy.

By the time she came back downstairs in a halter top and shorts that showed off her long legs, he was busy chopping vegetables for a salad. He didn't need the reminder, although he would have probably reacted in the same way toward her if she'd worn a sack. His memory was quite good. He knew exactly what she looked like without those few items of clothing.

In a bright tone, she asked, "What did you find for supper?"

"I'm steaming some veggies, making a salad. I wasn't sure if you'd want me to grill a couple of these chops so I thought I'd wait to ask."

"Not for me, but go ahead if you want one."

She sat down at the bar and he poured her a glass of iced tea.

"I've been doing a great deal of thinking since I saw you last," he said once she'd had a chance to sip the cool drink.

He watched her tighten her hold on the glass. Without looking at him, she said, "Oh?" as though she wasn't particularly interested in what he'd been thinking.

Too bad. "I've got several ideas I want to run past you."

Now she definitely looked wary. "Such as?"

"Oh, about what I can do to make your life a little easier in the next few months. I imagine you're going to want to continue working for a while. That being the case, I thought I might take over some of the chores around here. I can run the vacuum and keep things picked up, throw in a load of laundry whenever it's necessary, help with the meals and grocery shopping. You know, that sort of thing."

Tess couldn't believe what she was hearing. This was Craig Jamison talking! "I don't remember a genie granting me three wishes," she finally replied. "Why are you offering to do so much around here? I may be pregnant, but I'm certainly not an invalid."

He grinned. "Well, since I can't carry the baby, the least I can do is some of the household chores."

She propped her elbows onto the counter and dropped her forehead into her hands. "I can't let you do this, Craig. I really can't. I appreciate your offer to help. Actually I'm touched more than I can say, but I know you. You'll hate being cooped up here all day. After a week or so you'd be planning your escape, booking a flight to Tahiti."

"Been there. It's overrated. Besides, I don't intend to stay here all day. I have a friend here in town I intend to look up. He's got his own studio and has asked me to work with him before. I have a hunch he can put me in the way of as much work as I can handle. Plus, I can set up some of my photo lab equipment here and continue with my own stuff. I've got several weeks of work ahead of me, developing the film I've taken recently."

"You've always hated studio work and you know it—taking pictures of babies and graduates and brides-to-be, not to mention all the actors' portfolios."

"It's not so bad, really. Besides, I'm going to want to get some practice taking baby pictures. After all, I'm going to have a new model coming along."

Tess made a muffled sound, but didn't look up.

"What?" he asked.

She shook her head. He leaned down, trying to see her face. "You're not crying, are you?" He'd been trying so hard to keep it light, but he knew tears would do him in.

She kept her head down. "My eyes seem to have developed an automatic watering system lately. Maybe it has something to do with hormonal changes or something."

After a long silence, he murmured, "Please don't cry."

She raised her head, fixing him with a damp glare. "I'll cry if I want to, darn it. You're going to have to get used to the idea that I can turn into a watering bucket at the snap of your fingers. Remember, I'm still adjusting to all of this. You seem to be taking it in stride better than I am." She watched him fill two plates with steamed vegetables, then place the salad bowl on the bar between them.

They ate in silence, each caught up in his and her own thoughts. After a while, Tess said, "Since you cooked tonight, I'll do it tomorrow, okay?"

"Whatever works for you is fine with me," he replied as casually as possible, relieved that she appeared to be accepting his presence there.

She smiled at him. "Are you always going to be this agreeable? You're treating me as though I have some life-threatening disease, Jamison. Lighten up."

"Now there's a switch." He leaned over and kissed her on the nose. "I enjoy pampering you, honey. Guess you'll just have to get used to it."

They were companionably cleaning the kitchen when Craig said, "Oh, by the way, the folks want to know when they can come to visit us. I've never seen them so excited. Who would have guessed how much they've been pining to become grandparents? Mom said she'd tried to put it out of her mind and thought she was reconciled to not having any. I swear she's close to doing back flips."

She covered her cheeks with her hands. "I was hoping you hadn't told them just yet."

"I really don't think we could have kept it a secret for long, do you? They wanted to know why I'd decided to move in with you, so I told them I was trying hard to convince you to marry me. My moving in was the first step."

She buried her face in her hands. "Oh, Craig, you didn't. Wasn't it enough to tell them you were going to stay in the States for a while without mentioning me?"

"I could have, I suppose. But the truth was much easier to explain."

"They think I'm awful, don't they?" she asked in obvious dread.

"On the contrary, they couldn't believe I'd take advantage of you in such a way."

"Oh, Craig, you didn't tell them how it came about, did you?"

"Of course I did. It was the truth. I did take advantage of your vulnerability that night. It was that more than anything that kept haunting me all the while I was gone. I finally had to come back, to see if I could make amends."

"You didn't take advantage of me, can't you understand that?" She tossed down the rag that she'd been using to wipe the counter, folding her arms and glaring at him. Now this was more like the Tess he knew, not that bright and friendly fake who had first greeted him.

Here was the person he'd always enjoyed teasing. "Oh, I realized it, finally. Once I really gave it some thought, I figured out what had happened. Some-

time during the course of that evening, you decided
to lure me into your web of seduction. Being the true
innocent I am, I didn't understand what was happening. It's my guess you doped up that last drink
you offered me so that I would be totally under your
spell with no mind of my own . . . no will of my own.
All you had to do was beckon and I was yours . . . just
your typical, ordinary love-slave there to do your
bidding." He lifted his eyebrows. "Wasn't that what
happened?"

She was laughing by the time he finished. "You are
crazy, did you know that? Absolutely crazy."

He slipped his arms around her and held her. This
was exactly where she needed to be. Why hadn't he
known that years ago? "I don't have a problem with
that. Do you?"

She shook her head, bemused. He couldn't resist
kissing her. He immediately felt her resistance. As
casually as possible, he stepped back, silently reas-
suring her that he was not going to pressure her in any
way.

"What did your folks say when you told them you
intended to move in with me?" She refilled their
glasses, handing him one while she led the way into
the den.

She sat down in one of the chairs, so he relaxed on
the sofa. "They're hoping that eventually you'll take
pity on me as well as give my innocent babe my
name." He eyed her over the top of his glass before he

said, "I told them not to hold their breath, that you were hoping for someone better than me in your life."

"That's not true and you know it, Craig! I'm trying not to make any hasty decisions that would have long-range consequences on everyone concerned. Surely you can understand that, can't you?"

"Just so that you understand that while you're weighing all your options, and analyzing the consequences of each and every decision, I'm going to be right here. Make no mistake about it, darlin'. Until that little one is here, you aren't getting rid of me. I intend to dog your every step, make certain you take care of yourself, as well as anything else I can do to make your life easier. That's one decision I intend to make."

"Do you really think this is necessary?" Tess asked two days later, looking around the mammoth display of bedroom furniture and mattresses in all shapes and sizes.

"Yes, actually, I do. I tried your suggestion, remember? I've slept on that couch. If you hoped that would get rid of me, it didn't work. So...we'll get a king-size bed and both of us will be comfortable. We'll each have plenty of room to sprawl if we feel the urge, and if you get scared in the middle of the night and need a strong arm to hold and protect you, well, hey, I'll be right there beside you, an eager volunteer."

"That's all well and good, but since you only intend to stay until the baby arrives, it seems silly to waste money on new furniture that I'm not going to need, especially with all the other expenses of having a baby."

"Would you care to run that by me one more time?" Craig asked, leaning his shoulder against a bureau and crossing his ankles.

"What part don't you understand?"

"The part that I intend to stay only until the baby arrives."

"Isn't that what you said?"

"No, but it's obviously what you heard."

"Now I *am* confused."

"Is that part of your hormone thing?" he asked with considerable interest.

"Of course not, you idiot. I was just—"

"Tsk, tsk, tsk. Remember who's listening?"

"Oh, good grief! You can be so-o-o irritating at times."

"I'm reading the most fascinating book about the life of the unborn child. It's amazing what they've learned about the little tykes."

She stared at him in astonishment. "You're reading a book about prenatal development?"

"Among other things. There's also one on how the mother's diet affects the infant, although you haven't said whether or not you intend to nurse him…or her. However, your diet affects him now, so you can't be too careful. Then there's the book on what one can expect from infants from birth to their first year, then—"

She threw up her hands and walked away, saying, "I give up."

"Good." He straightened and strode to where one of the salesmen hovered. "We'd like this set to be delivered as soon as possible." Craig pulled out his checkbook. "You'll take a check, I presume."

"On a local bank?"

"Yes."

"Certainly, sir." The salesman walked over to the counter and began to figure the tax and total.

"Craig!" Tess snapped at his elbow.

He looked at her and smiled. "Yes, dear?" He hoped that sounded solicitous and husbandly enough.

"I don't think we should do this."

"What you said was that you didn't feel we should spend the money. I understand. You've carefully budgeted and this wasn't part of it. However, I haven't been given the opportunity to budget so this is my contribution to the household. Fair enough?"

She shook her head.

With his most forlorn look, he said, "You're going to consign me to that couch?" He rubbed his lower back. "There's no sense in *both* of us suffering from back pains, is there? Especially when mine can be alleviated. And just think. As long as I'm lying there beside you, I can give you back rubs to help ease any discomfort you might have. Now if that isn't working everything out efficiently, I don't know what is.''

She turned away before she said something she'd later regret. Besides, the salesman was approaching them once again.

They were driving back to the condo before Craig said, ''You're being awfully quiet. Are you okay?''

''Not really.''

''What's wrong.''

''I'm feeling pressured, pushed and manipulated, and I *really* don't like the feeling.''

You had to ask, he thought to himself. ''Yeah. I can see where you could be feeling some of that—maybe the pressured and pushed part. I'm having a little trouble with the manipulated part, though.''

''You wanted the bed. You got the bed. You even made it sound like it was the only reasonable thing for us to do.''

''It wasn't?''

''We're not playing house, Craig. We're not back in elementary school. This isn't about where to build the clubhouse and how big it needs to be, and what kind of restrictions for new members we'll make up.''

''I know that.''

''Then why are you treating this like a game?''

''In what way am I treating it like a game?''

''Maybe game's the wrong word, okay? You're treating it like one of your adventures. None of this is real to you. We find out I'm pregnant, so you decide to become the hero and rescue me. Craig, I don't need rescuing, can you understand that?''

"Because you're tough, right? You don't need anybody...you've never needed anybody. Who do I think I am, anyway?'' he replied, pulling into the garage. He got out of the car and walked around to her door. She was already pushing it open. He held out his hand and she looked at it for a long moment before slowly reaching out and grasping it.

With a steady pressure he eased her from the car until she was standing a few inches away from him. "Was that so difficult to do?''

She could feel the trembling that had started deep within her in the store increase. He hadn't let go of her hand. Instead he continued to hold it while he draped his other arm around her shoulders and pulled her closer so that her nose was pressed into the curve between his shoulder and neck.

''You really don't have to convince me you can do this on your own. I know you can, but thank God you don't have to. Please let me be a part of this, okay? I'm not trying to rush you into some kind of relationship with me you don't want. So maybe the bed wasn't the greatest idea, but I'm not trying to take advantage of you, or planning to make any moves on you.'' He leaned back to see her face, saying, "Not unless I'm encouraged to do so, of course.''

She wouldn't look at him, nor did she answer.

He dropped his arms from around her and walked over to the door into the house. After holding it for her, he followed her inside.

"Look, I don't want you to take this the wrong way, but once you start putting on weight you might have a little more difficulty getting around. What if you slipped and fell some night getting to the bathroom and I wasn't upstairs to know that you'd fallen?"

"Believe me, you'd hear it. You'd probably think the ceiling was falling through—probably mistake it for another earthquake," she replied in a shaky voice.

He smiled, following her into the den and watching her needlessly straighten the magazines on the coffee table. "See there? You didn't lose your sense of humor... just misplaced it for a little while. It's going to be all right. All of this." He took her hand and coaxed her to sit down on the sofa beside him. He stroked her cheek. "Remember me? I'm your best friend, not some stranger trying to muscle in on your nice, orderly life. What I think you may be missing here is that I need to be a part of this."

She closed her eyes for a moment, as though gathering inner strength. "We're not a hundred percent certain I'm even pregnant, Craig. I just feel we're rushing things a little, don't you?"

"You know the truth, though, don't you? Just as I do. That's what called me back home. That's why you reluctantly agreed to let me move in with you. We both know what the doctor is going to say next week."

She leaned back against the sofa and sighed. "It's all a little overwhelming at the moment, I guess."

"I've got an idea. Why don't we watch some old movies tonight. You have a great collection. We share a lot of favorites, you know. As for feeling manipulated, if you don't want me sleeping upstairs with you, I won't." He patted the sofa. "It will take some getting used to, but I can deal with this. You'll need the larger bed in a few months, anyway."

"It isn't about the bed, Craig. It's about being a part of the decision-making process. You're used to being on your own, so you've never felt the need to consult anyone else. You weigh your options and make a decision. I understand that because I've lived the same way. You would not like it if I was making decisions that you had to live with without my consulting you, would you?"

"No. You're right. I wouldn't be comfortable in that sort of situation. I suppose, in my own defense, I'm carrying on this way because I'm afraid that if I leave it up to you, you won't allow me any part of your life, or the baby's. You don't want to marry me . . . you are merely tolerating my living with you. I feel as though I have to fight to maintain any contact with my own child. I guess I'm not handling it very well."

"Obviously neither am I or you wouldn't be feeling so threatened by all of this. At least we're admitting we both have fears going into this. I think that's a good sign."

"I never thought of it in those terms."

"Of course not. No self-respecting male is ever going to admit to being afraid of anything!" She patted his cheek consolingly and they both laughed. When she sobered, Tess added, "You and I both know that we can't share the same bed without adding tension to our relationship. I'm not certain I'm ready to add anything more in my life to deal with at the moment."

He held his hand in the oath-making position. "I do solemnly swear to keep my distance when we are in bed together. I will not venture past my half of the mattress unless I'm specifically invited. If I break any of these promises, you can send me back to this sofa for the duration." He tilted his head inquiringly. "Fair enough?"

She studied him carefully before holding out her hand. "It's a deal." They solemnly shook on their new agreement.

Chapter Five

It was during her fourth month checkup that they found out the rest of the story.

"Twins?" she repeated, staring at the doctor.

"That's right. There's two of them. No doubt about it."

Tess left the doctor's office dazed by his news. She was more shocked than when he'd confirmed her pregnancy two months ago. After all, she'd had a little time to get used to the idea before she'd seen him. But twins? This was news she'd never expected to receive. What in the world was she going to do?

Craig was out on a shoot today. She hurried home hoping to have some time to herself before she had to face him. She already knew that he would want to know everything she'd found out from the doctor, just as he had after each visit. He threatened to go with her if she didn't make a full report.

It was amazing how her life had changed in two short months. In some ways it seemed as though she'd been pregnant forever, and in others, that Craig had moved in only a week or so ago.

True to his promise, he hadn't badgered her about marrying him. He'd also made certain that he didn't take advantage of the fact that they were now sharing a bed.

She seemed to be more affected than he was. Sharing the bedroom had increased the intimacy between them, even though Craig was considerate about allowing her privacy. He, on the other hand, didn't appear the least self-conscious about her seeing him in all stages of undress. He slept in a pair of jogging shorts, he explained, since he didn't own a pair of pajamas and didn't intend to buy any. That was his only concession to her modesty.

She supposed she was getting more used to sharing her space with him, if that was what he'd hoped to accomplish. There were times when she couldn't figure Craig out. Lately she made less effort to try.

She let herself into the house. The doctor had warned her that her need for sleep would increase. He'd been right. She tired much easier now. She could just imagine what she would be doing in another month or so, carrying twins!

She went upstairs and changed out of her clothes and into her comfortable robe. She'd take a quick nap and then start dinner so that it would be ready when Craig got home. That was the last thought she had before waking up some time later with the most delicious smells wafting up from the kitchen.

Craig was home.

She sat up on the side of the bed, knowing better than to get up too quickly. Her body had certainly let it be known that she could no longer spring out of bed without falling on her nose.

She also knew to take it slow and easy down the stairs. When she walked into the kitchen Craig stood at the stove with his back to her. He must have heard her because he glanced over his shoulder and smiled at her. "Hi, sleepyhead. How's it going?"

She promptly yawned, then sat down at the bar. "Fine."

"That's all the doctor said? You're fine?"

She grinned. "Actually he did add another word."

Craig walked around the bar and gave her a hug, another thing she was getting used to. "What word?"

"Twins."

She watched his face as the word and its meaning registered. He sat on the stool beside her, just staring at her. The silence stretched between them. "Twins?" he finally said slowly.

"Uh-huh."

"Oh my God."

"My sentiments exactly."

They sat there staring at each other in silence. Then he grinned. "He's sure?"

"Positive."

"Wow," he whispered after another long pause. "You know what this means, don't you?"

"We double everything we have on the list for a newborn?"

"That, too. But I'm talking about the future. We're going to have to find a larger place to live. We can't have our children jammed into that little bedroom for long. We've got some time, but it wouldn't hurt to start looking."

"Craig...don't. This place is as much as I can afford. I'll be all right here."

He looked at her. "C'mon, Tess, don't start that all over again. Will you please get it through your head that I am not about to go off and leave you to cope alone? I am fully prepared to play responsible parent here. I'm also going to bring up the dreaded *M*-word again. Haven't I convinced you that we're going to make this work? I'm happy doing what I do here. I'm not making any demands on you. I—"

"I know that. It's just—" She didn't know anymore. She was so tired of trying to deal with everything she was feeling.

"What is it, honey? What are you so afraid of?"

"I don't know! Everything, I guess. But you're right. You've been wonderful to me these past few months, shamelessly pampering me. All I do is eat and sleep and get fatter and be grouchy and—"

"But you're supposed to eat and sleep and get fatter and you're not grouchy...unless you're tired...or hungry...or—"

"See what I mean? Face it. I'm a grouch."

"But you're a lovable grouch. You know, I've been thinking that it's probably past time for me to confess to something."

"What?" She was immediately suspicious.

"Has it ever occurred to you that the reason I came back from Tibet, before I knew you were pregnant, mind you, was to ask you to marry me?"

She chuckled. "No."

"Has it ever occurred to you that I might have discovered the last time I was here that I love you?"

"Now *that* I might believe since I love you, too. Why do you think I'm having such a struggle dealing with all of this? I can't forget how adamant you sounded that night about not being the marrying kind. You were very convincing."

"That's because I had convinced myself. But then we spent that night together. It was a magical time, Tess. Like no other I've ever experienced before. Now, to add to the magic, we find out that our night together produced twins. Even if you hadn't gotten pregnant, being with you that night opened my eyes to a lot of things. I think I've loved you for a long time and didn't recognize it. But I definitely recognized it after that night. I've been trying hard not to rush you into anything, not to push you, but Tess, I've gotta tell you, lying beside you every night has been a real test of my self-control. I made an oath to you and I won't go back on it, but what I want more than anything is to be married to you, to be able to make love to you, to plan for the future with you."

"It's been bothering you to sleep beside me every night and not make love to me?"

"Hell, yes. I'm human, and you're about the sexiest female I've ever known. It just took me a few years to grow up enough to appreciate that fact. I have to keep reminding myself that you are pregnant, that you—"

"The doctor said it was all right for us to have relations for the next few months, until the last several weeks."

"You mean you asked him?"

"Maybe I hinted or something. I don't remember, but he volunteered that information. He said that a woman sometimes feels her strongest urges now, when she knows she doesn't have to worry about pregnancy."

"And are you feeling some strong urges?"

"How should I know? I haven't much experience in that department."

He put his arms around her and nuzzled her neck. "We could certainly experiment and find out, if you'd like...in the interest of science, of course."

His whispered words caused a shiver to run down her back.

"After we're married, naturally," he said, straightening. "What would the children think if we became that intimate prior to the wedding ceremony?"

"Craig, don't be—"

"Why don't I call the folks and have them fly over here? We can have a private ceremony at the church. They'll love it. I think they were married there as well." Before she could say anything he said, "Don't worry, I'll take care of the details, you won't have to do a thing but show up."

"Craig, you're doing it again, making a decision for both of us without listening to me."

"Oops. You're right. Absolutely right. It was the talk about sex that scrambled my already rattled brain. Sorry."

"However, in this case, I happen to agree with you."

"You do?"

"I've had to face the fact that the only reason I've resisted marrying you was that I was afraid I'd become too attached to you. Then when you left, I'd—"

"I am not leaving you. Will you please get that through your stubborn head? You are going to get so sick and tired of my hanging around you that you'll plead and bribe me to go away and give you some space."

"I can't believe you think I'm sexy," she muttered, and he laughed, hugging her.

"Then you'll marry me?" he asked softly.

She nodded. "With the understanding that if you decide you can't take it any longer, that you'll tell me and we'll work out some kind of arrangement."

"You're already building in an escape hatch for me before we're even officially engaged?"

"I'm serious, Craig."

"I don't doubt that in the least, darlin'. It's just one of the many reasons why I love you."

"It's not completely unheard of that you might want to travel again, you know."

"Then we'll do it as a family. I'm not your father, Tess. I won't walk out on you, or die on you like your mother and grandmother did. Let me prove that to you."

Mention of her father brought tears to her eyes and a great deal of pain to her heart. Was that why she felt safer on her own, so that she wouldn't have to trust anyone else?

"Have I ever gone back on my word to you?" he asked.

"No."

"I'm not going to start now." He returned to the stove and began to place food on their plates. "We're going to do just fine together. Wait and see."

Phil and Susan Jamison were the only witnesses to their wedding ten days later. The pastor married them in his study, pleased that they had made this decision.

Susan was bubbling over with suggestions. She wanted to rush out and purchase all the baby furniture they could possibly use. She wanted them to immediately look for a home to buy. She wanted to plan a time for her to come over and help to care for the newborns.

Phil finally had to calm her down, gently pointing out that Craig and Tess appeared to have everything under control.

They flew back to Phoenix that afternoon, Susan still offering helpful hints to the mother-to-be as they were boarding. Tess could only laugh.

"I'm glad you find her amusing," Craig said, escorting her back to the car park. "Can you imagine what she would be like if they were still living next door? She'd probably be knocking on the door each morning to make sure you'd taken your vitamins and milk."

"I've known your mother as long as I've known you and I have never seen her this excited."

"I know. It was the thought of twins that put her into orbit. You would think they were the first pair ever to be born."

"She also seemed to be relieved that we decided to get married."

"I know."

He put her into the car, then walked around to the driver's side. "Well, Mrs. Jamison," he said, once they were away from the airport, "What would you like to do next on your wedding day?"

"It's been a rather full day. Would it be all right to go home and have an early night?"

"Are you uncomfortable? Do you think you over-did it today? Are you having any pain?"

"No. Now you're beginning to sound like your mother, Craig."

"Heaven forbid."

"Let's just have a quiet evening at home."

She was already half-asleep when he walked out of the bathroom and crawled into bed without saying anything.

"Craig?"

"Mmm?"

"We're married now."

"Did you think it might slip my mind?"

"You don't have to hug that side of the bed any-more."

"I thought you were tired."

"I'm not that tired."

He reached out and pulled her into his arms. As soon as she touched him she realized how aware of her he was. His heart was racing and his body radi-ated heat. "What a faker you are," she whispered, amused. "Pretending to be so nonchalant about to-night. Obviously your body is anticipating some-thing." She touched his rigid length and giggled.

"I've grown used to the condition. It set in permanently a couple of months ago."

"You never said anything."

"No."

"I'm glad."

"That I didn't say anything?"

"That you want me. I thought that I was no longer appealing to you."

"If you were any more appealing, I'd explode, which is still a very real possibility."

She turned to him, pressing herself against him. "Let's see if I can remember any of those things you taught me last spring."

From his reaction, she seemed to have remembered quite well.

The sound of a door quietly closing pulled Craig from a deep, satisfying sleep. He opened his eyes and peered at his watch. It was a little after five. Daylight was on the horizon but it was much too early to think about getting up.

He'd gotten used to Tess leaving their shared bed around this time each morning. Mother Nature definitely had her way when a woman was pregnant.

He doubled his pillow, propping himself up, waiting for Tess to return to bed. When she opened the bathroom door a few minutes later, he smiled at her.

"I'm sorry. I didn't mean to wake you."

He held out his arm to her. "Doesn't matter. Come here, you, and let me hold you. It's much too early to get up."

She eyed him warily. "You're certainly in a good mood this morning." She carefully lowered herself back into bed, then relaxed against his shoulder with a contented sigh.

"It's amazing how a good night's sleep can put a fella into a terrific mood. I haven't slept so well in months." He placed his hand possessively over her protruding stomach, still smiling.

"Oh? You always looked like you were sleeping all right to me. What was wrong?"

"Oh, I was probably asleep but my erotic dreams definitely disturbed my rest. Now I can admit it. Being in bed with you and not touching you was sheer hell."

"You're the one who set those rules, you know."

"Would you have let me stay here with you without them?"

"I don't know, to be honest. Things were happening a little too fast for me about that time. You may not have noticed but I was feeling a tremendous amount of pressure."

"Oh, I noticed," he replied with a grin.

He rubbed her shoulders, turning her into him even more so that he could stroke her back, kneading the muscles in the lower back area. He was rewarded with a soft crooning sound from Tess.

"I've been afraid to offer to rub your back for fear you'd think I was using that as an excuse to get my hands on you."

She looked at him, her eyes wide. "Me? Suspect your sterling motives? How could I possibly do that?"

Her teasing was greeted with a kiss that grew rather lengthy and provoked him into forgetting about the back rub.

Their lovemaking was lazy, full of exploration and discovery without being rushed. He loved bringing Tess to peaks of pleasure, basking in his power to provide her with these passionate gifts. He'd never known that the act could be so enthralling when he was with someone he loved as much as he loved Tess.

He would never tire of expressing his love to her and for her.

Later that morning, after a leisurely breakfast, they went out to work on her garden. While he was diligently pulling weeds away from her blooms, Craig asked, "Did you ever think about us being together like this when we were growing up?"

Tess sat back on her heels and adjusted her wide-brimmed sun hat. "If I ever did, I must have forgotten it by the time I was grown. You were always my favorite person when we were growing up, though. I suppose that should have been some kind of clue."

He helped her to her feet and they sat down on the lounge chairs arranged on the small, covered patio.

He poured them each a glass of iced lemonade. "I was sitting here thinking about the communication system we had at one time. Do you remember it?"

She laughed. "Of course. You strung twine from your bedroom window to mine with a bell attached to either end. Whenever we wanted the other's attention—"

"We'd pull on the twine. Yeah. I hadn't thought about that in years."

"I wonder why it never occurred to us that the phone would have worked just as well. Remember all the elaborate hand signals we had to use?"

"I remember I used to be teased by my buddies for teaching you some of our codes."

"You were always taking up for me."

"I thought I was supposed to. After all, you were just a girl. You couldn't help it, of course. You needed a rugged male to protect you."

She leaned over and poked him in the ribs and he laughed. "Too bad no one was protecting me from you!"

He took her hand and held it. "I want you to know that I'm not sorry about the way things have worked out. Maybe I wouldn't have wanted to settle down years ago, but we're both older now. We've each made a life for ourselves. I think we bring a great deal to this relationship. Just think of the stories we'll be able to tell our children."

"You've almost got me convinced, Craig. Maybe things do have a way of working out for people, after all."

Chapter Six

"Craig?"

"Mmm."

"Something's happening."

"What? What is it?"

"I think my water broke."

"Oh, no. It's too soon. You can't be going into labor. It's—"

"Maybe you'd better call the doctor. His number is by the kitchen telephone."

Craig raced downstairs and made the phone call. By the time he returned she was sitting up in bed. "He said he'd meet us at the hospital."

They stared at each other in dismay.

"I've got to change my gown. And I'm going to need something to stop this—"

"Hang on. I'll get it." He disappeared into the bathroom and was soon back. Then he found her another gown. "Do you have a bag packed?"

"No. I didn't think I'd need one just yet."

"Don't worry. I can always bring you something." He lifted her gown over her head, dropped the dry one over it, found her robe and wrapped her in it, then for good measure, placed the comforter around her as well.

"I'll carry you to the car."

"You've got to be kidding. You aren't going to be able to get your arms around all of this."

"Sure I will. Just watch." He scooped her up as though she weighed nothing, tucking the comforter around her before going down the stairs.

Craig fought to stay calm as they drove to the hospital. Luckily at that time of night, or early morning, there was little traffic. He pulled up at the emergency entrance and said, "Stay right there. I'll be right back."

"Don't worry. I'm not going anywhere."

The medics soon appeared with a rolling stretcher. They eased her out of the car and onto the stretcher. Once inside Craig gave admitting information at the desk while they wheeled Tess into one of the examining rooms.

When Craig went to look for her, one of the nurses stopped him.

"They've taken your wife upstairs to the OB ward, Mr. Jamison. The doctor is already there." She gave him directions to that floor.

When he stepped off the elevator, he looked around for the nurses' desk and explained why he was there. They pointed him to the waiting room.

"You don't understand. I'm supposed to be with her. I'm her coach. If she's actually going into labor I've got to be there."

"The doctor will be with you in a moment, Mr. Jamison. Please wait in there until he can speak with you."

Craig looked around the stark waiting room with its blank television, stacks of magazines and well-worn furniture. It was almost four o'clock in the morning. Much too early to call his parents. Besides, he had nothing to tell them at the moment.

He sank into one of the chairs. What seemed to be hours later, but in fact was less than fifteen minutes, her doctor appeared in the doorway wearing surgical scrubs. Craig recognized him from the last few visits when he'd driven Tess.

"It's too soon for the babies, isn't it?" he asked, immediately moving toward the door.

"We'll see, but we don't have much of a choice but to go ahead now. We're going to have to do a caesarean."

"Is she going to be all right?"

"She's hanging in there. Of course she's upset, but that's to be expected."

"What caused her water to break? Was it something we could have prevented?"

"No, not at all. These things just happen, sometimes."

"I thought I'd be with her through this part of it."

"Unfortunately that isn't possible. I'll be back to discuss everything with you as soon as I know more."

He nodded, then headed back through the swinging doors that led to the delivery rooms.

Craig had never felt more helpless in his life. Or more scared. He wanted to be with Tess. He wanted to reassure her that everything was going to be okay, even when he wasn't certain he believed that, himself.

He'd had six months with her. Only six months. That wasn't enough time. Look at all those years that he could have been with her and hadn't been.

He kept seeing her as that little girl with her hair in a ponytail, her front teeth missing. If anyone could pull through this, Tess could. She was a fighter. She'd show everybody.

And the twins? Could they survive such an early birth? He wanted them so much, but not at the expense of losing Tess. He couldn't imagine his life without her. She was just now beginning to trust that he loved her and would always be there for her.

It had taken him a long time to convince her of his total love and acceptance of her. As she steadily grew in size, she'd been adamant that nobody could possibly find her attractive. And yet she was absolutely beautiful, like a rose at full bloom, ripe and voluptuous.

They'd found a house they wanted in an older part of Pasadena. It had been built in a time of gracefulness and spaciousness. They had discussed terms with the owners, a couple who were retiring and who wanted to move closer to their children.

Craig explained about the twins and that it was too near Tess's time to consider a move immediately. Because there wasn't a compelling reason for the older couple to leave right away, they agreed to postpone the closing until after the twins were born.

What would he and Tess do if something happened to the twins? Their lives had revolved around that notion for six months. He thought he had Tess convinced of his sincerity about staying there with her. But if she lost the babies, would she remember that? Or would she think that he would want his freedom?

Freedom was what he'd always prized. It still was. Freedom meant different things to different people. In his case, it was his choice to curtail his photo-taking assignments and to remain with Tess.

He could no more imagine a life without Tess in it on a daily basis than he could imagine life on another planet.

Craig could not sit still. He walked down the hallway and found a coffee machine. He tried not to think about all the possibilities. Instead he concentrated on a successful conclusion to this harrowing night.

Almost two hours passed before the doctor reappeared. He looked as though he'd been through a marathon race, but he was smiling.

"Is she all right?" were Craig's first words.

The doctor nodded. "All of them are doing as well as can be expected. I think we're going to be able to pull the girls through. They're small, but all their signs are good."

"Girls?"

The doctor held out his hand. "You've got a household of girls. You'd better get used to lace and ribbons."

Craig laughed, elated. "Are you kidding? If they're anything like their mother, they'll be demanding footballs and track shoes!" He felt almost giddy with relief. "Can I see Tess now?"

"I'm afraid not for several hours. She's in recovery. We won't place her into her room until she's fully conscious."

"Does she know about the girls?"

"Not yet. We'll tell her as soon as she comes around." The doctor glanced at his watch. "You've got time to get a few hours of sleep before she'll be able to have company. Why don't you go on home?"

Craig took his advice, since it was less than fifteen minutes away. As soon as he got home, he called his parents, alerting them to the news. Then he fell across the bed and crashed, needing to deal with the idea that their wait was over. He was asleep in minutes.

"Have you seen them?" Tess asked as soon as he stepped into her room.

"You bet. Boy, does that one have your temper. She's letting everybody know that she isn't at all happy about the way things are run in there." He leaned over and kissed her. She looked pale, but her eyes were bright and her smile made him think of a child on Christmas morning.

"Oh, Craig. Where did you get the flowers?"

He glanced down at the delicate arrangement. "At the florist's downstairs. You had to have something to remind you that you're now a mommy." He placed the flowers beside the bed.

"Have you decided on names, yet?"

"Not really. We've talked about so many."

"How about Tiffany and Crystal?"

She arched a brow. "Sounds like a couple of burlesque queens."

"Come to think of it, that's probably where I first heard them," he replied, grinning.

She shook her head. "You're hopeless, you do know that, don't you?"

He took her hand. "All I know is that I've never been so scared in all my life than I was over this deal."

"Me, too. They're so small, Craig."

"But healthy. The doctor's reassured us on that one." After a moment, he said, "Is there anyone you want me to notify at your office?"

"That's okay. I can call from here. It will be fun surprising everybody with the news."

"The doctor said you're going to have to take it easy since you had surgery. You're not going to bounce back quite as quickly as you planned."

"It doesn't really matter. After all, I've got a husband who's going to pamper us. You've done a good job of convincing me that you can take care of us."

"Will wonders never cease? Does this mean that the self-reliant Tess Cassidy has officially tossed away all her reservations about hanging on to her independence? Gee, I must have done something right."

"You have. You've taught me about the kind of dad I never had. My girls are very lucky to have you in their life."

"Then you won't care if I teach them how to take photographs and wander the world with me looking for the next great shot?"

"Not as long as I'm along for the trip."

"Never fear, my love. I wouldn't want it any other way."

* * * * *

Dear Reader,

Once upon a time I gave birth to four sons in seven years. Looking back to that time in my life, I can summarize how I felt in one word: outnumbered.

I'd been raised an only child. Boys had always seemed to me to be a strange species filled with boisterous rowdiness. I've never had reason to change my original opinion.

In retrospect I realize that my sons taught me as much as I taught them. Seeing them today, I'm amazed that these four men were ever grubby little boys, demanding all of my time and attention, completely stealing my heart away in the process.

Motherhood is an ongoing process. The role changes as needs change. Of all the things I've been in my life— student, wife, mother, secretary, teacher, singer, actor, and author—being a mother was by far the most demanding.

I wouldn't have missed it for the world.

Annette Broadrick

SOUL MATES

Ginna Gray

Chapter One

"Bob and Susan are going to adopt a baby."

"Mmm."

A beat later, Jack Riley looked up from the papers he was studying and stared across his desk at Caroline Smithson. She sat curled in the corner of the leather sofa on the other side of his study, going through the day's mail. "What did you say?"

"Bob and Susan are adopting a baby."

"You've got to be kidding."

"Nope. We got an announcement. They say their son, Kevin, has added so much to their lives that they want to experience the joy of parenting to its fullest, and since Susan is unable to have more children they've decided to open their home and their hearts to a needy orphan.

"They're adopting a Eurasian baby girl named...mmm, let's see." Caroline scanned the joyously worded message again. "Ah, here it is. Kim Lee. She's two months old, half American and half Korean. She'll be arriving at Houston Intercontinental Airport next Thursday evening at seven. According to this, Bob and Susan would like for all their friends and family to be there to help them welcome their new daughter into their family."

"I don't believe it. I had lunch with Bob just yesterday. He never mentioned a word about it."

"I guess they wanted to surprise everyone."

Caroline stared at the pale pink card, aware of a strange sensation in her chest—an achy knot that sat just beneath her breastbone and made breathing difficult. Why, she wondered, was she so affected by the announcement? Why did she suddenly feel all teary and emotional? It wasn't like her.

"All I can say is they must be gluttons for punishment." Jack shook his head, dislodging the unruly black lock of hair that habitually tumbled over his forehead. He absently raked it back and returned his attention to the blueprints on his desk.

"Oh, I don't know." Caroline felt compelled to add. "You have to admit, Kevin is a darling little boy. And you always seem to enjoy being around him."

"Yeah, he's an okay kid. Now. But just give him a few years. One of these days he'll be a teenager and a royal pain in the butt. Then see if you think he's so sweet. The main reason I can have fun with the kid now is because he's theirs and not ours. When we go home, he stays with Bob and Susan."

The statement sounded flippant, even cold, but Caroline knew the pain that was behind it, and she gazed sadly at Jack's bent head. It wasn't that he didn't like children. He simply did not want to risk subjecting them to the kind of childhood both of them had endured.

She agreed with him totally. Even so, she could not let the matter drop.

"That's true. Still... they certainly don't seem to mind." What on earth was wrong with her? It wasn't as though she were pining away for a family of her own, God forbid.

"Yeah, well, that's because they're still living the fantasy."

"I suppose you're right."

Determined to shake off her maudlin mood, Caroline had replied briskly, but something in her voice must have captured Jack's attention. He looked up again and frowned.

"Of course I'm right."

Rising, he came around the desk and sat down beside her on the sofa. He put his arms around her, tipped her face up and smiled tenderly into her eyes. "I'm just glad that you and I never bought into the myth of marriage and children and all the baggage that goes with it. Look at us. We've been together for six years. We're proof that you don't need a piece of paper to be committed to each other. Right?"

"Right," Caroline agreed, but she knew her smile was wan. What was wrong with her? Of course she agreed with him. Completely. Their shared view on the folly of marriage was one of the things that had drawn them together in the first place.

They had both learned that lesson from their parents' frequent matrimonial mistakes. To date, be-

tween them, her parents and Jack's had already gone
through a total of eighteen marriages. Each time the
parent involved had fervently declared that this was
"the one," a match made in heaven that would last
forever.

"You don't sound very convinced."

"Oh, don't mind me." She sighed and flashed him
a wry look. "I guess I'm just feeling out of sorts and
ornery."

"Really? I'm sorry. What's wrong, sweetheart?"

Instead of helping, Jack's concern merely depressed her more. She'd been feeling restless for
months—out of sync and vaguely discontent, and the
devil of it was, she didn't know why. And it hurt that
he obviously hadn't even noticed she was not herself.

How could he love her as he claimed and not be
aware that something was bothering her?

Others had noticed. Her partner certainly had. But
then, she and Louise Ritter had been best friends
since high school, long before they opened Ambience and Caroline had met Jack. She and Louise
knew each other inside out.

Even so...she and Jack had been lovers for almost seven years. They had been living together for
six. By now he ought to be sensitive to the slightest
change in her moods.

Caroline experienced a spurt of anger, but before
she could reply he stroked her cheek and murmured,
"Poor darling. I think you've been working too hard.

I tell you what. As soon as I wrap up the Munich project, let's take a week or two off and get away together, just the two of us. How about it?''

His blue eyes caressed her and tenderness softened his roughly handsome features. Caroline gazed at that beloved face and felt the knot in her chest begin to ease. What a foolish woman she was. How could she feel even a moment's discontent when she had Jack?

Had she been able to make a list of the traits and qualities she wanted in a mate and custom order him, no one would have filled the bill as well. He was rugged and strong and so devastatingly masculine at times simply watching him move made her tingle all over. In business he was tough and knowledgeable, relentless when he had to be, but as a lover he was caring and passionate, and a wonderful companion. He had a sharp mind, a wry wit and an ability to laugh at himself, which was endearing.

He was, quite simply, everything to her. From the moment they met they had been perfectly attuned. They shared a spiritual affinity and a physical passion that bound them together like two halves of a whole. It was as though, in each other, they had found all the missing pieces of their lives—love, understanding, companionship. She could not imagine her life without him.

Her annoyance dissipated like smoke in the wind. Smiling softly, she reached up and threaded her fingers through his hair and pushed back the unruly ebony lock of hair that was forever defying control. She savored the feel of those silky strands against her skin, the warmth of his scalp. Even after all this time, touching him still brought a rush of pleasure so intense it made her warm all over.

"Oh, Jack," she murmured, loving him with her eyes. "You always know how to make me feel better. I can't think of anything I'd like more than to go away with you."

"Good. Why don't we sail the *Free Spirit* down to Mexico?" He brushed a soft kiss over her mouth, then her cheek. "We'll lay on the beach and drink Margaritas." He nuzzled her neck, and she closed her eyes and sighed, tipping her head to one side to give him better access. "Make love beneath the moon," he continued in that same, sexy murmur. The tip of his tongue traced a line from her shoulder to her ear, and a delicious shudder rippled through Caroline. "And in the ocean." His breath filled her ear, hot and moist and arousing. He nipped her lobe, then drew it into his mouth and soothed the tiny pain with a gentle sucking. Caroline moaned and clutched his hair with both hands.

Jack gave a throaty chuckle. "You like that, sweetheart?"

"Yes. Yes!" She pressed closer, desperately seeking his lips. "Kiss me, darling," she gasped. "Please ki—"

His mouth closed over hers, cutting off the fervid plea. The kiss was hot and deep and unashamedly carnal. The leather sofa crackled as they sprawled across the cushions. Small sounds issued from the pair—gasps and moans of pleasure and need, of want and frustration. Hands roamed and clutched, limbs entwined, their bodies strained closer.

Caught in the grip of feverish passion, at first Caroline did not notice the intrusive ringing. Jack raised his head and looked around, momentarily disoriented. She gave an anguished cry and tried to pull his head back down.

"No. No, let go, sweetheart. The phone—"

"Don't answer it."

"I have to. It might be important." He dropped a quick kiss on her lips. "I'll be right back." He pried her hands loose from his neck and bounded off the sofa, leaving her lying disheveled and bereft.

"Yeah, Riley here," he growled into the receiver. "Oh, hi, Melissa. What's up?"

The name hit Caroline like a dash of ice water. She closed her eyes, and struggled to catch her breath as she ground her teeth and mentally cursed the woman. As usual, Melissa's timing was impeccable. If Caroline hadn't known better she could almost believe Jack's assistant had bugged their apartment.

After a moment she sat up and straightened her clothes, and watched Jack. He sat perched on the corner of the desk, jotting down notes, the telephone clamped between his shoulder and jaw. His shirt was pulled out of his trousers and unbuttoned, the wrinkled tails hanging open around his hips, revealing a wide chest dusted with dark, silky curls and a rock-hard belly. His black hair stuck out in all directions where she had run her hands through it, but he didn't seem to notice. The woman on the other end of the telephone line held his undivided attention.

Melissa Atkins had been a thorn in Caroline's side ever since Jack had hired her. Blond, beautiful and brainy, she exuded a ruthless self-confidence and sex appeal. At twenty-five, she was eight years younger than Caroline.

Jack thought she was wonderful. Efficient, hard-working, smart, she had proved invaluable as an assistant, and he sang her praises constantly.

Caroline didn't trust her. Not an inch.

Melissa was ambitious and manipulative, the type that would stop at nothing to get what she wanted. Caroline didn't believe that Jack had any romantic interest in Melissa—not yet, at any rate—but Melissa definitely had her sights set on Jack.

As with most men when it came to conniving women, he was oblivious to the subtle jabs and sneers that Melissa sent her way. On the few occasions when she and Melissa had been alone, his assistant had not bothered to disguise her contempt for Caroline, nor her intention, but in his presence her manner was scrupulously cordial and businesslike. Only another woman would recognize the double meaning behind her polite words.

Caroline received the message loud and clear: Melissa Atkins wanted Jack Riley, and she intended to have him. She'd also made it clear that she did not consider Caroline a threat.

It did no good, however, to talk to Jack about the problem. God knows, she'd tried. At first he laughed off the idea. Caroline was imagining things. Melissa was his assistant, and a damn good one, nothing more, he'd insisted. When she had persisted, however, he'd gotten angry.

Just the week before when she'd complained about the woman's attitude they'd had a lulu of a fight—the worst they'd had in all their time together. Realizing she was playing into Melissa's hands, Caroline had vowed never to make that mistake again. Normally Jack was an excellent judge of character, but where Melissa was concerned he seemed to have a blind spot.

Caroline drummed her fingers on the arm of the leather sofa and cleared her throat. Jack didn't notice. Now and then he muttered a comment, but Melissa was doing most of the talking. Caroline waited for him to end the conversation, but when he gave no sign of doing so after twenty minutes, she stood and quietly left the room.

Propping her elbow on her desk, her chin in her palm, Caroline sighed. Though faint, the melancholy sound was full of despondency.

Louise Ritter looked up from the bundle of fabric swatches she was examining and frowned. "Don't tell me you're still depressed?"

"What?" Caroline blinked and gazed at her friend and partner across the elegant room that served as both the design center and office of Ambience, the interior decorating firm they had built together. "Oh. No. No, I'm fine."

"Don't give me that. This is me you're talking to, remember? You've been in a funk for weeks. I've been waiting for you to tell me what's bothering you, but I'm fresh out of patience, so just spit it out."

Despite her melancholy, the statement caused a faint smile to twitch at Caroline's mouth. As usual, Louise was as blunt as a sledgehammer. Patience and tact had never been virtues to which her friend could lay claim. That she had held her tongue this long was something of a miracle in itself.

Louise was wrong about one thing, though. This mood hadn't begun a few weeks ago; it had been creeping over Caroline for months now, robbing her of her concentration and sapping her energy.

She sighed again. "To tell you the truth, I don't really know what's wrong with me. I've just been feeling . . . I don't know . . . restless, I guess. Sort of, well, discontent." She spread her palms wide in a helpless gesture. "I don't even know why I'm so down, but I can't seem to shake the feeling."

"Mmm." Louise looked at her steadily, her mouth pursed.

"It's silly and stupid, I know. I have everything anyone could ask for—a loving relationship with a wonderful man, a successful business, good friends, financial security, good health. There is absolutely no reason for me to feel blue."

"There must be something bothering you, or you wouldn't be so down."

"Well . . . lately Jack and I—" Abruptly she waved her hand and shook her head. "Oh, never mind. It sounds so trite when you say it out loud."

"What? *What?* C'mon, Caro, you can't just start something and then stop like that. Spit it out."

"It's just that . . . the magic seems to have gone out of our relationship. There, I told you it would sound stupid. Satisfied?"

"Hey, it's not stupid. That sort of thing can be a real problem." Louise fiddled with the paperweight on her desk, then sent Caroline a cautious sidelong look. "Uh, are you saying there's trouble . . . you know . . . in the bedroom?"

"No! Not that. Not at all." Hardly, Caroline thought. Jack's desire for her had not waned in the least. Their sex life was as lusty and satisfying as ever. That was the one thing that was right about their relationship. "It's just that lately it seems that he's been taking me for granted. He is completely wrapped up in the Munich project."

"Humph. Is that all? Heck, that's not so surprising. Or unusual. After all, Jack is in charge of building that factory. He's always put in long hours when working on a big project for his company. It's never bothered you before."

"I know. But this time it's different. It's like he barely knows I exist. Even when he's home, he's working. If I didn't keep him company in his study, I'd never see him. He used to be so attentive, so attuned to my every mood, but for the past few months he's been so preoccupied he hasn't even noticed that something is bothering me.

"And then there's Miss Hot-to-Trot Atkins," Caroline added sourly. "He spends more time with her than with me these days. The woman never misses an opportunity to be with him. And I swear, I think she makes up excuses to call him at home."

"Boy, you do have a bad case of the 'poor me's,' don't you?" Louise rose from her desk and walked over to stand in front of Caroline's with her hands on her hips. "As far as Miss Hot Pants is concerned, you have only yourself to blame if she steals Jack right out from under your nose. After all, he is a single man."

Caroline shot her a stern look. "Don't start, Louise."

Her friend shrugged. "I'm just stating facts. You and Jack aren't married or even engaged. As far as Ms. Atkins is concerned, that makes him fair game."

"Maybe so, but Jack loves me. We're committed to each other."

"Caro, you know that I like Jack, but he's a virile, good-looking devil, and it's not all that unusual for a man to get itchy when a couple has been together for as long as you two have. Especially when a young, beautiful woman makes a play for him. He loves you, but still, when temptation presents itself, in the back of his mind, sitting there like a little escape clause, is the knowledge that you're not married."

"Well, thanks a lot. That really makes me feel better."

"I'm just trying to make you wake up and face reality."

"You're wasting your time. Jack and I are just fine the way we are."

"Look, just because—"

The front door opened, and both women looked up as their former receptionist, Stephanie Baker, walked in.

"Steph. What a nice surprise," both women said in unison.

"Oh, look, Caro. She brought the baby."

"Hi. Actually, Amy and I just came from getting our six-week checkup, and since we were in the neighborhood, I thought I'd drop by and show you how much she's grown."

Laden with a voluminous diaper bag, a huge purse and a baby carrier, Stephanie looked as though she was about to topple over. "Here, let us help you."

Louise, the original Earth Mother, made a beeline for the baby and scooped her up out of the carrier. Caroline lifted the huge bag off Stephanie's shoulder and nearly staggered. "Good grief! What's in this thing? It weighs a ton."

Stephanie laughed. "Just the bare essentials. You would be amazed how much paraphernalia is required to care for a baby."

"Oh, aren't you just the most precious thing," Louise cooed. "Caro, look. She's adorable."

Caroline doubted that. She and Louise had visited Stephanie at the hospital following the birth. The baby had been red, wrinkled and as scrawny as a plucked chicken. Caroline had dutifully complimented the young mother and said all the right things, but privately she had wondered how anyone could go gaga over such an unappealing scrap of humanity.

Stepping closer, she peered at the pink-and-white bundle in Louise's arms, and received a shock. The baby had filled out into a beautiful little cherub with chubby cheeks, a rosebud mouth and the biggest, most beautiful dark blue eyes Caroline had ever seen.

"Oh, my," she whispered. "Why, she's...she's perfect." The baby fixed her with an unblinking stare, and Caroline felt an odd warmth steal into her heart. Golden fuzz covered the baby's head and her fingers were the size of matchsticks. Unable to resist, Caroline reached out and stroked her cheek then those tiny fingers. Her skin was warm and as velvety soft as rose petals.

With amazing speed, the infant's tiny hand wrapped around Caroline's finger. "My goodness. Her grip is so strong."

"I know." Stephanie smiled at her daughter with motherly pride. "When she grabs hold of something you have to pry her loose."

"Here, why don't you hold her, Caro," Louise suggested.

"What? Oh, no. No, I wouldn't know how. I might hurt her."

"Nonsense. You'll do fine. Here." Louise stuffed the infant into Caroline's arms before she could back away. The baby fixed her with that unblinking stare that seemed to look right into Caroline's soul.

"Why don't you hold her up against your shoulder? She might need to burp," Louise advised, and Caroline shot her a terrorized look. "Oh, go on. She won't break."

Cautiously she lifted the baby to her shoulder, one hand cupped around the tiny bottom, the other splayed over her back and the base of her head. Flaying her little fists, Amy made a gurgling sound and burrowed close.

Caroline caught her breath. A sweet pressure swelled her chest and made her feel warm all over. She wanted to cry and laugh at the same time.

She hadn't realized how tiny a baby was, how helpless, how incredibly soft and warm.

Obeying an urge she didn't understand, Caroline stroked the downy head with her fingertips and snuggled her face against the baby's neck. She sighed and closed her eyes as the wonderful smell of baby filled her senses. Her heart ached and her throat grew so tight she couldn't speak.

"You know, Stephanie, if you change your mind and want to come back to work, your job is waiting," Louise said. "We haven't found anyone to fill the position yet."

"Thanks, Mrs. Ritter, but I don't think so. I've got the most important job in the world already, taking care of Amy. It's a little tough, making ends meet on just one salary, but Dave and I agreed that it's best for Amy to be cared for by her mother. Speaking of which, I'd better run. By the time I get home it will be time to nurse her."

Caroline reluctantly surrendered the infant to her mother. She was surprised at how empty and cold her arms felt without that squirming little bundle.

When they left Caroline returned to her desk, but instead of working she stared out the window at nothing in particular. Why, she wondered, did she feel so odd?

Several seconds passed before she realized that Louise was standing in front of her desk, watching her with a cat-that-ate-the-canary look on her face. Caroline raised one eyebrow. "What?"

"I've changed my mind."

"Oh? About what?"

"It's not Jack's neglect or Miss Hot Pants' poaching that's giving you the blue devils. The problem is, your biological clock is ticking."

"*What?* That's the most preposterous thing I've ever heard."

"You wouldn't say that if you could have seen your face when you were holding Amy. You want a baby, and you want it bad. If you had a lick of sense you'd marry Jack and start a family, before it's too late."

Panic fluttered through Caroline. As a result her voice was sharper than she intended. "Don't be ridiculous. I'm not in the least maternal. Even if I were, marriage is out of the question. You know how Jack and I feel about that. Of all people, we know that so-called 'wedded bliss' is a crock. Jack's mother is currently married to her fifth husband and his father has been married and divorced four times. As we speak, my own mother is honeymooning in the Caribbean with husband number six. Who, I might add, is eleven years her junior."

"What about your dad? Charley certainly seems happy, and he and Alma have been married for twenty-three years."

"Ah, yes, Dad. The third time does seem to have been the charm for him, doesn't it?" Caroline drawled, shooting her partner a dry look.

Caroline had always been much closer to her father than her mother, but her love for him did not blind her to his faults.

"You're so cynical. There are plenty of successful marriages around. Take Roger and me, for instance. Hitched ten years, two kids and I love the big lug more every day."

"Yes, well, you and Rog are the exceptions."

Louise huffed and rolled her eyes. "I don't care what you say. I know you, Caroline Smithson. Regardless of your background, and this stupid agreement that you and Jack have, you want what most women want...a family of your own—a husband, a baby or two, a house in the suburbs with a swing set in the backyard, maybe even a dog, the whole she-bang. The trouble is, you're too scared to admit it, so you're trying to pretend that something else is getting you down."

"Oh pul-leeze. *Me?* That's absurd."

"Uh-huh. So you say. But how are you going to ignore that sound?"

"What sound?"

Smirking, Louise leaned across Caroline's desk and said softly, "Tick. Tick. Tick."

Chapter Two

Over the next several weeks Caroline told herself that Louise was wrong. The very idea was ridiculous and totally off the mark, merely another of her friend's misguided attempts to steer her toward the altar. Louise was happily married, therefore she thought everyone else, especially her closest friend, should be as well.

What she ought to do, Caroline told herself, what she fully intended to do, was forget the whole thing.

That, however, proved impossible. She found herself thinking about Louise's theory constantly. She would be browsing through a bundle of upholstery swatches, or studying a customer's floor plan, or haggling with a supplier, and the next thing she knew her mind had wandered off to babies and wedding rings.

It didn't help that every time she got anywhere near Louise, her friend would get that sly smile on her face and whisper under her breath, "Tick. Tick. Tick."

Dammit! She was happy with the arrangement she and Jack had, Caroline staunchly repeated over and over. They were the envy of everyone who knew them, for heaven's sake! They had it all—a loving relationship, success in fascinating careers that they loved, good health, a fabulous apartment, even a luxurious forty-foot cabin cruiser. Unemcumbered by children, they had the time, money and freedom to enjoy an idyllic life-style. Only a fool wouldn't be happy in her shoes.

It didn't help. Finally, deciding it was time for a sharp reminder of why she had always avoided marriage, Caroline took her father out to lunch.

Punctual, as always, Charley Smithson arrived at the restaurant before she did. "Hi, Dad. Sorry I'm late."

He rose at her approach, and Caroline's heart swelled with pride and love. Still slender at sixty, with his silver hair and blue eyes and rugged masculine features he was Paul Newmanish handsome. He was also one of the sweetest men she'd ever encountered. She had never been able to understand why her mother had left him for someone else. Lilah seemed to be one of those pathetic women who measured her own worth by how many men she could attract and to deny her advancing years by seeking out younger and younger companions.

"Hi, pumpkin. How's my favorite daughter?"

Caroline shot him a wry smile and took the seat he held out for her. "I'm fine. And since I'm your only daughter, your only child, for that matter, that's not much of a compliment, you know."

"Ah, well, beautiful as you are I'm sure Jack gives you plenty of those. How is he, by the way." A slight edge entered her father's voice at the last. He liked Jack a lot, but he was old-fashioned about some things, and he had never reconciled himself to their living arrangement.

"He's fine. Working hard right now on the electronics factory in Munich." The waiter handed them menus and rattled off the luncheon specials, then discreetly faded away. "How is Alma?" Caroline asked while perusing the menu.

"Right as rain." Her father's face softened noticeably when he talked about his third wife. Alma was short, plump and motherly, and her father adored her.

"She's volunteering today at the hospital, otherwise she would have joined us. She sent her love, though. And said I was to tell you that she'd like for you and Jack to come for dinner one night next week. She wants you to call her."

"I will. That would be nice." Caroline liked her stepmother, but she was glad Alma hadn't joined them this time. She needed to talk to her father alone.

"So how is Lilah?"

"Fine, I guess. She's still sailing the Caribbean with her child groom. You know..." She batted her eyelashes and imitated her mother's breathless gush, "Robbie, darling."

"Now, Caro, don't be snide. Maybe this time she really will find happiness."

"Maybe," she agreed grudgingly, but she wasn't going to hold her breath. Had her mother been in town, Caroline would have gotten a reality check by taking her out to lunch. In the marriage department Charley Smithson was a piker compared to his first wife. Lilah Smithson-Grant-Webster-Adamson-Hewlitt-Collins-Robakowski had made a career out of getting married. Still . . . her father had been to the altar three times himself.

The waiter returned and took their order. The moment he left her father took a sip of wine and smiled at her over the rim of the glass. "Speaking of happiness, when are you and Jack going to get married and give me a grandchild or two?"

Caroline looked up sharply and narrowed her eyes. "Has Louise been talking to you?" Though her father's feelings on the subject of her and Jack were no secret, he rarely addressed the matter directly or prodded her in any way. Given the state of her emotions lately, this was just a bit too uncanny for coincidence.

"She may have mentioned that you were feeling down, lately."

"And, I suppose, she also told you her little theory as to the reason," Caroline said huffily. Just wait until she got back to the office. She was going to tear a strip off Louise.

"Would that be such a bad thing?" he asked gently. Reaching across the table, he took her hand and patted it, his eyes warm. "Louise is your friend, sweetheart. She's concerned about you. And I happen to think she's right."

"Well, you're both wrong. I have no desire to get married. Or have children." She felt suddenly teary and tried to hide behind flippancy. "Heavens, I learned that lesson watching you and mother. Why would I want to mess up my life that way?" she said with a little chuckle and an airy wave of her hand.

"I was afraid you felt that way." His hand squeezed her tighter. "Caro, sweetheart, not all marriages are doomed. Just look at Alma and me. We've been married twenty-three years."

"But before that you had two failures."

Her father frowned and shifted uncomfortably. "Sweetheart, listen to me. I don't want to blame your mother, but I won't pretend I understand what drives her. All I know is I loved her very much, and I was hurt and angry when she ran off with another man. I should never have married Nancy, especially not so soon after Lilah divorced me. It was unfair to her and stupid of me. My only excuse is my pride had taken a beating and I guess I was trying to strike back at your mother. But when I met Alma I knew I had found the right woman.

"Just as Jack is the right man for you. Please, Caro, don't deny yourself happiness just because your mother and I made mistakes. Marriage with the right person can be wonderful. Take it from me, I know."

Her father's words touched something deep inside
Caroline. She tried to dismiss the advice. She told
herself he was just being a protective father, that she
didn't need the traditional trappings. She was con-
tent with her life exactly as it was.

The more she tried to convince herself, however,
the more unhappy she became. Eventually the avowal
rang false, even to her own ears, and she was left with
no choice but to do some honest soul-searching.

Was she truly happy?

She and Jack had been living together for six years.
On the surface they had the ideal relationship. God
knew, she loved Jack Riley with all her heart. He was
her soul mate.

Yet Caroline could no longer ignore the truth; in
her heart of hearts, she felt incomplete. Something
was missing. Something vital.

Was it possible this undefined need that gnawed at
her constantly was for something as ordinary as a
husband and a stable family of her own? Even though
she knew, firsthand, just how difficult that was to
achieve?

The very idea scared her witless. She tried to reject
it, but she could not. For one thing, she couldn't forget how she'd felt holding Stephanie's baby. A sweet
rush of emotions, like nothing she'd ever experienced, had run through her in a warm flood. How
profoundly moved she had been just to cradle that
tiny human to her breast. And Amy wasn't even hers.

How much more acutely would she be affected by a child of her own?

Also, replaying over and over in her mind was Stephanie's comment that raising a child was the most important job in the world. It was true, Caroline realized with a sense of wonder. She found the enormity of that truth both daunting and exciting. She couldn't help but think that if her own mother had felt the same how different her childhood might have been.

Over the weeks following Stephanie's visit to Ambience and the lunch with her father, it seemed to Caroline that suddenly everywhere she looked there were babies. Or pregnant women. Or married couples who looked, not just in love, but truly happy with one another.

When shopping in department stores she always seemed to wind up in the infant department, gazing with undeniable longing at lacy little dresses and tiny booties.

The first thing she turned to when reading the newspaper was the pictures of engaged or newly married couples. Once, a picture and small article about a couple celebrating their fiftieth wedding anniversary filled her with such choking emotion she had to leave the room before Jack noticed. She had locked herself in the bathroom and wept, though for what, she could not have said. Not then.

Gradually, however, Caroline came to a painful acceptance. Though she and Jack claimed they were committed to each other, deep down in the core of her being, she didn't truly feel secure. She didn't feel a sense of permanence, a sense of being half of an unbreakable whole.

Whenever she closed her eyes and tried to imagine them together, as they were now, in twenty or thirty years, she could not, and that frightened her.

They loved each other, but they hadn't enough faith in the permanence of that love to defy the odds and make those solemn vows, before God and the world, that would bind them together as life partners.

Caroline was not a naive romantic. She knew full well that wedding vows did not keep a couple together, but it was that lack of faith in their love that ate away at her.

Finally she could no longer deny the truth: Louise was right. Her biological clock was ticking loudly, and she could no longer ignore it. She wanted marriage and a family and all the traditional things that went along with them.

The question was, could she convince Jack to want the same things?

Caroline stewed over the problem for three days before she worked up the courage to broach the matter to Jack. Her hands were sweating and her stomach felt as though it were tied in a knot when she entered their apartment that evening, but she was determined to get her feelings out in the open. Now that she'd made up her mind, she was conscious every minute of time inexorably slipping away, and a sense of urgency consumed her.

"Hi. I'm home," she called, and winced at the nervous quiver in her voice.

"Back here," Jack answered.

Caroline closed her eyes for an instant, then drew a deep breath, crossed her fingers and headed down the hall toward their bedroom.

"Jack, there's something important I wa—"

She stopped cold in the doorway. "Where are you going?"

Jack looked up from placing a stack of shirts in one of the suitcases spread across their bed. The ever-present and endearing errant lock of hair dangled over his forehead. With his necktie and collar loosened and the sleeves of his white dress shirt rolled up he looked so devastatingly masculine Caroline's heart gave a little bump.

"Munich. We've got a problem at the site."

"When are you leaving?"

He straightened and glanced at his watch. "My flight leaves in just over two hours."

"Two *hours!*"

"I know. I'm sorry, sweetheart. I hate to leave you in such a rush, but this is important."

"But . . . but I need to talk to you about something, Jack. It's important, too."

"Okay. Go ahead. I can talk and pack at the same time." Detouring by the door, he bent and bestowed a quick but stirring kiss on her lips. His eyes caressed her warmly when he straightened. "But hurry, will you? I'm hoping to squeeze in enough time for a proper goodbye before I leave," he murmured with a lecherous glance at the bed. He smiled and chucked her chin, then strode to the dresser and scooped up a stack of underwear from a drawer.

She watched him recross the room, panic tightening her chest. "Jack, this is not something I want to rush. This is serious. It's something we need to sit down and discuss thoroughly."

"I'm sorry, darling, it's either now or when I get back. Unless you want to talk about whatever this is over the telephone."

"No. No, I don't want that." She sat down on the edge of the bed, and watched him disappear into the closet, a feeling of despair edging in on her. She didn't want to put this off. Now that she'd made up her mind, she was anxious to get it all out. "How long will you be gone?" she asked when he emerged carrying an armload of suits.

He dumped them on the bed and began to fold one of the coats with his usual quick efficiency and neatness. "Oh, about six weeks. Two months, tops."

"Two *months!* You've never been gone that long at a stretch before. Not even on jobs much bigger than this one."

"I know. But Melissa pointed out that by the time I get this problem settled, we'll be about ready to wrap up the project, and I need to be there for that. It would be pointless for me to fly home for a few days, then turn around and fly right back."

Caroline clenched her jaws. *Melissa*. She should have known.

"So what is it that's got you so wound up? You look tense, sweetheart."

Caroline twisted her hands together in her lap. She had no choice but to tell him now. She couldn't possibly wait two months. She'd burst if she tried.

"Jack, I...I don't know any other way to say this but to come straight out with it."

He glanced her way as he placed the last of the suits in the case and frowned. "Sounds serious. Is something wrong?"

"No. At least...I hope you won't think so. I..." She sat up straighter and unconsciously squared her shoulders. "I want us to get married."

"What?" He couldn't have looked more stunned if she had suggested they jump out the window of their ninth-floor apartment. "You *can't* be serious."

"I am. Very serious."

"Good grief, Caroline. Why? We agreed years ago that neither of us wanted to make that mistake. Why would you change your mind now?"

His tone was harsh and exasperated. Caroline felt the knot in her stomach squeeze tighter. "For several reasons," she replied, powerless to control the quaver in her voice. "For one thing, I love you and I want to be your wife." Her chin began to wobble, and she had to stop and press her lips together to control it. Tears threatened, and she looked at the ceiling and blinked hard. "I . . . I want to be connected to you in a real way."

"You are!"

"No." She shook her head and gazed at him sadly. "No, I'm not. Not really."

"Caroline, you—"

"And there's another reason." She cut in before he could launch a full-fledged rebuttal. She swallowed hard and forced herself to look him right in the eyes. "I want to have children."

"Good God."

The exclamation came out low and a bit breathless, as though he'd just had the wind knocked out of him. Caroline's hopes sank like a stone in a pond.

Raking a hand through his hair, Jack turned away. She stared at his tense back. She thought she heard him cursing under his breath, and her heart broke a little.

He swung back abruptly and pinned her with a hard look. "This doesn't make any sense. You and I know how meaningless marriage is. How precarious. We've talked about it a hundred times or more. Good Lord, Caro, we both grew up enduring a stream of stepparents, constant squabbling and fighting between our parents and their spouses of the moment.

"That is, when they were there. Hell, I saw more of my baby-sitter when I was young than my parents. Then when I was old enough it was off to boarding school and out of their hair. Your childhood wasn't any better. Do you really want to run the risk of subjecting a child to that?

"And when it's all said and done, what are we talking about, really? A few words on paper that costs you a fortune in attorney's fees to nullify. The result is the adults take an emotional and financial beating, the kids get hurt and the attorneys get richer. Well, no thanks."

His words hit her like a slap in the face. Tears welled in Caroline's eyes, but she raised her chin and struggled to hold them in check. "It doesn't have to be that way. A lot of couples stay married and raise happy, well-adjusted children. To most parents, children are a blessing they would not trade for anything in the world.

"But you obviously expect us to part someday." Her voice cracked on the last and her chin began to wobble even more, but she forced herself to continue. "I never realized that before. Sorry. My mistake."

"Dammit, I don't think any such thing. As far as I'm concerned, you and I are forever. But splitting up is always a risk in any relationship. Highly unlikely in our case, but no matter how small the risk, it's not one I'm willing to inflict on a child. Not now, not ever."

He turned away and started slamming and banging drawers and snatching up items and dumping them into his bags willy-nilly.

"I see," Caroline murmured past the lump in her throat. She stood as still as a statue and watched him stomp back and forth across the room, his face like stone. His image became a blur as tears banked against her lower eyelids and slowly spilled over.

"Then you're not even willing to discuss this?" she asked in a forlorn little voice.

"No. We made an agreement and we're sticking to it."

Caroline winced. She felt guilty about trying to change the rules at this late date, but she couldn't help it. She wanted this. She needed it. "Jack that was six years ago. Things change. *I've* changed."

"Well, I haven't."

"But Jack—"

The doorbell rang, and she groaned. The last thing they needed was an interruption.

"That'll be Melissa." Jack snapped the cases closed and glanced at his watch. "She's half an hour early."

"Early for what? What is she even doing here? I'll take you to the airport. I always do."

"No need. Melissa and I are sharing a cab."

She stared at him in disbelief. Fury began to build inside her. "You mean, *she's* going with you to Germany?"

"Don't start, Caroline," he warned. "I can't deal with your unfounded jealousy on top of everything else right now."

He could have saved his breath. After their last fight over Melissa, Caroline had vowed to keep her suspicions to herself. She couldn't make Jack understand that she wasn't jealous; she simply didn't trust Melissa. This, however, was too much.

"She's never gone out of town with you before. I thought her job was to keep things at the office running smoothly while you were away."

"Normally that's true. But I'll be gone a long time, and Melissa will be a big help to me."

"I'll just bet she will. And let me guess. This was Melissa's idea, too. Right?"

"Yes, but—"

"Good grief, Jack, will you wake up? Can't you see, the woman has her sights set on you?"

"Caroline, stop it." He grasped her shoulders and gave her a little shake. "You're upset and overemotional. I love you. Only you. Melissa is my assistant and a competent professional, and I'm damn lucky to have her, but there is nothing going on between us."

"Not yet. But if she has her way, there will be before you get back from Germany."

His face tightened. Caroline knew he was furious. "I thought you trusted me."

"I do. It's her I don't trust."

"Hell, there's no talking to you on this subject." He released her, snatched up the cases and stalked out. The doorbell rang again as he headed down the hall with long, angry strides.

Caroline darted after him, following right on his heels like an angry terrier. "I don't believe this. You're furious with me for wanting to marry you and have a baby. Yet I'm not supposed to object to you going on a two-month trip with another woman?"

"Melissa isn't another woman, she's my assistant. This is a business trip, not an illicit tryst."

"Ha!" Caroline huffed and planted her fists on her hips. "The woman's a female shark. Dear heaven, why are men so blind?"

"That's enough, Caroline. Hopefully, by the time I get back you will have cooled down. Maybe then we can discuss this like two rational adults."

Before she could respond he jerked the door open.

Surprise flashed across Melissa's perfectly made up face. As usual, not a single blond hair was out of place and she looked chic in a fitted designer suit that showed off a body kept trim and tight by four-a-week visits to a fitness center.

Caroline had never seen her looking any way but exquisite. By comparison, after a long and tiring day dealing with picky customers and inept suppliers, she knew she probably looked as though she'd been jerked through a knothole backward.

Melissa blinked and opened her mouth to speak, but Jack stepped out into the hall, tucked one suitcase under his arm and grasped her elbow. "C'mon. Let's go."

"But, Jack...I came early so we could go over a few things."

"We'll do it on the plane."

"Oh. Yes, of course. Whatever you say." She looked curiously from Jack to Caroline, but she went.

Caroline stepped into the open doorway and watched them, disbelief and despair settling over her like a sodden cape. A few feet down the hallway, Jack halted abruptly, released Melissa and plunked down the cases and stalked back. Without so much as a word, he snatched Caroline into his arms and captured her mouth in a long, angry, but soul-stirring kiss.

When he released her she was so addled she could only stare after him as he stalked back to Melissa. "C'mon, let's go."

Looking back over her shoulder, Melissa aimed a triumphant smirk at Caroline. "Don't you worry about Jack, Ms. Smithson. I'll take good care of him.''

"Jack, did you hear me?"

A few seconds passed before it registered on Jack that Melissa was speaking to him. "What?" Reluctantly he dragged his gaze from the pitch-black sky on the other side of the jet's window. "Sorry. What did you say?"

"Jack, is something wrong? You've been distracted ever since I picked you up. You hardly said two words in the taxi."

Normally he did not discuss his personal life with anyone, but Caroline's bombshell had hit him like a fist in the gut. Her jealous outburst about Melissa hadn't helped, either. He was still reeling, and Melissa's sympathetic expression was a balm. "Caro and I had a disagreement, is all," he muttered. "She wants to get married and have a baby."

"Ah, I see."

He scowled. "I wish to hell I did. I just don't get it. From the beginning we both said we didn't want children or marriage, and she's always been perfectly happy with that. Now, all of the sudden, she does an about-face. This isn't like Caroline."

"I take it you refused to go along with the idea."

"Damn right."

"You know, Jack, this sort of thing is really not that uncommon for a woman Caroline's age. After all, she's...what? Thirty-six? Thirty-seven?"

"She just turned thirty-three."

Melissa arched one eyebrow. "Really. Hmm, I thought she was much older. Anyway, she's probably become aware of her biological clock ticking down and she's panicked that her youth is slipping away."

"Hmm. I hadn't thought of that."

"It's a perfectly normal thing for older women like Caroline. Although, I must say, I'm glad you didn't let her trap you into marriage."

Jack frowned. *Trapped* was not a word he would ever use in relation to Caroline. She was the best thing that had ever happened to him. Hell, if she were shackled to him hand and foot for the rest of his life he wouldn't feel trapped.

Muttering a noncommittal reply, Jack shifted in his seat and returned his gaze to the night sky. He regretted now mentioning their fight to Melissa. That he had made him feel vaguely disloyal.

"What do you mean, you're moving out?" Louise jumped up and stalked across the studio to stand in front of Caroline's desk. Hands on her hips, she glared, shock and angry disbelief all over her face. "Have you completely lost your mind? Good Lord, Caro, when I encouraged you to get married and have babies, I meant with Jack. I thought you would bring him around to your point of view. I certainly never dreamed you would dump him and go out looking for another man to father your children. That's crazy. You and Jack are perfect for each other.''

"I know. But since he refuses to even consider marriage, much less a family, that hardly matters, does it?''

"Well...you caught him off guard, is all. Once he's thought it over he may feel differently. Give the man a chance.''

"I have. He called me when he arrived in Munich, but when I tried to talk to him about it he just got angry all over again and flatly refused to consider it.''

"That's been what...a week ago?'' At Caroline's nod, Louise leaned forward and planted her palms on her friend's desk. "There you go, then. He's had a time to think about it, and if you let him know how important this is to you, I'm sure he'll come around. Jack adores you. He wants you to be happy.''

"That's just it. I want him to be happy, too. I don't want to coerce him into something he truly doesn't want.'' Even if she could persuade him to get married and start a family, which was a very big if, given the lackluster state of their relationship these days, he would be doing it under protest. She didn't want that.

Louise rolled her eyes and sighed. "Are you kidding? I've seen Jack with kids. He'd make a terrific father.''

"I know, but that's not what he wants." A dull throbbing had begun in Caroline's temples. She gritted her teeth and tried to ignore it. "The devil of it is, I, better than anyone, know why Jack feels this way, and I understand and respect his opinion. I simply no longer share it."

"At least promise me that you'll try to work this out with Jack one more time before you do anything drastic."

Giving in to the persistent ache, Caroline massaged her temples with her fingertips. God knew she didn't want to leave Jack; it would be like ripping out her heart. But, she was afraid if they simply continued the way they were and she denied herself her heart's desire, she would end up blaming Jack, perhaps even hating him someday. That would be horrible.

It would be better to part friends now and get on with their lives, while they were both still young enough to start over with someone else.

The thought of Jack with another woman was like a stab in her heart, but Caroline squelched the pain. If she and Jack had to part, she would deal with the hurt then. She didn't have much hope that he had changed his mind, but Louise was right; she had to find out.

With a sigh, she raised her head and met her partner's anxious stare. "All right. You win. I'll try to talk to him about it one more time. He's so busy it's difficult to track him down during the day. I'll call him tonight. It'll be early in the morning in Germany. I'll catch him before he leaves to go to the site.''

Melissa checked her appearance in the mirror one last time and smiled. Perfect. The rose silk blouse and form-fitting skirt were seductive without being obvious. Pulling out the V neckline of her blouse, she spritzed perfume down her cleavage, then behind each ear and on her wrists. Then for good measure, on the backs of her knees. Satisfied, she fluffed her blond page boy, picked up her purse and briefcase and let herself out of the hotel room.

A little frown creased between her eyebrows as she walked swiftly down the hall to Jack's room. If he hadn't been so obtuse, by now they would be cozily sharing a room instead of having the entire width of the hotel between them.

Bypassing the company's travel department, she had personally made their reservations and had requested adjoining rooms with a connecting door. However, when they had checked in and Jack had discovered the arrangement he assumed the hotel had made an error and insisted that they be put on separate floors. However, the only room available had been at the opposite end of the hall from his.

Jack finally answered his door after her third knock. ''Melissa!'' He ran a hand through his messy hair and glanced at the clock on the bedside table. "What are you doing here so early?"

He looked deliciously rumpled and sleepy... and unbearably sexy. Crease marks from the pillow still crisscrossed one cheek and a dark stubble shadowed the lower half of his face. The maroon silk robe he'd hastily put on gaped wide all the way down to the low-cinched belt, exposing a beautiful male chest covered with a mat of black hair and an intriguing mole about a quarter inch to the upper right of his navel. Her fingers itched to delve through the silky thatch and stroke that velvety dot.

She smiled pleasantly. "I thought it would save time if we ordered room service and went over these changes you're putting into the finished work during breakfast." Without waiting for an invitation, she stepped inside, sidling around him, close enough that he couldn't possibly miss her perfume.

"At six in the morning?"

She turned and gave him an ingenuous look. "Oh. I'm sorry, is this too early for you? I'm such an early bird, I sometimes forget that other people aren't. I can come back later, if you'd like."

Jack hesitated, then shrugged and closed the door, tightening the belt on the robe as he walked barefoot back into the room. "No, that's okay. Now that I'm up I couldn't go back to sleep anyway. Just give me a few minutes to shave and shower. While I do, you can order breakfast for us."

"Certainly. Do you have a preference?"

"Make mine two eggs, over easy, and all the trimmings," he called from the bathroom.

A few minutes later she had just hung up after placing the order with room service when the telephone rang.

Melissa's gaze narrowed on the instrument. Only one person would be calling Jack at that hour. Deliberately making her voice husky, she picked up the receiver and murmured a sleepy, "Hello?"

A moment of heavy silence followed, then a hesitant, "I'm sorry. The operator must have put me through to the wrong room. I was calling Jack Riley."

"Wait! Don't hang up. This is Jack Riley's room."

The silence again, longer this time. Melissa smiled. "Miss Smithson? Is that you?"

"Yes," came the dull reply.

"I'm sorry, Jack can't come to the phone right now. He's in the shower." Melissa glanced at the closed bathroom door. From the other side came the sound of water running. "I am glad you called, though. I want to thank you."

"Thank me? For what?"

"For pressing Jack to get married and start a family. It was just the push he needed to make the break and do what he's been wanting to do for months."

"And that would be?"

"Why, turn to me, of course." She waited a beat to let that soak in, then added. "I'm very grateful. By the way, that mole just above his belly button is delicious, isn't it."

With a quiet click, the telephone went dead.

Chapter Three

With Louise's reluctant assistance, Caroline moved into her new apartment the next weekend. All she took with her, other than her personal belongings, were a few dishes, the furniture from the guest bedroom and a chair from the living room, all of which she intended to return as soon as the new furniture she had ordered was delivered. When they had unpacked and stowed everything the place looked empty and forlorn.

"This is downright depressing," Louise grumbled, looking around. "You sure you don't want to change your mind? We could take it all back and Jack would never know."

"No. I've made up my mind. This is for the best."

Louise sighed, but she didn't argue. She knew Caroline too well for that. When she decided on a course of action she saw it through.

They both knew it had been Caroline's strength, her determination and grit, that had allowed them to make a success of the business they had started on a shoestring ten years before. Many times in those early years, Louise would have given up and thrown in the towel had it not been for her. They were the same traits Caroline called on to solve her current dilemma.

Parting with Jack was the hardest thing she ever had to do, but it was necessary—for both their sakes. The simple truth was, they had come to a point in their lives where their desires and needs had taken separate paths. It hurt—oh, how it hurt—to know that he had turned to someone else without being open and honest with her, but she knew that anger sometimes clouded judgment. And Jack had certainly been angry when he left—and, in all honesty, she supposed he'd had every right to be. She, after all, had been the one reneging on their agreement.

Even though her heart was breaking, she had no intention of standing in the way of Jack's happiness. Nor would she let him stand in the way of hers.

Caroline and Louise spent the next hour clearing the apartment of boxes and packing material and cleaning up. The sudden ring of the telephone just after midnight made both women jump.

"Good heavens," Louise exclaimed, fluttering her hand over her heart as Caroline headed for the telephone. "If that's Roger tell him I'm on my way."

"Hello."

"Hello, sweetheart."

Caroline's voice frosted over and her hand tightened around the receiver. "Hello, Jack."

"Jack!" Louise exclaimed in a loud whisper. "Uh-oh. It's going to hit the fan now."

"Thank God, I finally caught you at home. Where've you been? I've been calling you every day, at home and at Ambience, but you're never at either place. And you never called me back. Didn't you get the messages I left with Louise?"

Oh, yes, she'd gotten them all right...and promptly tossed them into the trash. "Sorry. I've been busy."

A beat of silence followed. "Caro? Is something wrong? You sound...different. You're not still upset over that little disagreement we had, are you?"

"It hardly matters, one way or the other, does it?" she replied in the same cold voice. *Little* disagreement? That *little* disagreement changed the course of her life. Jack's, too. He just didn't know it yet.

"Of course it ma—"

"I'm tired, Jack. I really don't feel like talking. Besides, shouldn't you be getting back to Melissa?"

"Ah, c'mon, Caroline," Jack groaned. "Don't start that again." She could almost see him shaking his head and grinding his teeth. "Dammit, I didn't call you long-distance to fight."

"Then perhaps we should hang up."

"Okay, I get it. You're still angry. Fine. When you get over your pout, give me a call."

He hung up before she could reply, but as she returned the receiver to its cradle with more force than necessary she muttered, "Don't hold your breath."

"How did Jack get this number so fast?" Louise asked, watching her with a worried expression. "What did he say? Was he furious?"

"He doesn't have this number. I'm having the calls to our apartment forwarded to this phone."

"Then, he doesn't know yet that you're leaving him?" Louise rolled her eyes when Caroline shook her head. "When, pray tell, do you plan to tell the man?"

"I'll explain everything to him as soon as he returns. There's no point in telling him now. He's in the middle of wrapping up a major project. He doesn't need any more problems at the moment. Besides, he's got Melissa, so what does it matter."

"Caro, are you absolutely sure there's hanky-panky going on there? Maybe there was a perfectly legitimate professional reason for her being in Jack's room that morning."

"At six in the morning? While he was in the shower? Oh, please."

"Well...there could have been," Louise persisted, but her sulky voice lacked conviction.

"Oh really? And what about Jack's tummy mole? I suppose there's a perfectly logical and professional reason why she would know about that, too."

"Sure...well...maybe. Oh, I don't know. My point is, this seems a cold way to end a seven-year relationship."

"Not at all. This is perfect. When Jack and I got together we promised each other that if at anytime either of us wanted out, for whatever reason, we would make the break quick and clean, and it would be amicable—no recriminations or anger or arguments.

"When he returns the whole thing will be a fait accompli. By then I will have established myself as a single woman and gotten on with my life and he'll discover he's free to make whatever changes in his that he wants. No mess, no emotional turmoil, no lingering regrets on either side. Don't worry, he'll accept my decision without a fuss. With Melissa in the picture, he'll probably be grateful."

Louise snorted. "Yeah, right."

After living seven years as half of a couple, adjusting to the single life wasn't easy. It was, Caroline discovered, downright depressing.

Word of their breakup spread fast among their friends and acquaintances. With the exception of a handful of people, she told everyone that the parting had been a mutual and amicable decision. Everyone was shocked. Most, it seemed, had thought of them as the perfect couple.

Several unmarried friends volunteered to help her ease back into the swing of things. One night she went with two of them to a singles' bar but she stayed less than an hour. She had never seen so many people working so hard to convince themselves they were having a good time. The atmosphere of manic desperation and false gaiety saddened her, and not even under pain of death would she have gone out with any of the men who approached her.

Another well-meaning friend invited her over for dinner to meet her cousin Harry, an accountant. He was a nice enough man, but he had the personality of a mud fence and at forty-one he still lived at home with his mother.

A single man in her building asked her out but something about him made Caroline nervous—he was too eager, too friendly too soon. She could easily picture him turning into a stalker.

She went to church socials, museums, parties, wine tastings, a ski weekend for singles. Once, she even went to a Laundromat, an experience that weeks later still made her shudder to think of it. Nowhere did she meet anyone who remotely measured up.

"You know what your problem is, don't you?" Louise commented when Caroline finished one of her laments on the single scene. "You're comparing every man you meet to Jack. Face it, Caro, not many men can measure up to a hunk like that."

It was true, Caroline realized. While not male-model handsome, Jack possessed rugged looks and a potent masculinity that drew stares from women. An intensely sexy and sensual man, he was also intelligent, articulate, warm, thoughtful and even tempered—unless provoked. Then he exploded with a wrath that made grown men quake.

Louise was right: Jack Riley was going to be a hard act to follow. But surely there was someone out there who could. Caroline refused to believe otherwise.

However, five weeks after moving into her own apartment, she was no closer to meeting someone with whom she might possibly build a future than she had been the first day. It was depressing. She was beginning to think she might have to consider going to a sperm bank in order to have the child she wanted so much. Half a dream was better than none, after all.

A few well-meaning friends offered to fix Caroline up with blind dates but she declined. She wasn't that desperate. Not yet.

In all that time she had heard nothing from Jack, but that didn't surprise her. When he bowed his neck the man was mule stubborn. He was so sure she would reconsider and call him.

Caroline knew Jack too well to believe he would two-time. He probably had the brush-off speech he intended to give her ready. No doubt, he placed the blame for their breakup on her shoulders, she thought sourly.

Keeping her anger whipped up helped her deal with the pain of losing Jack, but it did not banish it completely. She missed him terribly—missed seeing that rugged face, that untamable lock of hair dangling over his forehead, missed touching his sandpapery jaw at the end of the day, running her fingers through his black hair, missed the deep rumble of his voice, the smell of him. She even missed the clutter of his masculine accouterments on the bathroom counter, and having to put the toilet seat down a dozen times a day.

Most of all, dear God, how she missed making love with him.

When the yearning got too strong she reminded herself of why she was putting herself through this torture. She could have Jack, or she could have a family, but not both. She had made her choice, and though her heart ached, deep down Caroline knew she had made the right one. Even without Melissa in the picture, she would still have made the same decision.

"I can't believe it," Melissa enthused. "We're almost finished, and we're coming in ahead of schedule. Everything is up and running. Just a few more days of testing and the factory will be operational and we turn it over to Cyber-Tech."

"Um," Jack grunted, and pushed through the front door of the hotel. He strode across the lobby to the desk, barely aware of Melissa at his side, almost trotting to keep up.

He retrieved a stack of messages from the desk clerk and began going through the slips of paper on the way to the elevator, his frown deepening when he failed to spot Caroline's name on any of them. Dammit, he hadn't heard a peep out of her in five weeks. This wasn't like Caroline to hold on to anger this long. Wadding the messages, he stuffed them into his trouser pocket. Dammit. He'd had enough of this.

He left the elevator and stalked down the hall to his room. Inside, he marched straight to the bed, sat down on the edge and reached for the telephone. He hadn't realized that Melissa had followed him inside until she spoke.

"For heaven's sake, Jack, did you even hear what I said?"

He looked around at her and frowned. "Melissa. What're you doing in here? I thought you were going to your room."

"I am. But first I wanted us to make some plans."

"What kind of plans?"

"Well, first of all, I thought tonight maybe we could celebrate the end of the project with a cozy dinner and dancing."

"Dancing?" He raised his eyebrows, then shook his head. "I don't think so."

"Oh. I guess you're tired. Well, then, how about this. We have some free time while the testing is being done. Why don't we book a trip?" Smiling seductively, she stepped closer and ran her fingertips along his shoulder and down his bicep. The look in her eyes invited. "We could travel around Germany, just the two of us, see the sights, maybe stay in a romantic castle. What do you say? It would be fun. I promise you."

Jack's eyes narrowed. He shifted on the bed, breaking contact with that exploring finger. "Sorry. I can't."

Melissa's expression changed instantly from coaxing to sulky. "Why not?" she whined.

"Because those are the kinds of things I only do with Caroline."

"Oh, for heaven's sake! Caroline, Caroline, Caroline! I'm sick to death of hearing that name. There are other women in the world, you know. I've been trying to call that to your attention ever since you hired me. I thought this time together would finally open your eyes, but for five weeks you've been so preoccupied over your little argument with Caroline you don't see what's right under your nose."

Jack got to his feet slowly. He stood with his hands on his hips and studied her. "My God. Caroline was right about you all along. You are trying to seduce me."

She gave her blond hair a defiant toss and raised her chin. "What if I am? What's wrong with that? It's not as though you and your precious Caroline are married or anything." Her expression underwent another rapid change, and she stepped forward, pouting prettily, and placed her palms flat on his chest. "You and I will be terrific together, Jack," she murmured in a husky, hot voice. "I promise."

She started to slide her hands up over his shoulders, but Jack caught her wrists and pushed her away. "Go pack your things, Melissa. You're flying back to Houston on the first available flight. As of this moment, you're no longer on my staff."

"*What!* You can't fire me! I'll...I'll sue you for unlawful dismissal if you even try it."

"I'm not going to fire you." Stepping around her, Jack went to the door and opened it wide. "But I am going to transfer you to another department. Effective immediately upon your return to the home office. Now please leave."

Melissa hesitated only a moment, just long enough to catch that implacable glint in his eyes.

With another toss of her hair, she puffed up like a toad and stomped past him. She was so angry she looked ready to explode.

"Oh, by the way, Melissa," Jack said in a silky voice. She halted a few feet down the hall and cast a sullen look over her shoulder. "I'd be careful about threatening to sue if I were you. Just remember, sexual harassment runs both ways these days."

It took Jack forty-nine hours to shake loose from the Cyber-Tech project and fly back to Houston. Technically he should have stayed in Munich for the formal ribbon cutting and transfer ceremony, but for weeks he'd had a gut feeling that something was wrong at home. The scene with Melissa had only served to increase his uneasiness.

He landed in Houston a little before six, and it took another hour to clear customs, retrieve his bags and get a taxi home. The instant he let himself in the front door he knew he'd been right to worry. There were no lights on and there was an unnatural silence in the apartment. Something was definitely wrong.

Jack flicked on the entryway light, then the ones in the living room. "Caro? You here?"

The sound of his voice seemed to echo through the apartment, mocking him. Where was she? Had she gone out with friends or a client? Maybe she was working late at Ambience.

Jack glanced into the living room and frowned. Something wasn't quite right there, but he didn't waste time ferreting the work out exactly. Maybe she had fallen asleep when she got home from work. He strode down the hall, turning on lights and calling, "Caroline? Caroline, where are you?"

Just inside their bedroom he jerked to a stop and stared across the room at the dresser. His heart began to boom. The top of the polished cherry-wood piece of furniture normally held Caro's jewelry box and her collection of perfumes. The heavenly, feminine scents coming from that collection of cut-crystal atomizers were a sensual delight that he had always found provocative and arousing. Now the dresser top was empty.

Slowly his head swiveled, taking in the rest of the room. Not a single item belonging to Caroline was in sight.

Clenching his jaws, Jack stomped across to the gigantic walk-in closet they shared and jerked the doubled wide doors open. His heart boomed harder, as though it were going to bludgeon itself right out of his chest. Caroline's side of the closet was empty. All that was left were a few empty hangers and a torn dry cleaner's bag lying on the floor.

She was gone. Caroline had left him.

A vicious pain sliced through Jack. Following hard on its heels was fury.

"The hell she has," he growled as he spun and stalked out of the room.

Twenty minutes later he burst through the door at Ambience, sending it crashing back against the wall. Louise nearly jumped right out of her chair.

"Jack!"

"All right. Where is she?" he demanded after one quick glance at Caroline's empty desk.

"I . . . uh . . . she, uh . . . that is . . ."

"Spit it out, Louise."

"She, uh . . . she we-went home early to get ready for a da— Uh, for an appointment."

"And just where is 'home' for Caroline these days?"

"Well . . . I'm not sure I should—"

"Give it to me, Louise. Now!" He banged his fist on her desk to emphasize the last, and Louise jumped and quickly scribbled the address on a slip of paper.

Jack snatched it out of her hand and whirled around without a word.

Wide-eyed, Louise watched him stomp out. She flinched when the door crashed shut behind him. "Whooie, Caro, are you ever in for it now."

Chapter Four

A blind date. Caroline groaned. Oh, Lord, what had she been thinking? She couldn't believe she had actually agreed to go out on a blind date. The act of the truly desperate.

Caroline grimaced at her reflection in the mirror as she slipped her earrings on. "It's going to be a disaster. You know that, don't you? In six weeks you haven't met anyone you would give a second look. What on earth makes you think your friends can do any better? This is pathetic, Caro. Really pathetic."

Her date was Lester Killibrew. She rolled her eyes. Heaven help her, even his name sounded nerdy.

The doorbell rang, and Caroline jumped. She pressed her palm to her abdomen. Oh, Lord, she felt nauseated.

Gritting her teeth, she headed for the front door. Before she could get there the bell rang again. Oh, great. The impatient type.

She paused in the small entryway, drew a deep breath and pasted a smile on her face. Then she reached for the knob. "Good eve— *Jack!*"

"Yes, Jack." Before she could stop him or even think, he stepped inside, took the door from her nerveless hand and slammed it shut with enough force that it banged against the frame like a pistol shot. Caroline jumped and took a step backward. Jack advanced, his head thrust forward.

"Now, my darling. Would you care to explain just what the bloody hell is going on?"

He was angrier than Caroline had ever seen him. Fury darkened his face and a muscle jerked and quivered along his clenched jaw. Low pitched and rough, his voice reminded her of the ominous rumble that precedes an earthquake. Had he been a man prone to violence, Caroline would have been terrified.

As it was, she was so uneasy she felt as though she were about to jump right out of her skin.

That did not, however, prevent a burst of joy from swelling her heart. She gazed at that beloved face, fierce now and tight with rage, and wanted to cover it with kisses. Her fingers itched to smooth back that inevitable dangling curl over his forehead, to winnow through that thick shock of hair and explore the warmth of his scalp.

His scent tantalized her, dark and musky, and uniquely Jack. Like the moon's inexorable pull on the tides, his body drew hers. Between them, from the moment they met, there had always been this magnetic attraction, and neither time nor rage nor all the intellectualizing in the world could diminish it. Every cell in Caroline's body quivered. She had to grit her teeth and curl her hands into fists at her sides just to stop from flinging herself into his arms.

However, no matter how glad she was to see him, she was not about to let him barge in and steamroll over her. Jack was a take-charge, dominant man. It was his nature to assume command. The only way to prevent that was to stand toe-to-toe with him.

Caroline stuck out her chin. "I should think that's obvious."

"All that's obvious is I leave for a few weeks, and out of the blue, you pack up and move out of our apartment. No explanation, no discussion, no nothing. You didn't even have the decency to tell me you were leaving, much less why!"

"I told you why. I want to get married and have a baby. You made it clear both times I tried to talk to you about it that I couldn't expect either of those things from you."

"That's it? This nonsense about motherhood and happily ever after? That's the reason you left me? I don't believe this! Have you gone nuts? You're willing to throw away what we have for marriage and diapers and a home in the suburbs?"

Caroline's chin went up another notch. "It isn't nonsense. And there's also the matter of Melissa."

An odd look flashed across his face. "Look, about—"

The doorbell rang. Jack whipped his head around and scowled at the wooden panel. "Who the hell is that?"

"That's, uh...well...that's probably my date."

His head snapped back. "Your *what?*"

He didn't wait for a reply. Taking a quick step to the door, he jerked it open.

"Beat it!" he barked, and slammed the door in the man's face.

Caroline caught only a glimpse of a bouquet of flowers and a startled expression. "Jack! What do you think you're doing?"

"I'm doing the guy a favor."

"This happens to be my—"

The bell rang again, and his scowl darkened.

"I'll get it. Jack, don't you dare—"

Ignoring her, he snatched the door open again and thrust his face into that of the other man. "Listen, you. Either you get out of here right now under your own steam or I'm going to beat the living hell out of you and throw you out. Got it?"

"Wh-who *are* you?"

"I'm Caroline's lover. And I don't share what's mine. Now hit the road."

Lester Killibrew looked shocked and flustered, but he gamely glanced over Jack's shoulder and caught Caroline's eye.

"Ms. Smithson?"

Color flooded her face. Wincing, she gave him a chagrined look. "I'm terribly sorry about this Mr. Killibrew. Honestly I am. But...well...perhaps it would be best if you do as he says."

"Are you going to be all right?" he asked tentatively, which Caroline thought was very sweet, given the fact that Lester was a good five inches shorter and at least fifty pounds lighter that Jack.

"Yes. I'll be fine. Don't worry."

Looking unconvinced, Lester shifted from one foot to the other. Finally he attempted to hand Caroline the bouquet, but Jack blocked the move. Jutting his face forward until his nose was barely an inch from the smaller man's, he growled, "Git. Now. And take your damn posies with you."

"Jack Riley, that was the most uncouth, rude, disgustingly overbearing thing you have ever done!" Caroline raged the instant he turned from slamming the door in Lester's face for the second time.

Ignoring the scathing reprimand, Jack launched an attack of his own. "So this is what you've been up to while I've been gone. While I've been missing you and working my buns off just so I could get back sooner and patch things up between us, you've been trolling for a husband to replace me. Just how many men have you been out with in the past six weeks?"

"That's none of your busi—"

"How many?" he roared, and Caroline jumped.

She clasped her hands together to keep them from trembling and raised her chin. "Actually...Lester was the first."

"And he's damn well going to be the last."

"Now see here, Jack Riley—" she began, but he stomped past her and into the living room.

In the middle of the floor he stopped and raked a hand through his hair. "Damn. I should have known you wouldn't let go of this marriage business. Once you get an idea in your head, you're as tenacious as a damn terrier."

He swung back to face her, his expression accusing. "But why this way, Caro? Why didn't you wait and talk to me about this? How could you just move out behind my back? How could you do that to me? To us?"

Caroline chewed her lower lip as guilt flooded her. *Because, God help me, I knew if I didn't you would talk me out of going,* she thought with despair. *The way you've always been able to persuade me to do whatever you wanted.*

"I tried talking to you. Remember?" she said in a shaky voice. "But you wouldn't listen. And you made it clear that you wouldn't change your mind. Since I won't change mine either, I saw no point in prolonging my decision.

"I planned to tell you as soon as you got back. I thought you would call and let me know when you were arriving so I could pick you up at the airport, like always. It was never my intention for you to come home and find me gone.''

"Thanks a lot. Why the hell didn't you just call me in Germany and break the news?'' He snorted and shot her a scornful look. "Hell, I would have thought that would have been the easiest way out.''

Caroline wrung her hands. "I wasn't looking for the easiest way out, Jack. Just the quickest and most painless for both of us. I...I figured you had enough to worry about with the Munich project.''

He went utterly still, as if he were a predator spotting a weakness in his prey. "So...you're saying that even when you were walking out on me you were concerned about me?'' The slow smile that curved his mouth was rife with triumph. "You still love me, Caroline. That proves it. Don't try to deny it.''

"Oh, Jack. Of course I still love you.'' Her voice held a wealth of sadness. So did the look she gave him. "I suppose I'll always love you. This has nothing to do with my feelings for you.''

Instead of discouraging him, he looked even more pleased and started toward her with a seductive smile. Caroline frowned, realizing the admission was a mistake. Show Jack the least vulnerability and he used it to his advantage. She quickly changed tact, resuming an annoyed expression.

"Anyway, I don't know why you're making so much of this. We agreed from the start that if either of us wanted out, no matter the reason, we would be free to leave, no questions asked and no hard feelings.''

That stopped him in his tracks. "To hell with that!" he roared. "I don't give a good tinker's damn what we said six years ago. I'm not giving you up without a fight, no matter what screwy, hare-brained notions you've gotten into your head. I don't know how you could even think for a minute that I would."

"Given your affair with Melissa, it wasn't difficult to imagine, I assure you."

"My *what?* Dammit, Caro, I didn't have an affair with Melissa." He gestured sharply with his hands. "All right. Let's get this business out of the way once and for all. I'll admit, I owe you an apology. You were right. She was on the make. When I finally tumbled to that, I got rid of her. I had her transferred to the Los Angeles office. If I hadn't been worried she would sue the company for wrongful dismissal I would have fired her.

"I'm sorry I didn't listen to you and that you were upset, but believe me, sweetheart, you never had anything to worry about. So can we just forget about Melissa? She's out of our lives and no longer a factor in this situation."

"Jack, please. Don't treat me like an idiot. I called your room one morning at six and Melissa answered the telephone. You were in the shower."

"What? She never told me you called!"

"Yes, well, even if the hour and the circumstances hadn't convinced me, she made sure I knew that you were lovers. She even knew about the mole by your belly button."

"That bitch. That dirty, rotten..." Biting off the vile epithet, he stepped closer, grasped her upper arms and looked her in the eyes, his gaze direct and intense. "Caroline, have I ever lied to you? Have I?" he demanded when she hesitated.

She shook her head slowly. "No."

"Right. And I'm not lying to you now. So get this through your head—I am not having, nor have I ever had, an affair with Melissa. Or anyone else, for that matter. I love you. You're the only woman I want." She searched his face and that intense blue stare and saw the honesty there, and a sweet relief swept through her. "Do you believe me?" he asked finally.

She nodded slowly, her eyes sad. "Yes. I believe you—at least, I believe *you* believe what you're saying."

He scowled. "What the hell does that mean?"

"Just that I think we've grown apart. Lately...I've felt that you don't love me as deeply as you once did—"

"What! That's crazy! Dammit! I adore you, woman!" he insisted in a decidedly unloverlike roar that made her jump.

"Jack, for the past year you were hardly ever around and when you were here you were so wrapped up in your work I could have tap-danced naked on top of your desk and you wouldn't have noticed."

An arrested look came over his face, and she got the distinct feeling he was picturing that scenario. She was certain of it when a glint of wicked amusement softened his scowl ever so slightly. "Believe me, sweetheart, I would have noticed. I would have had you on your back before you completed three steps."

She chose to ignore that. "The point is, you say you love me, but I think you're just used to me. I've become more of a comfortable habit in your life than anything else." Her shoulders lifted in a disconsolate little shrug and she looked away to keep him from seeing the pain in her eyes. "Quite frankly, it occurred to me that, once you got over the shock of me leaving, you might actually be relieved."

"What?" He looked thunderstruck. "Dammit, Caroline, that's insulting! Look, I know the past year has been difficult. I'll admit I've been busy and preoccupied with the Germany project, but I had no idea you would interpret that to mean I was losing interest in you! I don't get it. I've been wrapped up in projects before and it never bothered you. Why now?"

"I don't know. It was just...different this time. You were constantly distracted. And there was Melissa always hovering around. You spent more time with her than with me."

"Ah, I see. You were feeling neglected. And maybe even jealous. That's what this is really all about, isn't it?"

Caroline shook her head sadly. "You really don't understand, do you? Those things were just secondary. Perhaps they provided the push I needed to make the break, but I would have come to the same decision eventually, regardless.

"Jack, I want the white picket fence and the two o'clock feedings and crayon drawings on the refrigerator. I know that you don't want that, and I don't expect you to understand, but I've reached a point in my life where I *need* those things."

"I do understand. You're running up against that biological thing. It's that sneaky, maternal urge that Mother Nature programmed into women rearing its head. But, honey, these yearnings will pass. It's just a temporary thing, you'll see. We'll work through it, Caro. Together. And once we get past it you'll be glad you didn't succumb. I promise you."

"Oh, Jack." Caroline looked at him sadly. "You're so wrong. This isn't some whim that's going to blow over with time. This is a longing so basic and so strong that I can't ignore it. Believe me, I've tried, but it won't go away.

"I want the total commitment of marriage, Jack. And I want at least one child—someone to nourish and cherish and love and mold into a fine human being. Someone who is a part of me. I would like for my baby to be a part of you, too, but since that isn't what you want, I have to find someone else, and I have to do it now. Time is running out for me."

"Come on, Caro. Is having a kid really more important to you than us?"

"Not more important, but just as important. I wanted you and marriage and a family, but I finally realized that I had to choose one or the other."

"So you chose having a kid," he said with unmistakable anger.

"Only because I was afraid that if I didn't, I would always regret it, that I might even end up resenting you, even hating you for it. I didn't want that."

"It would never happen. I wouldn't let it," he said with all his natural arrogance. "Look, I think you've blown this all out of proportion, Caro. You've been upset with me and unhappy and you're letting it cloud your judgment. I'm not going to allow you to throw away what we have together over some illogical, irrational hormone-driven urge."

Irrational and illogical, was she? Caroline's chin came up. "I'm afraid you don't have any choice. I've made the break, and it's final. You and I are through."

"Oh, yeah? Why don't we put that to the test."

She didn't like the sound of that—or the sudden predatory look in his eyes. "What do you me—?" Her eyes widened as he took off his coat and tossed it onto the sofa. "What're you doing, Jack?"

Calmly, never taking his eyes from her, he slipped off his tie and tossed it on his coat, and went to work on the buttons of his shirt as he started toward her. Caroline backed away warily. "Now, Jack, you just stay away from me."

He shook his head slowly, a diabolical gleam in his eyes. "Uh-uh. Not on your life."

Caroline's heart stuttered, then took off at a gallop. She knew that look. It was the same one that he always got when he came home from a trip. Jack was a highly sexed and sexy man, but he was also faithful, and after prolonged periods of abstinence he always fell on her like a hungry wolf, dragging her off to bed the instant he walked in the door.

She backed away another step—two, then three. "Now, Jack, stop this right now."

His throaty chuckle sent prickles racing down her spine. He stalked her as if he were a big, sleek cat, his loose-limbed stride fluid and relentless.

Caroline knew if he touched her she would be lost. Jack could turn her into a mass of quivering jelly with one kiss, or merely a look. Her pride told her to stand her ground and defy him, but she knew a lost cause when she saw one.

She backed into the sofa, and quickly sidled around the end. Jack followed.

"Jack will you listen to reason?"

"When you're willing to be reasonable, yes."

The backs of her calves hit the footstool and she nearly toppled backward. Flailing her arms, she regained her balance and quickly scooted around it to take refuge behind a Queen Anne chair.

Jack kicked the stool out of the way and kept coming at her with that same purposeful stalk, that same wicked gleam in his eyes.

"Jack, this is silly."

"This whole damn situation is silly. That's why I'm going to put an end to it."

"Now, Jack, I'm warning you..." She gripped the back of the chair tightly, watching him closely to see which way he skirted around it, preparing to go in the opposite direction. Her eyes widened and she gasped when he simply grabbed one arm and shoved it aside, sending it tumbling as easily as he had the footstool

Caroline gave a little squeak and turned to run, but she was too late. Jack snagged her wrist and whipped her around, using her momentum to propel her up against his chest and into his arms.

The impact was stunning. The feel of that familiar, masculine body against her softness was heavenly. On principle she splayed her hands on that broad chest and strained against his hold, but in her heart of hearts she knew it was useless. It felt too good already, just being back in his arms, and he hadn't even kissed her yet.

His scent surrounded her, a heady maleness that made her head spin and started a quiver deep inside her. It felt wonderful being held in his arms again. She looked up into those vivid blue eyes, watching her so intently, and felt her heart turn over. It had been six long weeks since she'd seen him, since she'd touched him, and, Lord, she had missed him so.

Immediately she reminded herself that she had better get used to being without him.

She pushed harder at his chest. "Jack, this isn't going to solve anything. Let me go."

"No. Never." His gaze roamed her face, hot and hungry and shockingly possessive. "You and I were meant for each other, Caro, and you know it. I love you now more than ever, and I'll go right on loving you until the day I die." His gaze zeroed in on her mouth, and he tipped his head to one side, bending closer. "You're not a habit in my life, my darling," he growled against her lips. "You're an addiction. One I can't live without."

A moan tumbled from Caroline's throat, part ecstasy, part despair. Jack caught the sound in his mouth as his lips settled over hers.

The kiss seared her all the way to her toes. It was openmouthed and wet and greedy and hot, shimmering with pent-up passions. Caroline could no more have resisted than she could have flown to the sun. With a desperate little whimper, she clutched his open shirt in both hands and sagged against him. She felt as though every cell in her body was melting.

A low sound of satisfaction rumbled from Jack's throat. Tightening his arms around her, his mouth still fastened to hers, he sank with her to the floor.

Caroline felt the soft nap of the oriental rug against her back above the scoop neckline of her dress, against her calves, prickling slightly in the mesh of her stockings. She didn't resist or even question the foolishness of making love on the floor when there was a bed just a few steps away. Her defenses breached, she was as frantic and desperate for him as he was for her. It had been so long, and she had missed him so.

"Oh, sweetheart, I missed you." Jack ground out the words in a guttural voice, echoing her feelings. "I can't get enough of you. I'll never get enough of you."

"I know. I know," Caroline agreed breathlessly. Something niggled at her mind, as her head rolled from side to side in restless passion. Something important she needed to tell Jack, but she couldn't think when he was touching her like that . . .

"I love you, Caro. I need you."

Her eyes opened and a groan slid from her throat as she remembered what it was. Her fingers dug into his shoulders. "Jack . . . Jack, we can't. I . . . I'm not on the pill anymore."

He stilled, and she felt the quivering tautness of his muscles as he fought for control. He raised himself and looked at her. His eyes blazed and his face was flushed and rigid with desire. Breath left his lungs in ragged gasps and his nostrils flared. For an instant she thought he would withdraw from her, and she braced for it, but instead he bit out a vicious curse and growled, "We'll have to risk it. I have to have you, dammit. Now."

"But, Jack—"

His mouth closed over hers, ending the protest, and Caroline was lost. Whatever tiny amount of sanity and willpower she possessed went flying right out the window.

She pulled his shirt free of his trousers and ran her hands beneath it, clutching his shoulders, his back. When her hands encountered his trousers she tried to run her hands beneath the waistband but there wasn't room, and she frantically sought his belt buckle.

In response to her silent quest, Jack rolled with her until they were lying on their sides, facing each other. Sucking in a sharp breath, he went utterly still as her deft fingers dealt with buckle, button and zipper. Slipping inside, her hands stroked over the bulge beneath the white cotton Jockey shorts, then slipped beneath the elastic waistband and cupped him. Jack growled and yanked down the zipper on the back of her dress and unfastened her bra.

In a frenzy of tugging and fumbling, they worked to rid each other of their clothes. Jack managed to work Caroline's arms out of the sleeves of her dress. He climbed to his knees and with a furious yank, he peeled the garment, along with her bra, down her body. In the next instant both went sailing over his shoulder. Moments later her black lacy garter belt and panties followed. The panties floated to the rug with a whisper, but the garter belt landed on a blade of the ceiling fan and dangled provocatively.

Breathing hard, his hot gaze fastened on her, stretched out before him on the exquisite oriental rug, he snatched off shoes and socks and shucked out of his trousers and underwear with one mighty shove.

Then he was there with her, his big body stretching out over her, bare flesh touching, feverish and delicious. Their mouths met in a searing kiss. Caroline made a frantic sound and coiled her arms around his neck. Their bodies strained together, unable to get close enough, both wanting, seeking, needing more. There was a wild hunger raging in both of them, wanton and out of control.

They touched and kissed and stroked until they couldn't stand it a moment longer. "Ah, sweetheart, you drive me crazy," Jack declared in a shaken voice as tremors racked his body. He raised himself partway and looked at her flushed face, his eyes blazing. "Tell me you want me. Tell me."

Clutching him, her nails digging into his taut flesh, Caroline sobbed, "Yes. Yes. I want you. Please, Jack! Hurry!"

Responding instantly to the frantic plea, Jack took her with wild abandon. He thrust deep, loving her with a ferocity and power that bordered on despera-

tion, and Caroline responded with all the pent-up
need and longing that had eaten at her for the past six
lonely weeks, matching his boldness and driving their
passions higher and higher, until they were spinning
out of control.

"Jack! Oh, Jack!"

He raised himself over her on stiffened arms. His
eyes locked with hers. "Could you give up this?" he
growled as he drove her to the brink.

Caroline made a desperate sound and pleaded with
him with her eyes, with her body, but he held back.

"Could you, Caro? Tell me."

"No! No! Oh, Jack, please!"

Jack smiled, a hard, satisfied smile, and took her
with him into sweet oblivion.

A short while later, as their racing hearts slowed
and their breathing returned to normal, Jack lifted up
on his forearms, taking most of his weight from her
body. He cupped her face between his palms and
studied her. "You did mean it, didn't you?" he asked,
needing desperately to hear her say it again.

Her heavy eyelids lifted. She looked at him for so
long, Jack's heart began to thud again. Then she
raised one hand and pushed the dangling curl off his
forehead, smiling a little wistfully. "Yes. I mean it,
Jack," she said quietly.

Jack watched her closely, his chest tight. The admission pleased him immensely, but the aura of sadness and defeat that surrounded her made him uneasy.

Chapter Five

"Well, well, look who's here," Louise said.

Caroline looked up from the stack of invoices she was checking and was surprised to see Jack striding across the showroom toward her. Dressed in a dark blue suit, crisp white shirt and a blue-and-magenta tie he was so ruggedly handsome he took her breath away.

"Well, hi. What are you doing here?"

"Can't I stop by to see my lady if I want to?" Before she could answer he came around her desk, put a hand under her chin and raised her face for a long and thorough kiss.

With exquisite delicacy, his mouth rocked over hers, lingering like a gourmet savoring a particularly fine dish. Slowly his lips plucked at hers, rubbed, pressed. His tongue teased with tiny forays and butterfly touches. The moist warmth of his breath skated over her cheek in little gusts as their breathing picked up speed.

Through it all Caroline gripped the edge of her desk with both hands, so tight her fingers whitened. He was touching her with only those wonderful, wicked lips, but that slight contact sent fire streaking through her.

The outdoorsy smell of his masculine after-shave blended with that scent that was solely Jack, and the combination was devastating. He tasted of peppermint and coffee, a combination to which Caroline had grown accustomed over the years. Jack had a weakness for both.

When at last he raised his head his blue eyes were hot and his smile was a seduction in itself.

"It's about time you two came up for air," Louise grumbled. "I thought I was going to have to throw cold water on you."

Neither of them paid the slightest attention to her.

Caroline sat slumped in her chair, weak as a kitten. She lifted her heavy eyelids and met his seductive gaze and smiled. "That was nice." She ran the tip of her tongue over her lips and twinkled up at him. "Hmm, peppermint."

He smiled and kissed the end of her nose before straightening. "Now that's what I like," he murmured. "That well-loved look."

"Would you two kindly remember that this is a place of business," Louise grumbled, tongue in cheek.

Jack looked at her and winked. "Don't worry, I don't have time for anything serious. I've got an appointment in twenty minutes. I just stopped by to see if Caroline would like to go out to dinner tonight. I thought we'd try that new place on Westheimer. I hear they've got great food and a pretty good combo for dancing.'' He raised his eyebrows and looked at her warmly. ''How about it, sweetheart?''

''It sounds lovely, but...would you mind very much if we skipped it tonight? I'm just not up to it. Maybe we could just order in.''

''Are you still feeling under the weather?''

''No. I'm just terribly tired. I want to go home, have a long hot soak, maybe some Chinese food and sleep for about twelve hours.''

Jack searched her face, a frown creasing his brow. ''Are you sure? You look pale, and you've been feeling below par for over a week now. Maybe you should go to the doctor and get a checkup. Could be you're anemic or something.''

''Nonsense, I'm fine. Just a little tired is all. All I need is rest.''

He didn't look convinced, but after searching her face one more time he nodded. ''Okay. But I'm giving you fair warning, if this keeps up, I'm taking you to the doctor myself. And I'm sitting in on the diagnosis, too, so don't think you can pull the wool over my eyes.''

''All right, all right,'' she said, laughing. ''Since I'm certain I'll feel better after I've had some rest I'll agree to those terms. Now shoo. Go to your appointment, before you're late.''

He bent and kissed her again. ''I'll pick up the food on the way home. See you tonight, sweetheart.''

"So. The honeymoon is still going on," Louise drawled when he had gone.

Caroline smiled and glanced at the bouquet of flowers on her desk. Jack had sent them the day before for no reason at all except, according to the card that came with the bouquet, to say that he loved her. "Yes. It appears so."

"I'll say one thing, when you flew the coop you woke that man up good. Maybe it wasn't such a bad idea after all."

"Except that wasn't why I did it."

"Who cares, when you're getting these results? Hmm. I wonder if it would work with Roger?" Louise appeared to consider the idea, then shook her head. "Naw. If I left him alone with the kids there wouldn't be a stick of my house left standing after six weeks."

Caroline laughed. "Why would you bother? Roger's crazy about you and you know it. I'll bet he makes plenty of romantic gestures."

The comment was mainly to bolster Louise. Personally, Caroline could not picture her partner's ex-pro linebacker husband sending her flowers on an impulse or bringing her coffee to bed or taking her dancing at a romantic little bistro. Roger was a nice guy, but suave sophistication and finesse weren't exactly his style.

"Oh, yeah, like taking out the garbage and bathing the kids when I come home bushed." Louise's expression turned thoughtful. "You know, come to think of it, that is pretty romantic." A wicked gleam entered her eyes. "I think I'll go home tonight and seduce the big lug."

Caroline chuckled, and went back to checking invoices—at least she tried. She had barely gotten started when Louise came over and stood beside her desk. Caroline looked up and found her studying her intently. "What? Do I have dirt on my face, or something?"

"No. I was just wondering. Are you happy with your life, Caro?"

The question caught her by surprise. For an instant, she was tempted to pretend, but this was her dearest friend and confidante. This was the woman who listened to her troubles and shared her joys and was always there when she needed her. Louise deserved the truth.

Caroline's shoulders slumped and a fluttery smile wavered around her lips. She looked at Louise with sad eyes, then looked away into the distance.

"As happy as I can be, I suppose. In some ways I'm very happy." Her gaze strayed to the bouquet on the corner of her desk again, and she smiled wistfully.

In the six weeks since Jack's return from Germany their lives had settled back into the old routine, only now, to his credit, he was doing everything in his power to make up for his previous neglect and show her how much he cared. He was constantly surprising her with flowers and little gifts and thoughtful gestures.

There had been romantic, candlelit dinners on their terrace, cozy Sunday mornings cuddled together reading the papers, weekends on the cabin cruiser. Their lovemaking, always deeply satisfying, was steamier than ever. Except for the dull knot of sadness that seemed to be permanently lodged in her chest, she was happy.

"Jack showers me with love and attention and gifts, and he spends as much time with me as he can. I have to admit, I adore that. And I adore sharing my life with him. But..."

"But you still want babies and marriage, right?"

Caroline's smile was wan. "I guess I'm just greedy. Anyway, I have to accept that it's just not going to happen. I can't give up Jack. I tried, but I just can't. I love him too much."

"Of course you can't give him up. You two were meant for each other. Any fool can see that. I swear, I could just thump that hardheaded Jack Riley."

That roused a weak chuckle out of Caroline. "I'd let you if I thought it would help. I've tried talking to him, but he won't budge. I've finally given up."

"Can you live with that?"

"I don't seem to have any choice."

"Hmm." Louise was quiet for a moment, then she asked, "What's this about you feeling poorly? You never mentioned that to me."

"It's nothing. Don't pay any attention to Jack. He's being a worrywart. I'm just feeling a little tired and washed out lately is all. It'll pass."

"Hmm. You do look kinda peaked." Louise's eyes narrowed, and she studied Caroline intently. "Tell me, do you want to sleep a lot?"

"Constantly."

"Uh-huh. And are you emotional? Do you get teary for no reason?"

"How did you know that?"

"Are your breasts tender?"

"Louise!"

"Are they?"

"Well . . . yes, a little, I guess."

"How about morning sickness? Has that started yet?"

"Morning sickness? Why would I have mor—" Caroline's eyes widened. "Oh, no. You don't mean— It can't be— There was just that one time when I was unprotected."

"Honey, where were you during junior high school sex education class? One time is all it takes."

"No. No, I don't believe it. It would be just too bizarre. And unfair to Jack." She put her hand over her mouth, her eyes going wider still. "Oh, my Lord. Jack. He would be livid." Caroline shook her head vigorously. "No. I am definitely not pregnant. I can't be pregnant."

The next morning, the instant she sat up on the side of the bed, the nausea hit her. There was no time to control it or even to respond to Jack's throaty "Good morning" as he leaned over in the bed and nuzzled her neck from behind. Her eyes widened, and with a moan she shot off the bed and raced for the bathroom with her hand over her mouth.

"What the hell?" she heard Jack growl behind her, but she hadn't time for an explanation. She barely made it as it was.

Seconds later he came tearing into the bathroom and found her on her knees with her head hung over the toilet bowl, retching.

"All right. That's it. I'm taking you to a doctor," he declared as he stepped closer and held her head for her.

"Nooo, I don't need a doctor," Caroline groaned, but the protest had barely left her lips when another powerful wave of sickness rolled over her, and she began to heave again.

When she was finally done she was as weak and limp as the wet cloth Jack used to wash her face, but even as he lifted her from the floor and led her back to the bed she argued. "I'm fine, Jack. Really. It was probably just the Chinese food."

"Uh-huh. Then why am I not sick? Now you just lie there and rest while I call the doctor's office. Then I'll be right back and help you get dressed."

"No, Jack, don't," she protested weakly. "I don't need to see a doctor."

"Tough. You're going. We're going to find out what the hell is wrong with you."

That was exactly what Caroline was afraid of.

Jack looked as if he had been turned to stone. He stared at the doctor across the wide desk, unblinking, every muscle in his body taut. "Pregnant?"

"That's right. Ms. Smithson is approximately six weeks pregnant. The symptoms she's experiencing, while annoying and unpleasant, are not at all unusual at this stage of her first trimester, I assure you. The nausea and the extreme fatigue will pass about the time she enters her second trimester."

"Pregnant?" Jack repeated as though he had not heard a word. "She *can't* be pregnant."

"I assure you, she is."

Caroline sat beside Jack, gripping the arms of her chair, her lips folded together, watching him apprehensively. Conflicting emotions roiled through her as violently as the sickness had earlier. How, she wondered, was it possible to feel so terrible and so happy all at the same time?

On one level, she felt wretchedly guilty, though why she didn't know. She'd tried to warn him that night

he'd come storming into her apartment and arro-
gantly set aside all her plans, but he had refused to
listen.

On another level, she was so thrilled and elated she
wanted to shout. She was going to have a baby. Jack's
baby. She couldn't believe it! It was what she wanted
most in the world. How could she not be happy?

Jack was not. That much was painfully obvious.
He sat in stony silence while Dr. Lawson gave Caroline instructions and brochures on prenatal care and
wrote out a prescription for vitamins.

Jack did not utter so much as a word until they
were in the car, driving home. He wouldn't even look
at her. Miserable, Caroline stared straight ahead, her
hands clasped tightly in her lap. She could not think
of a thing to say.

Neither could Jack. He was too busy trying to come
to terms with the burst of elation and pride he'd experienced when Dr. Lawson had delivered his stunning piece of news.

It had caught him completely by surprise. It wasn't
logical. Once he'd gotten over his shock he'd finally
chalked it up to nothing more than a primitive reaction designed into the male psyche to ensure the con-
tinuation of the species—much the same as Caroline's
ticking biological clock. Viewed in that light, he could
understand it and control it, which eased his mind
somewhat.

That did not, however, solve the problem of Caro's condition. He glanced at her out of the corner of his eye. She was tense and apprehensive. Probably wondering what he was going to do.

Hell, he didn't see that they had any choice. He cleared his throat and gripped the steering wheel tighter.

"We'll get married right away."

That snapped her head around. He could feel her staring at him.

"Wh-what did you say?"

He glanced at her, and felt a stab of concern. She looked so pale and vulnerable. Childbirth was difficult, sometimes even dangerous for women Caroline's age. "I'm assuming that you won't consider giving the child up for adoption or having an abortion."

"No! Of course I won't! I don't know how you can even ask such a thing."

"I was just checking." He would have been surprised if she had. He realized, with a rush of confusion, he would have been disappointed in her also. He hadn't wanted—*didn't* want—this baby, but it was his and he would take care of it. Jack Riley was not a man who shirked his responsibilities.

"Well, I'm having this baby whether you like it or not."

"If that's your decision, then for the child's sake, we'll get married as soon as we can make the arrangements."

"We'll do no such thing." She shot him an appalled look. "I will not trap you into marriage, Jack, and that's that."

"Dammit, Caroline, you're not trapping me. You warned me that you weren't protected, and I wouldn't listen. Although, if you hadn't pulled that dumb stunt of moving out to begin with, none of this would have happened."

"It was *not* a dumb stunt. It was a logical and well-thought-out plan."

"Whatever. The fact remains that I took a chance and lost." His mouth tightened, and so did his grip on the steering wheel. "Now I'll just have to pay the price."

"Well, thank you so much. How charming," she snapped with searing sarcasm. "You can take your noble sacrifice and stuff it, Jack Riley. The answer is no."

"No? For God's sake, Caroline, you've been after me to marry you for months. And now you're saying no?"

"Because you're doing it for the wrong reasons. I *want* to be your wife and have your baby. You don't want either of us, but you'll grit your teeth and marry me because you feel responsible. Well, forget it. I won't be anyone's obligation. And I will not have my child grow up knowing his father resents him. You and I both know what that feels like," she declared, and promptly burst into tears.

Jack was flabbergasted. Caroline had never been a weepy woman. Except for a few sniffles during sappy movies, he couldn't remember ever seeing her cry before, but she was bawling as if her heart was broken. If he hadn't been on the damn freeway he would have pulled over immediately and taken her into his arms.

"Take it easy, Caro. Aw, c'mon, honey, don't cry like that. Please. You're going to make yourself sick again."

His pleas were useless. He wasn't even sure she heard him. Jack checked the traffic in the mirrors, whipped the car through three lanes of traffic, earning a chorus of horn blasts, and exited the freeway at the next ramp.

He pulled into the parking area in front of a strip center on the corner of the feeder street, zipped into a parking slot and switched off the engine. Quickly he unlatched both their seat belts and reached for her.

"Don't! Leave me alone! I don't want you to touch me!" Caro wailed, slapping at his arms. She was so upset she couldn't think. She felt raw and vulnerable and hurt and she hated it! She hated Jack!

"Tough." Hooking his hands under her arms he lifted her over the Jaguar's console and dragged her onto his lap.

She twisted and pushed, but she was crying too hard to escape him. Jack wrapped his arms around her and held her tight against his chest. After a while Caroline gave up the fight and collapsed against him, her fingers curling into the fabric of his shirt as another paroxysm of weeping seized her. She sobbed and hiccuped and her breath hitched with each watery sniff.

"Take it easy, sweetheart," he crooned. "Come on, now." With a hand on the back of her head, he cradled her face against the hollow of his neck beneath his jaw and ran his other hand up and down her back, his movements slow and hypnotic, his murmured words soothing. After several minutes she began to quiet, and she lay still against him except for intermittent shudders, the ragged remnants of spent tears.

"Here." Jack stuffed a snowy white handkerchief in her hand. "Now blow."

Caroline did, noisily. She was in the middle of a particularly loud honk when someone rapped on the driver's window at her back. She jumped and cut loose a choked scream.

"Take it easy, honey." Jack's right arm tightened around her as he pushed the button to roll down the window. Caroline twisted around on his lap and looked right into the bright blue eyes of a policeman.

"Yes, officer?"

"Everything okay here?"

"Everything's under control. My wife's just up-set, officer," Jack said with a friendly smile. "She's expecting, and she's a little emotional."

"Is that right, ma'am? This man's not abusing you, is he? Or holding you against your will? I saw him jerk you out of your seat."

Caroline hastily wiped away her tears with her fingers even as her cheeks flamed. She shook her head. "No, officer. I'm fine. Ju-just a bit up-upset is all," she said over another ragged hitch of breath.

"You sure?"

She nodded. "Ye-yes, sir."

He looked from her to Jack, then touched his forefinger to his hat. "Okay, then. Sorry I bothered you."

"What did you tell him that for?" Caroline demanded the instant the policeman was out of ear-shot. "I'm not your wife."

"You soon will be."

"Jack, I told you, I'm not going to marry you just because I'm pregnant."

"Can you think of a better reason?"

"Yes! Love!"

"Dammit, Caro. You know that I love you more than life itself. And don't you dare start crying again," he ordered with an edge of panic in his voice when fresh tears filled her eyes.

She scrambled out of his lap and back into the passenger seat. Her chin still wobbled but she raised it and shot him a cold look. "That's not why you're insisting on marriage, though, is it? Well just forget it. I can take care of my baby just fine without you."

"I'm sure you can, my sweet, but you're forgetting one thing—this is my child, too. I'm responsible for its conception and I'll be responsible for its welfare once it arrives, and it's damned well going to be born with my name."

"Oh." She looked at him and chewed her lower lip. She hadn't thought about that aspect. She mulled it over a moment, then nodded. "All right. I'll marry you so the baby will have your name, but we'll live apart."

"Wrong again. We'll continue just as we are. At least, until the baby gets here," he added with a grimace.

He started the Jaguar again, reversed out of the parking slot and merged into the traffic headed south on Fannin. "It's true, I don't want this baby," he continued with his eyes on the streaming traffic. "But there appears to be nothing I can do to prevent it from getting here. Its arrival is going to change our lives, and there's nothing I can do about that, either, but I'll be damned if I'll let it rob me of you."

"You don't have any say in the matter. You can't make me stay with you, Jack," she challenged bravely. "And I won't raise a child in a home where it isn't truly wanted and loved."

Jack listened to the edict with tight-jawed anger. He turned his head and jolted her with a sizzling look from those blue eyes. "We'll see."

Caroline did not give up. Jack had known that she wouldn't. When she set her mind on something her tenacity was mind-boggling. Over the next several days he tried everything—reason, pleading, even seduction—but she still insisted that they would have to part once the baby got there. Worried about upsetting her again, he didn't push. The pregnancy had put Caroline's emotions on a permanent roller-coaster ride, and her mood swings concerned him.

After one particularly bad bout with morning sickness, her emotions hit a low ebb, and she suggested that it really would be best if she simply moved out again and got out of his hair. Jack's patience came to a screeching halt.

"The hell you will! You're staying right where you are where I can look after you. Furthermore, we are getting married immediately. No more delays."

He would not listen to any more of her foolish arguments.

The wedding took place three days later, a brief, dismal affair in a justice of the peace office. The only guests were Louise and Roger and Caroline's father and stepmother.

Caroline expected to feel different, to feel somehow like a married woman, but the ceremony was over so quickly and was so impersonal, all she felt was depressed.

Afterward they went to Vargo's for a champagne brunch, mainly for the sake of her father and stepmother. They were thrilled about the marriage, although in an aside, her father had gently scolded her about the hurried ceremony.

"Really, Caro, a justice of the peace? I would have been happy to give you a proper church wedding with all the trimmings. You are my only child after all."

"Don't fret, Dad. This was fine." She kissed his cheek. "The important thing is Jack and I are married, just as you've always wanted."

He beamed. "Yes, that's true. I suppose I shouldn't complain."

Caroline felt guilty for misleading her father. He thought his daughter was at last settled into a marriage to last a lifetime. She didn't have the heart to tell him it was just a temporary arrangement.

Caroline sat through the interminable brunch torn between nausea and heartsickness. Her father and stepmother were so happy. Even Louise and Roger seemed upbeat, though she'd explained the whole thing to her partner.

When she'd told her that she and Jack would be parting after the baby's birth, Louise had merely given her a long, pithy look and murmured, "Oh, yeah, right," and went back to work, with what looked suspiciously like a smug grin.

Finally the brunch was over and, after Caroline and Jack received numerous hugs and kisses and congratulations, plus an unexpected pelting of rice, they all went their separate ways.

Leaning her head back in the Jaguar's buttery leather seat, Caroline closed her eyes and sighed. "Thank goodness that's over."

"Tired?"

"Drained is a better word."

"Did you tell your father about the baby?"

"No, not yet. There's plenty of time for that. He was so happy, I saw no point in ruining this day for him."

Rolling her head to the side, she opened her eyes and gazed at the scenery whizzing by. It took her a moment to realize that they weren't heading back to the apartment.

She frowned and sat up straight. "Where are you going?"

"To the airport."

"What for?"

"So we can catch a flight. We're going on a honeymoon."

"What? Jack, that's crazy. The kind of wedding we had doesn't call for a honeymoon. I'd feel like a fraud. Besides, I don't have any clothes with me."

"Yeah, you do. I packed your bags last night while you were sleeping the sleep of the dead. They're in the trunk. And I checked with Dr. Lawson. He said there was no problem with you traveling. In fact, he thought some R and R would be good for you. Louise assured me she could take care of Ambience by herself for a few days.''

She looked at him, shaking her head. "You've gone to a lot of trouble to arrange this. Why?"

"Because we just got married. Because you need to take a break and rest. Because it seemed appropriate. Because I want to. All of the above. And if you need any more convincing, think about long, lazy days in crystal water and laying in the sun on a white sand beach. Waiters plying us with Bloody Marys, in your case, Virgin Marys. Room service," he added in a seductive murmur.

Caroline groaned. "You convinced me. Where are we going?"

"Antigua. Most beautiful beaches in the Caribbean."

Their hotel room turned out to be a small but luxurious cottage, one of several tucked away among the tall palms and gardens adjacent to the main hotel.

"This is gorgeous." When the bellhop left, Caroline rushed to the French doors and threw them wide. From the private terrace she could see lacy whitecaps lazily rolling in to the shore and the glowing moon reflecting on the surface of the water. The palm trees were undulating purple shadows against a star-bright sky. The waves swished against the sand, and from somewhere farther to the left by the main hotel, she heard the faint strains of a steel drum band.

Coming to stand behind her, Jack slipped his arms around her waist and nuzzled his jaw against her temple. Caroline sighed and leaned back against him, resting her forearms atop his, enjoying the slight scratch of crisp suit sleeves against her skin. Simply being close to Jack gave her pleasure.

"There's chilled champagne waiting. Nonalcoholic, but it's the symbolism that counts. And I turned on the water in the bath." He bent his head and nibbled her ear. "I got you a new nightgown and negligee," he murmured, and she shivered as his hot breath filled her ear. "It's white satin and lace." His teeth nipped. "And *ve-ry* sexy."

Caroline was both touched and saddened. "Oh, Jack, that was sweet, but you shouldn't have gone to so much trouble. This is really more of a vacation than a honeymoon."

Grasping her shoulders, he turned her slowly but firmly until she was facing him. His blue eyes glittered beneath half-closed lids and the seductive curve of his mouth sent her heart caroming. He stroked his fingertips up the side of her neck, making her tremble. "You're wrong, my darling," he said in a husky murmur as his gaze lowered to her mouth. His head tipped to one side and began a slow descent.

Caroline waited in trembling anticipation, her breathing shallow, her skin tingling. Her mouth parted slightly as his drew near, and as her heavy eyelids drooped her breath came out on a sigh.

His mouth hovered a hairbreadth from hers. The tip of his tongue touched her lower lip, and a hard shudder rippled through her. Her breasts grew heavy.

His scent went to her head like fine wine, and she could feel his heat all along the front of her body. With a little moan, she tried to lean closer, but his hands gripped her upper arms, holding her back.

"You're so very wrong," he whispered against her lips. "This is definitely a honeymoon."

Then, with skill and stunning passion, he proceeded to prove it to her.

Chapter Six

For Caroline, the first three months of marriage passed in a blur of retching and bone-weary lethargy. The so-called morning sickness hit her at all hours of the day and night and lasted well into her second trimester. When she wasn't hanging over the toilet bowl all she wanted to do was sleep. She could barely manage to drag herself to the studio every day, but she did. Even at that, though she tried to keep up with her share of the work, most of the load fell on Louise's shoulders.

Caroline felt terrible about that, but whenever she mentioned it or tried to apologize, Louise cut her off bruskly.

"Nonsense. That's what friends are for. Partners, too, for that matter. Besides, you did the same for me twice in the last ten years."

"Yeah, but I don't remember you ever being this sick or draggy," Caroline moaned. "Most of the time I'm almost comatose. I'm almost no help to you at all."

Louise laughed. "Your own pregnancies always seem worse than anyone else's, but believe me, I went through pretty much the same thing. Just keep reminding yourself that it will soon be over."

Caroline groaned and put her head down on her desk. "I feel like I've already been pregnant a year."

If Jack had had his way, Caroline would not have gone to work at all. He was appalled by the relentless nausea, sure that no one could be that ill for that long without something being terribly wrong, and the acute lethargy worried him almost as much. He watched her like a hawk and called Dr. Lawson if she so much as coughed. He nearly drove her crazy with his fretting.

For the first time in all the years that Caroline had known him he did his best to avoid making business trips, sending underlings on his staff whenever he could.

Though Jack's insistence that she stay in bed held great appeal in her listless state, Caroline would not hear of letting Louise carry the load alone. As a compromise, Jack set up a daybed in the storeroom at Ambience and made Louise promise that she would see to it that Caroline took at least one nap every day.

By the time Caroline was into her fourth month her waist had thickened but her tummy had only a slight pouch. However, her breasts had increased two cup sizes and were ultrasensitive, changes which Jack found endlessly fascinating.

Jack was a lusty man with a healthy sexual appetite, but during the first few months when she was so dreadfully ill he did nothing more than hold her in his arms while she slept. Once the sickness eased off and her body began to change, he made love to her very gently, being careful of her, restraining his power and natural drive. He worried about hurting her and treated her as though she were made of delicate crystal.

Caroline loved the tenderness, but she missed his vigorous and earthy lovemaking, and for that reason she was at times anxious for the baby to arrive ... until she remembered that once it had, unless a miracle occurred, she and Jack would go their separate ways.

Whenever she tried to bring up the subject of their parting after the baby's birth, he changed the subject or refused to discuss it, but they both knew he was merely putting off the inevitable.

Jack had been wonderful through the whole affair, looking after her, humoring her through her mood swings and caring for her through the awful sickness. He was a man of integrity and he was determined to do the right thing by her and the baby, but she knew, if he could wave a magic wand and put things back the way they had been he would in a heartbeat.

That saddened her, but she understood. He had not wanted to become a husband and father, and she was not about to shackle him to a life-style he detested. More importantly, she would not raise her child in a home where it was not totally and unconditionally loved and wanted by both parents.

At five months Caroline's belly had a definite ripe roundness, and by the time she was six months along, she was bemoaning her shape.

"I look like a basketball with legs," she groaned, looking at herself in a three-way mirror as she and Louise were shopping for maternity clothes one evening after work. "I was doing fine, then all the sudden I ballooned. I've gained thirteen pounds just since Jack left three weeks ago. I can't even see my feet anymore!"

"It goes with the territory, kiddo," Louise said heartlessly. "I hate to tell you this, but it's going to get worse before it gets better."

"Oh, thanks loads. Already my back aches, my legs ache, my ankles swell. Shaving my legs and putting on panty hose are major ordeals, both of which involve unbelievable contortions. Everything I eat gives me heartburn, and to top it all off, I feel like someone parked a truck on my bladder. And you tell me it's going to get worse?"

"Uh-huh. Pretty soon you'll move on to feeling like a beached whale. You'll waddle like a duck, and by the end of the day your feet will be so swollen your toes will look like little sausages. Then there are broken veins and stretch marks and—"

"Oh, stop. Stop! I get the picture. I don't want to, but I get it."

Louise laughed. "You know what they say, 'Be careful what you wish for because you might get it.'

Well, you wanted a baby, and this is the price you pay, my friend. But don't worry, I promise you it will all be worth it once you have your baby in your arms.''

"I know. That's the only thing that keeps me going. But in the meantime I look like a blimp."

"So what's your problem? Jack doesn't seem to mind."

"Jack hasn't seen me looking like this. He's going to be shocked at what a difference a few weeks can make."

"Hmm. When's he due back?"

"In about a week." Caroline turned sideways and looked at her burgeoning shape in the mirror. She rolled her eyes. "God alone knows what I'll look like by then."

The elevator stopped on the ninth floor, and Jack hefted his cases and stepped out, weary but relieved to be home. It had been a hellacious flight. What should have taken three hours had taken almost ten, thanks to a four-hour delay, a missed connection and turbulent weather. To top it off, an obnoxious drunk for a seatmate had made the last leg of the journey seem twice as long as it actually was.

An appropriate ending, he supposed, for what had been an even more hellacious business trip.

Of course, that was his own fault. He had worked his buns off, and those of the entire Detroit office staff, in order to cram four weeks of work into three.

In the future they would all probably run for cover whenever they saw him coming.

Jack's mouth twisted wryly as he set one suitcase down and fished into his trouser pocket for his key. He'd done it to get back to Caroline quicker. He unlocked the door, picked up his case again and stepped inside, shouldering the door shut behind him. He stopped in the entryway and breathed a sigh of relief. Home at last.

He had never liked being away from Caroline, but he liked his job, and travel was an important part of it, so he'd accepted the separations as necessary and endured them by burying himself in the work.

That, however, was before she became pregnant with his child. Now he worried about her too much. What if there were complications? What if she had trouble while he was gone? What if she fainted? What if she hurt herself? The anxiety was just too much. Which was why he'd already told his boss at Tilson and Dodd Engineering that he would not make any more trips over the next three months. If something came up, they'd just have to send someone else. He wasn't budging from Houston until Caroline had the baby.

The lights were on in the living room but there was no sign of Caroline when he peeked in. Down at the far end of the hall he could see light spilling from their bedroom as well, and he heard faint sounds of Caro moving around. And apparently, grumbling to herself. Grinning, he headed that way.

As he reached the door he opened his mouth to call out a greeting, but the words died in his throat when he spotted her. She was standing in front of the full-length cheval mirror wearing only a pair of practical white knit panties with an elastic maternity panel in the front and a white cotton maternity bra.

A sweet pressure filled his chest. Damn, it was wonderful to see her. He never felt truly comfortable without her.

He studied her with a bemused expression. As he had been leaving the Detroit offices, one of the engineers who had met Caroline called out to him to give his best to his wife, and the statement had jolted him. Watching Caroline, Jack smiled wryly. His wife. He still hadn't gotten used to thinking of Caroline as that, but he had to admit it had a possessive ring to it that he liked.

He watched her pick up a dress from the pile of clothes on the chair and toss it over her head. From the size of the pile, Jack gathered that she had been shopping. She turned this way and that, checking out how she looked in the voluminous dress and frowning.

"Blimp," she muttered, and Jack's lips twitched.

She whipped the garment off over her head and reached for another one. For a few seconds she stood again in only her panties and bra, and when she caught sight of her reflection she turned sideways to check her shape and immediately made a face. "Oh, yeah. Definitely a beached whale."

Another grin started, but Jack's amusement evaporated when he got a good look at her in profile. He stared, amazed. The little pumpkin tummy she'd had when he left three weeks ago was now the size of a bushel basket. Good Lord, she had almost three months to go! If she kept expanding at this rate she'd pop!

He stared at her for a long time as she exchanged one garment for another, that familiar confusion tightening his chest. It was strange. He had fully expected to have to grit his teeth and endure Caroline's pregnancy. He'd even expected he would have to fight feelings of resentment and had been braced for it. Instead he found that he was becoming totally involved in her pregnancy and enthralled by the whole process.

For months he'd held her head and wiped her face while she was sick. Nowadays he massaged away her leg cramps, dealt with her erratic mood swings, cajoling her whenever she was blue and consoling her through irrational bouts of crying, laughing with her when she was on top of the world.

His mouth twisted when he recalled how, with rueful humor, he had dutifully trudged out in the small hours of the morning for weird food when she was craving, hauled her out of chairs when she couldn't struggle out on her own and out of bed when the pressure on her bladder forced her to visit the bathroom several times each night.

And through it all, that tiny flare of pride he'd experienced on learning of the baby stubbornly hung on, resisting his efforts to snuff it out.

It was stupid. Why should he feel proud just because he'd managed to impregnate a woman? It wasn't as though he'd accomplished anything truly unique or performed any sort of spectacular feat or worked a miracle. His part in the whole thing had amounted to a few moments of intense pleasure. Big deal.

It was foolish to let yourself get caught up in the romanticism of impending parenthood. Realistically the child was a responsibility, and that's how he was determined to think of it. After all, he hadn't wanted this baby. He still didn't. He'd liked the life he and Caroline had just fine and had no desire to change a single thing about it. Certainly not to bring a third person into it.

That was what he'd always felt as a child—odd man out.

From the time he had hit puberty and learned where babies came from he had known that he did not want children. They were a nuisance and a burden— that was the message he'd gotten, loud and clear, from both his parents and a string of stepparents.

Which had caused him to wonder why anyone voluntarily saddled themselves with offspring.

However, like it or not, a child was on the way. Caroline, with her usual determination and tenacity, had dug in her heels; she wanted this baby, and he either went along with that decision or he lost her.

Jack shuddered. The mere thought put an icy knot of fear in his gut. He'd as soon cut out his heart with a dull knife.

As yet, he didn't know how he was going to handle being a father. Caroline was right. Children deserved to be loved and wanted. Intellectually he knew that. Hell, hadn't he longed for those very things as a kid? But he just couldn't seem to muster those feelings.

In that respect, Jack feared he was very much like his old man—closed off, remote, self-involved— which was what he'd always worried about, and was the main reason he hadn't wanted to stick any kid with himself as a father.

Oh sure, he was fascinated by the physical changes in his wife's body and the baby's rapid development but that was simply natural curiosity. He certainly didn't have any particular paternal feelings.

He'd have to muddle through somehow, though, or he'd lose Caroline.

She had declared her intention to leave him after the baby was born in a moment of extreme emotion, and at first he'd dismissed it. Now he wasn't so sure. Caroline had tried to broach the subject several times, but so far he'd managed to avoid that conversation, but the threat was always there, hovering between them.

She was so wrapped up in this baby and so intent on doing the right thing for it, she just might cut him out of her life, even though he knew damn well that would hurt her as much as it would hurt him. Hurt, hell, it would kill him.

Before he'd let that happen, he'd grit his teeth and bear anything, including marriage and parenthood. Caroline would just have to provide the kid with enough love for both of them because he wasn't letting her go.

Caroline stripped off another tent-type dress, and the muffled sounds coming from the folds of cloth as she dragged the garment over her head sounded amazingly like "hippopotamus in a muu-muu." She slung the dress down in disgust, but when she started to reach for another she stopped suddenly and placed both hands on her swollen abdomen, a startled look on her face.

Jack stiffened and snapped out, "What is it? What's wrong, Caro?"

Caroline jumped as though he'd tossed a lit firecracker into the room. "Jack! You scared me half to death! What are you doing here? You weren't due back until next week."

Ignoring her questions, he strode across the room with a long purposeful stride, his gaze fixed on the hands splayed across her belly. "What's wrong?" he demanded again.

"Wrong?"

"You stopped suddenly and grabbed your belly."

"Oh, that." She chuckled and looked down at the turgid mound. When her eyes met his again they were soft with wonder. "I just felt him kick."

Jack stopped cold, his expression a mix of horror, surprise and curiosity. "Really? You mean a real kick?"

She had been feeling slight movements before he left for Detroit, but those had been merely vague flutters.

"Uh-huh. Pro punter class. Oh, my. There he goes again."

As though in a daze, Jack stepped close and laid his hand on her distended abdomen. Caroline moved it a few inches and held it there. For a second there was nothing, then a definite thump against his palm.

Jack's eyes widened and his gaze met Caroline's. "Good God! Doesn't that hurt?"

"No," she said with a laugh. "It just feels ... peculiar." Her smile was radiant and her eyes shone with such indescribable joy, Jack felt it like a punch in the gut. In that moment, for the very first time, he began to realize just how much having this baby meant to Caroline.

She looked as though someone had just given her a slice of heaven. This wasn't just a vague, biological urge or a whim. This was vital. This was her heart's desire.

Which was what she'd been trying to tell you all along, dumb ass. It made him feel slightly sick to think that he had tried to deny her this.

The baby kicked against his hand again, three times in rapid succession, and Jack caught his breath. He met Caroline's look of dreamy happiness and smiled. "Lie down," he whispered.

"Jack, really, it doesn't hurt. Honest. Anyway, just let me put on my robe." She reached for the wrap as she spoke.

"No. I want to look at you," he said in a seductive voice, pushing it out of reach as he eased her onto the bed.

"Oh, but, Jack—" She tried to cover her abdomen with her arms, but that was a futile effort.

"What's the matter with you, Caro? Don't tell me you're shy? With me?" Her pained expression gave him his answer. He stared at her, astonished. Then he burst out laughing. He couldn't help it. "Hell, honey, I've seen, touched and kissed every square inch of your delectable little body."

"It's not so little anymore," she muttered unhappily, trying to drag the corner of the bedspread over herself.

"Ah, so that's the problem," Jack said with a sage nod, trying to pry the bed cover out of her hands.

"Jack, stop it. I've gotten as big as a house, and I don't want you to see. Jack! Give me that!" she wailed.

"Shh. I want to look." Tossing the spread aside, he raised up on one elbow and gazed intently at the protruding mound of her stomach. He ran his hand over it, marveling at how firm and taut it was, how warm. Not satisfied, he hooked his fingers under the elastic and started to push the panties down. Caroline grabbed his hand.

"Jack, no!"

"Caro, don't be silly. This is me, remember." He grinned. "Your husband. We don't have any secrets from each other."

"But—"

"Shh." Ignoring her moan, he slipped the panties down until they cupped under her abdomen. Jack went utterly still and stared. Caroline closed her eyes and bit her bottom lip to still its quivering.

Jack felt as though a giant hand were squeezing his heart. He had never had anything affect him so profoundly as the sight of her belly swollen with his child.

Tentatively he put out his hand and laid it on that milky white swell, and a tremor rippled through him. The taut skin was so warm, and as smooth as silk. His hand glided slowly, almost reverently over her, and the sight of his dark hand, with its sprinkling of black hairs on the back against the silvery sheen of her stretched skin was incredibly erotic.

A welter of emotions swirled within Jack—pride . . . foolish, maybe, but still there—amazement, pleasure, fear . . . and hot, greedy lust.

"Beautiful," he murmured.

Caroline's eyelids lifted a fraction, and she looked at him suspiciously through narrow slits. "I'm as big as a house and ugly."

"No. You're the most beautiful thing I've ever seen."

"You're just saying that to make me feel better."

He had to smile at her sulky tone. He started to refute the statement but that pouty mouth begged to be kissed, so he obliged.

Caroline responded with a sigh and slid her hand around his neck, her fingers spearing into the short hairs at his nape as her soft lips parted for him. As usual, the kiss set off a fire storm of desire sizzling between them.

When Jack ended the kiss he looked down into her glazed eyes. "I said it because it's true. You're gorgeous."

"I'm a big, shapeless, sexless blob. It probably disgusts you to look at me."

"Are you kidding?" He took her hand and pressed it against him. "Does that feel like I'm disgusted?"

Shock widened her eyes. "Jack!"

"A sexless blob? Hardly." He ran his hand over her again. "Honey, your ripe little body is the most erotic thing I've ever seen. Just looking at you gets me all hot and bothered."

"Oh, Jack, do you mean that?"

"Oh, yeah. I mean it. Lift up a second." She obeyed automatically, and in a deft move, he slipped her panties down her legs and off. He unhooked the front closure on her bra and spread the cups wide, and her engorged breasts spilled into his waiting hands.

His smile was devilish, but his eyes burned with passion. He bent his head and lathed each pouting nipple with his tongue, raking it across the sensitive tips until she arched her back and cried out. Then he kissed her neck, her swollen belly, and ran his tongue down the silky line at the juncture of her thigh.

Caroline moaned and writhed, her head thrashing against the pillow. When she was almost out of her head with wanting, Jack sat up and quickly removed his clothes.

Then he stretched out again and moved between her thighs. He paused over her, his face rigid with desire. "Lord, I want you," he growled, and entered her with a slow, silken thrust that wrung a cry from Caroline.

Chapter Seven

Jack took his eyes off the rain-slick street just long enough to glance at Caroline. "You doing okay? The evening didn't tire you too much, did it? I know the Bainbridges are a dull couple, but he's an important client."

She smiled softly. "I'm fine."

"You sure? I hate to subject you to these boring business dinners, but I'm just not comfortable leaving you alone when your due date is only a month away."

"Don't worry about it. I'm perfectly happy."

A tiny smile tugged at Jack's mouth. That was the God's truth. Caroline radiated happiness. She had ever since she emerged from those first few months of sickness. It shined from her eyes. It was in her laughter, her smile, in every small graceful movement and look. Seeing that inner joy left no doubt of how much having a child meant to her.

The changes in Caroline, physical and emotional, amazed and fascinated him. In the last month, she had bloomed. A peacefulness had settled over her, a Madonna-like serenity that gave her an ethereal glow. Her beauty had always beguiled him, but now she took his breath away.

Far from being turned off by her ripening figure, which, to be honest, was what he had expected, he found it highly erotic.

Jack gave a little snort. For all the good that did him. Now that she was in her ninth month, lovemaking was no longer advisable. However, her burgeoning figure fascinated him in other ways, as well. Whenever he felt the baby move inside her he experienced a welter of strange, new feelings, so acute and overwhelming they were almost painful.

Frowning into the rain-dark night, he took his foot off the brake and stepped on the gas as the traffic light up ahead turned green. So far he hadn't analyzed those feelings too closely. He wasn't sure he wanted to know what they meant.

They were halfway through the intersection when the screech of tires interrupted his thoughts.

"Dammit!" Jack did not have time to do anything other than grip the steering wheel tighter. The jarring impact knocked them to the side against their seat belts. Accompanying the crash was a loud bang, followed instantly by the sound of breaking glass and crumpling metal and Caroline's high-pitched scream.

Jack fought for control, but the Jaguar slewed around on the slick street and went skidding, doing slow revolutions as it glided toward the curb as though it were floating.

There was more rending metal and shattering glass as the rear of the Jag on Caroline's side clipped a parked car and sent them spiraling out into the street again, and more squealing tires as oncoming traffic slammed on brakes and struggled to miss them.

They finally came to a stop, facing in the wrong direction, when they slid into a curb almost a block from where they were hit.

There was a moment of magnified silence as Jack, still gripping the steering wheel tightly, tried to orient himself. Then his gaze jerked to Caroline, and fear shot through him.

Blood ran down her face from a cut just below her hairline and her skin was parchment white. But it was the way she clutched her abdomen with both hands that sent ice shooting through his veins.

"Caro! Oh, God, darling, are you hurt?"

She turned her head and looked at him, her face contorted with excruciating pain, her eyes filled with horror. "The baby," she gasped. "Jack, help me! I'm losing my baby!"

The ride in the ambulance to the hospital seemed interminable. By the time they arrived Caroline was in so much pain and so frightened that Jack was nearly out of his mind with worry and was ready to let fly at someone—anyone.

Dr. Lawson had been notified of the accident as soon as the call for the ambulance had gone in, and he was waiting at the emergency room entrance along with the trauma team of nurses and doctors. The minute Jack spotted the obstetrician he began a combination of autocratic orders and abject begging.

"You will save them, doctor. Do you understand me? You will damn well save both of them. You got that?" He ran alongside the gurney, holding Caroline's icy hand as the team of nurses and doctors pushed it at a run. Dr. Lawson was so busy trying to evaluate his patient he was hardly aware of Jack's rantings.

"Do you hear me? Dammit, I can't lose them! Oh, God, please don't let me lose either of them. Please."

"Come, Mr. Riley, you can't go in there." His upper arms were grabbed and he was jerked away from the gurney. "Why don't you come along with me, and we'll get your wife admitted."

"Let me go!" He stared as Caroline was wheeled away through a set of double doors. "I've got to be with my wife! Let go, dammit!"

"I'm sorry, Mr. Riley, but no one is allowed in surgery but the doctors and nurses. As soon as we fill out all the necessary forms, you can come back here. There's a nice waiting room right through those door."

Jack stood in the middle of the hall and stared at the still-swinging double doors. "Oh, God."

An hour later he sat on a bench inside the surgery waiting room. Leaning forward with his elbows resting on his knees, his hands were clasped together in a fisted prayer. *Please, God, let them be all right. Please.*

In that horrible first instant, when he'd realized that he might lose not only Caroline, but their child, as well, it had hit him like a fist to the heart that he wanted the baby desperately. He loved Caroline with all his heart and soul, and the child she was carrying was the product of their love, a blending of the two of them, and he loved the unborn baby as much as he loved his wife. If they lost it, the blow would be devastating—to Caroline and to him.

"Take it easy, Jack. You've got to have faith." Louise sat down beside him and put her arm around his shoulder. He barely remembered calling her, but he must have, because she had come bustling into the waiting room barely thirty minutes after they had wheeled Caroline away.

"It was my fault. I should have been more careful. I should have seen the guy coming and avoided him somehow."

"Jack, the guy ran a red light going fifteen miles an hour over the speed limit on a wet street. There was no way you could have avoided him. So would you please quit torturing yourself?"

"Maybe if—"

He broke off and lurched to his feet when Dr. Lawson appeared in the doorway. "How is she? How's the baby? Will they be all right?"

"Calm down, Jack. Other than a few stitches and a slight concussion, your wife is fine."

"And the baby? Is it . . . ?"

"Alive? You bet. We tried to stop the labor, but we couldn't. About ten minutes ago your wife gave birth to a healthy, beautiful six-pound girl."

Jack stared at the doctor and swallowed hard. "A girl?" he croaked, and swallowed again. "A girl! Did you hear that, Louise? Caroline and I have a daughter!"

"I heard," Louise said, smiling indulgently.

Jack got his first look at his daughter a half hour later when he was finally allowed into his wife's room. Caroline was propped up in the bed, looking down at the tiny pink-and-white infant cradled in her arms. His breath caught at the sight. She looked like a breathtakingly beautiful Madonna, her face aglow with love.

Standing quietly in the doorway, Jack watched her. He was gripped with an emotion so strong it was almost suffocating. *His wife and daughter.*

Caroline's soft expression held him entranced, and he stared at her, marveling at the tenderness that radiated from her, the inner glow that lit her face. She was the essence of womanhood. Feminine. Maternal. Loving. Jack knew that for as long as he lived he would remember this moment.

An aching tightness squeezed his throat, and he swallowed hard. Never taking his eyes from her, he walked into the room. "Do you have any idea how lovely you look?" he asked quietly, and Caroline looked up with a joyous smile.

"Oh, Jack, come see her. She's so precious."

Jack stopped beside the bed, and as he gazed at his daughter for the first time he felt as though someone had tied a half hitch around his heart. Love came gushing up from the center of his soul, swelling his chest until he could barely breathe. Then this was why, no matter how dismal and insane the world got, generation after generation, people had children, this sweet, painful, overwhelming feeling of love and hope.

"She's beautiful," he said around the lump in his throat and touched the baby's downy head.

"Oh, Jack, do you really think so?"

The anxiety in her voice almost made him wince. He dragged his gaze from his infant daughter and looked at his wife. "She's gorgeous," he whispered. "So are you."

He touched her cheek with the tips of his fingers. "Oh, Caro," he said in a shaken whisper. "I was so scared I'd lose you both."

Her eyes widened. "Both? Does that mean...?"

"That I've finally realized what an idiot I've been? Yes. I love you, Caroline. And I love our daughter."

Tears filled her eyes, and one by one they spilled over. "Oh, Jack."

As they gazed at each other the air vibrated with poignant feelings too deeply felt and too beautiful to express. Caroline's gaze was filled with love and wonder and a dreamy softness, Jack's with awe and adoration and a fierce possessiveness. "Caroline," he whispered again. With the baby between them, he bent and took her lips in an exquisitely soft kiss that sent shudders rippling through them both.

Their lips clung sweetly, but after a moment the baby began to squirm and make sharp little grunting noises. Jack lifted his head and grimaced wryly. "I think we're being scolded."

Smiling, Caroline stroked her daughter's cheek, and both she and Jack laughed when the little rose-bud mouth made a sucking motion.

Sitting down on the edge of the bed, Jack picked up his wife's hand and held it between both of his. He looked straight into her eyes. "Caroline, love of my life, will you marry me?"

Her mouth dropped. "Marry you? But...we're already married," she protested weakly.

"Legally, yes. But this time I want to do it right, and for the right reasons. In church with all the trimmings, and all our friends and...yes, dammit, even our families there. I want the whole world to see how much you and our daughter mean to me."

The declaration, made with such heartfelt sincerity, left Caroline so choked with emotions she could not speak. She could only gaze at him over the top of their daughter's fuzzy head and nod as tears streamed down her face.

Six weeks later, on Mother's Day, in a flower-bedecked church filled to capacity, with Jack's father acting as best man and Matron of Honor Louise, holding Anna Beth, Jack and Caroline pledged their love to each other and exchanged the vows that bound them together in marriage. Forever.

Dear Reader,

Is there any feeling as intense or all-consuming as that rush of fierce love that overwhelms you when you hold your newborn in your arms for the first time? I don't think so. From the instant of birth, those tiny fingers clutch your heart and never let go. The love you feel for your child is absolute, unconditional, and never-ending.

I was especially intrigued when my editor suggested I write a story from the hero's perspective—something on the father's reaction to impending parenthood.

Men experience the same awesome feelings as women when they become parents. Many times, however—perhaps because they are not as in touch with their emotions as women, or because of some misguided notion of masculinity imposed on them by society—they are not as receptive to the idea in the beginning.

When we married, my husband wasn't sure he wanted to be a father. He had not had much experience with children and he wasn't convinced that he would be a good parent. (Of course, we women know that it's the men who care enough to worry about such things who are the very ones who *should* be fathers.)

When our daughter was born he was so overwhelmed with love for her he instantly forgot every doubt he ever had about parenthood. That love and concern and caring has not diminished one iota over the years. He was, and remains, the kind of father I wish every child could have—loving, protective, supportive and giving of himself. He is eternally thankful that he did not deny himself the great joy and blessing of fatherhood.

That was the lesson my hero, Jack Riley, had to learn. I hope you enjoyed his struggle to arrive at that awesome and indisputable truth.

Ginna Gray

THE BABY INVASION

Raye Morgan

To Marie Ferrarella, for trying hard to
understand the secret life of dogs.

Chapter One

MANY CONDOLENCES DEATH OF BROTHER.
BABY'S THERE ONE WEEK. INTERNATIONAL
AIRPORT, NEXT SATURDAY.
NURSE'S DELIVERY. THANK YOU.

Matt Temple sat at his desk and stared at the telegram for a long time. Cryptic though it might have seemed to some, he knew exactly what it meant.

"It means," he said aloud, more in wonder than in fear, "I'm about to have a baby."

"Did you say something, Mr. Temple?" Shayla Conners, administrative assistant extraordinaire, was passing his open office door. She stuck her head in and looked at him questioningly.

"No," he said slowly, then looked up and realized she was the very person he needed. "I mean, yes. Come in, Conners. I have a little problem. Maybe you can help me deal with it."

Shayla stepped into the oak-paneled office, pulling a pencil out of the bun at her nape. She took a seat across the wide, cluttered desk, her pencil poised, her notebook ready. She was used to judging her boss's mood and could tell there was something different about him today. That put her on edge and on her toes, like a tennis player ready to receive the serve and deal with it brilliantly.

Matt turned in his seat and pinned her with his steely ice-blue gaze, using a stare that often turned opponents into blithering idiots, shaking in their expensive loafers.

"Well, Conners," he stated firmly, his rock-solid jaw jutting. "Tell me this. Have you ever had a baby?"

Shayla Conners did not quail under his piercing stare. Actually something close to amusement was flickering behind the owl-shaped lenses of her glasses. A personal question—and this from the man who treated her as though she had no existence outside of this office. She lifted her chin and said calmly, "No, Mr. Temple. I've never had a baby."

"Damn," he said, grimacing, his wide, exquisitely chiseled mouth twisted, his blue eyes troubled. "I was hoping you could help me out here." He frowned, searching her clear gaze. "Are you sure?"

Shayla nodded her neatly coiffed head, wanting to smile but holding it back. "It's not something a woman easily forgets," she advised him.

"I suppose not." He gave an exasperated sigh and sat back, flexing his wide shoulders beneath the expensive Italian suit, his square, expressive hands flattened against the desktop as he contemplated his options. "This is damn awkward, Conners, but I've got baby problems."

"Have you, sir?" The amusement died in her violet gaze and something frosty took its place, directly mirroring the chill that had crept into her heart. A quick glance into his eyes told her he wasn't joking. "Is it the Carbelli woman you've been dating lately?" she asked, attempting to keep up a cool, disinterested front.

"What?" He looked at her blankly. "What does Pia Carbelli have to do with this?"

Thank goodness for that, she thought to herself. Pia Carbelli had the motherly instincts of a half-starved cobra. "I see," she said quickly, keeping the stiff upper lip intact. "Then it's one of the others."

He stared at her for a moment as though he were afraid she'd lost her mind, then realized what she was getting at and barked out a short laugh. "No, Conners. None of my girlfriends are in the family way." He looked slightly offended. "I don't do things like that, you know. Any man with half a brain knows how to keep that from happening."

Shayla uncrossed her legs and crossed them again, a burning curiosity shining just behind the bland expression she kept on her face as if it were a mask. It was no secret her boss dated beautiful women. And it was also pretty plain he wasn't the marrying kind. So just where babies fit into his life, she couldn't imagine. "Then I'm afraid I don't understand, Mr. Temple," she said simply.

But Matt wasn't really listening. Instead he was studying his assistant as though he'd never seen her before. His attention had been caught by her tone and suddenly, he began to notice things about her—things such as her pale, strangely colored eyes with the heavy fringe of dark lashes and how the line of her neck curved gracefully into the white collar of her sensible blouse. She was a woman, and that was a fact he hadn't really registered much in all the months she'd worked for him. And not a bad one at that, in a chilly, reserved sort of way.

Not his type, however, and that, of course, was fortunate. He wouldn't want to be distracted by having stray thoughts about his assistant—especially this one. She was too important an employee to risk losing that way. He shoved the thought away immediately.

"Never had a baby, huh?" he mused, still examining her and wondering why he hadn't ever paid this much attention to her as a person before. "Are you married?"

She stared at him, and now outrage was beginning to form in that misty place behind her eyes. She'd been working for him for almost a year, noticing every single detail about him and about his life. She'd always known he basically saw her as an extremely efficient android. But this was taking things too far. He was looking at her as though he couldn't quite remember why she was here. Where had he been all this time? "No," she told him icily.

He shrugged. It wasn't the sort of thing he would have noticed. To him, work and play were entirely separate, and that was the way he meant to keep things.

"No baby, no husband." He frowned, his gaze taking in her flawless skin, her red, perfectly shaped nails, and the modest cut of her linen suit and cotton blouse. "And yet I have this feeling that you have a whole secret life I know nothing about."

She held his gaze and didn't waver. He was a tough boss but she'd never knuckled under to him. Their relationship was a precarious balance between his barked orders and her tart replies, but it seemed to work for them. Still, she resented the fact that he hardly seemed to know she existed in any capacity other than as a well-oiled part in his business operation. It stung to think he hadn't even bothered to remember if she were married or not.

"I have no other life, Mr. Temple," she said sweetly, leashing her irritation for the moment. "What I do when I leave here is go home and hang from the ceiling with my wings folded and wait for the dawn, like a reverse vampire bat."

He grimaced quizzically. He was used to her quick rejoinders. "You joke, Conners. But I think you're covering up for something." His eyes narrowed, assessing her in an infuriating fashion. "Care to comment?"

No, she did not, and now she was beginning to think he was toying with her. Snapping her notebook closed, she rose and turned toward the door. "Will that be all, Mr. Temple?" she said evenly.

He hit the flat of his hand on the polished mahogany of his desk with a smack that echoed against the walls. "No, dammit, it won't. I want to confide in you." He blinked rapidly for a moment, then looked up at her again. "I'm sorry if I've offended you, Conners, but I'm not thinking very clearly this afternoon. My brother has just died and I feel the need to unburden my soul. Unfortunately there is no one else around to unburden to. You'll have to do."

"Oh." She dropped back into her chair, horrified, her cheeks burning. She'd had no idea. The two of them often sparred. It seemed to be part of the natural rhythm of the way they dealt with each other. But now she felt nothing but remorse for having treated him so coldly.

"Oh, Mr. Temple, I'm so sorry," she said, her eyes misting, her compassionate nature coming to the surface without hesitation. She just barely resisted the urge to reach out and touch him with a sympathetic caress. "I . . . what can I do to help you?"

His mouth twisted. "That's very kind of you, Conners. But there's no need to get maudlin."

She sat back quickly, feeling rebuffed.

"He was a half brother, I should add. That's not to say I'm not upset at his loss," he said quickly, and a faraway look clouded his eyes. "We never spent much time together, but he is my flesh and blood. Partly. And he didn't deserve to go that young."

He paused, shaking his head, and she steeled herself against feeling sorry for him again. It was tough not to. He had a look on his face she hadn't seen before, and it touched her deeply. Why was he trying to put up this facade of unconcern? Was he afraid of appearing weak in front of an employee? She wouldn't put it past him, and she bit her tongue, holding back the sympathy.

"Are you with me, Conners?" he asked softly, glancing at her again.

She nodded, holding her notebook closed in her lap.

"Okay, here's the deal," he said, leaning forward, his eyes strangely veiled. "Remy had been fooling around in South America for years and he finally got himself killed in a plane crash. His wife died with him, but according to the lawyer who called me last night, there was a baby left at home, and therefore very much alive. I'm this baby's oldest living relative. So I'm elected. I get custody."

It took a moment for the details of the situation to fully form in her mind, but once they did, the horror of it all overwhelmed her. What on earth was this confirmed bachelor going to do with a baby?

"You, sir?" she murmured, thinking fast. She was his administrative assistant and he was used to turning to her for advice. He was asking for her help, so he must be trying to think of a way to get out of taking the baby. And that was exactly as it should be. Matt Temple with a baby in his arms—it didn't work for her. And it certainly wouldn't work for the poor baby.

"Yes, me," he responded. "And I guess I'll have to keep the little tyke. Family feelings and all that. So there's only one question. And that's what I want your help with."

She blinked at him, thrown a bit off guard again. "And what is that, sir?"

"Why, it's obvious." He looked at her expectantly. "I need a wife. Do you know where we can get one quickly?"

Shayla's mouth dropped open. For once, he'd floored her. She was speechless.

But Matt didn't notice. He went on, looking thoughtful. "I figure she ought to be good-looking, because after all, if I'm going to be married to her, I'll need to feel some sort of attraction, don't you think? And educated. I like a woman who understands the issues of the day and can hold her own at dinner parties." He shook his head. "But other than that, I just don't know. You're a woman. Maybe you know these things. Why don't you make up a list of specifications and call an agency and round up some candidates. We can start holding interviews..." He flipped through his calendar. "How about Thursday?"

She was still finding it difficult to react. She'd always thought he needed the right kind of woman to take care of him. Though he was a bold, decisive man who overcame obstacles and challenged danger constantly, she thought she could see a hint of sadness in his eyes at times, a suggestion of a loneliness that seemed to touch a chord in her. He needed someone. But not this way!

He wanted to hire a wife. In all the months she'd worked for him, she'd always considered him a very smart man. How could he have gone so wrong? Coughing to buy time, she came up with the most delicate solution she could think of offhand.

"But, Mr. Temple... If you really think you need a wife, wouldn't you prefer to pick from among the women you see socially? Someone you know?"

He looked at her as though she'd suggested sending away for a mail-order bride. "Hell, no. Those women aren't domestic. They're only for dating."

She opened her mouth and then closed it again. This was impossible. *He* was impossible—one of the original Neanderthals still in existence. There was no point in feeling outraged. He was what he was and she certainly wasn't going to change him.

"Mr. Temple," she said, more in despair than anything else, "why are you taking on this baby? Don't you have a sister or something?"

"No sisters. Only brothers." He raised an eyebrow and gave her a questioning look. "Why? What's wrong with me taking on this baby? Do you think women are the only ones who can nurture?"

She licked her upper lip and tried to be diplomatic. "I think they have a heck of a lot more practice at it than men do."

He grinned at her suddenly, as though she'd said something that tickled him. But he challenged her. "I consider that a sexist remark," he said. "But I'll overlook it for now." He looked at her sharply. "Besides, how would you know? We're both in the same boat. You've never had a baby and neither have I."

"True," she responded. How could she deny it? "But I grew up in a large family and took care of plenty of babies in my time."

"Ah-hah!" His smile was triumphant. "I knew it. You're going to come in handy after all. You always are my best resource." She tried to protest, but he didn't give her time. "Okay, argue with me on that later. We've got too much work to do to get tangled up in that right now." He glanced at the clock. "I've got a meeting with the Bradley people at two. Get right on this, would you? Get me a list of prospects by say...four this afternoon. We'll go over them and..."

"Wait." She put up a hand as though to stop the flow of this river of words. "I'm not sure that's possible. Agencies don't handle things like that. They're not matchmakers. They don't find partners for people."

He was not convinced. "Oh, sure they do. They must. There must be men who need them all the time. Nowadays, with all these mothers going off and leaving their husbands stuck with the kids..."

Stuck with the kids. She groaned. This entire situation was doomed. It would never work. This was a man who worked long, hard hours and partied seriously whenever he got the chance. A little person was about to come into his life, a baby who needed constant care and lots of love. He didn't have a clue about what raising a child would entail. Shayla looked at him and shook her head. She'd helped him out of scrapes before. She was going to have to help him out of this one—even if he didn't think he needed help at the moment. He would, soon enough.

"You know, there's something about your attitude," she told him severely. "I think you'd better mull this over again. You don't seem to realize what you're getting yourself into."

But then she looked into his face again, and her asperity melted. For once, his blue eyes held a candid look. She saw things there she'd never seen before, things that surprised her. The hardness was gone, the tough, biting intelligence was muted by something else. He was thinking about the baby who was coming, and his face held a look of wonder that set her back on her heels. She'd never realized he might have a tender side, and for once, she seemed to be getting a glimpse of one.

"I have no choice, Conners," he was saying softly. "The baby is as good as mine already." He shrugged. "I'm going to have to learn how to live with it."

That stumped her. He really meant what he'd said, she could see it in his face, and immediately, her instinct was to soften toward him. But she fought it this time, kept it inside. He was a complex man, and over the past few months, she'd learned the best way to handle him was to keep her guard up at all times. Instead of giving in to sympathy, she hardened her heart and tried to think of some way to convince him he could no more raise a baby than she could swim the Atlantic. There had to be a way to get through to him.

Matt was waiting. He could tell she was against his plans and he often trusted her judgment. So he waited for what she had to say, and while he waited, he looked at her again, gave her a good scan in a way he almost never did. She wasn't bad looking, despite the glasses and the severe attitude. He noticed the trim line of her ankle. She was wearing dark stockings and conservative pumps with only the barest suggestion of a heel. She dressed, he realized suddenly, to turn male attention away.

"Don't you like men, Conners?" he asked. He was accustomed to saying what he thought when he thought it, and he saw no reason to hold back now.

"Sir?" she asked, startled, and shocked at the fact that her heart was suddenly beating very hard.

He frowned, puzzled by her. "Do you date much? Do you ever try to make yourself attractive to men?"

That was enough to raise permanent hackles. She gritted her teeth and gave him a frigid smile. "You've asked an awful lot of personal questions today, Mr. Temple," she noted icily.

"That's right." He gave her a quizzical look. "And you haven't given me a satisfactory answer to one of them."

She shifted her position, unconsciously broadcasting how uncomfortable he made her. "What kind of answer are you looking for?" she said evasively.

He smiled. For once, he'd put her on the defensive. It was an unusual moment for him. "I want to get to know you, Conners," he said smoothly, picking up the first thing that popped into his head. But then he went on more sincerely. "You're the best administrative assistant I've ever had, and I realize I hardly know you."

The compliment seemed to smooth back her ruffled fur, at least a bit. "Thank you, Mr. Temple," she said quickly.

He leaned toward her, giving her his most sincere look. "No, I mean it. You're darn good at what you do."

To her chagrin, two bright spots of color appeared in her cheeks. She could feel them glowing there warmly, and she cursed them silently. But it didn't seem to help.

"Thank you very much, Mr. Temple," she said, averting her eyes and hoping for the color to die down.

He was still staring at her and suddenly she realized he was waiting for something. "Well?" he said impatiently.

She looked up, blinking at him, bewildered. "Well, what?"

He shrugged, looking hopeful. "What about me? What do you think about me as a boss?"

"You?" She hesitated. He was just so darn sure of himself, she could hardly stand it. He wanted her to drool all over him, and she flat refused to do it. "I'd prefer not to answer that question," she said at last, rising.

"What? Why not?"

She smiled at him, enjoying the look of surprise in his eyes. "The evaluation is still pending," she told him briskly. "I'll let you know. Stay tuned." And with one last flip smile in his direction, she strode out of his office.

Matt sat back in his chair and laughed softly. He wasn't used to a woman who didn't use flattery to get her way with him. *But wait a minute,* he told himself. How could he say that? Conners always acted that way. Funny. He'd accepted it without question as a co-worker, but he couldn't quite handle it as a man-woman thing. Mainly because he'd never thought of her in those terms before. Why was that?

But he had no time to puzzle it out. His mind was already shifting gears. Picking up the telegram, he frowned at it, his gaze cloudy. For just a moment he saw the silver plane, flashing in the sunlight, plummeting to earth as if it were a wounded bird, and he winced.

"Hey, Remy, old man," he said softly, as though his half brother might be nearby, just waiting for a word from him. "We were never close, but we were brothers." Something burned in his throat and he paused, trying to swallow it. But it wouldn't leave and he accepted that, thinking of Remy again.

"I'm going to do this for you," he told him. "You didn't get a very long run in this life, but your kid is going to be taken care of." He clenched his fist, crumpling the yellow paper in his hand. "And he's going to be raised a hell of a lot better than we were." He ground out the words, his eyes lit with an icy fire. "That much I promise you."

Chapter Two

Shayla Conners sat at her desk and stared at the telephone. She'd already called four employment agencies. At each one, she'd had exactly the response she'd expected—plus a few guffaws. The question was, would Mr. Temple accept four rejections and call it quits? *She* was certainly ready to.

Shrugging, she turned to her computer keyboard and typed up a complete report, every word of the answers she'd received, including the obscenities, and put the memo on his desk, just as she would have done with any other project.

And that made her realize the flaw in this entire operation once again. Finding a mother for a baby was not an office project. You couldn't treat it like a new assignment. There was just something missing.

"Heart," she mused aloud, balancing her pencil on her finger and watching it wobble. That was it. Where was the heart?

Only Matt Temple would come up with such a crazy scheme. You didn't hire a wife the way you hired a receptionist. But surely he knew that. He made a distinction between the women he worked with and the women he dated. It was obvious. He worked with a lot of women, but the women he

worked with were all business while the women he
dated were all entertainment. He saw the difference
and used it to his advantage. His dates were young,
shapely and utterly brainless. His employees were
nothing like that. Shirley, his secretary, was a grandmother many times over, and had an advanced degree in abnormal psychology. Carol, the receptionist
with the motherly attitude, had a loving husband and
five children who called constantly once school was
out in the afternoon. And if that weren't enough, she
was taking legal writing at night school. Shayla herself had a degree in business management and was
probably the youngest on his immediate staff.

"And I suppose he took one look at me and
thought, 'I'll never be attracted to this one,'" she
mused as she packed up her things and prepared to
leave for the evening. And he was right. He hadn't
been. She'd worked there for months and he hadn't
shown one spark of interest. "And I haven't shown
one spark of interest in him," she lied to herself.

She stopped, as though something in her conscience were chiding her. She knew what she'd just
told herself wasn't true. She'd seen potential in Matt
Temple from the first time she'd interviewed with
him. How could a woman not respond to those eyes
that were as blue as northern lakes, that wavy dark
hair that sometimes fell boyishly over his forehead
when he got excited, the tall, strong body of an ath-
lete, the engaging grin, the dangerous scowl, the...

"Stop it!" she told herself fiercely, tearing a stack of papers and dumping the remnants into the trash.

She was a thirty-year-old professional woman without a husband or a family of her own, and the last thing she was going to let herself do was begin fantasizing that there was something going on with her boss. She knew women who did that, women with no real lives of their own who lived in a dreamworld, pretending some movie star or singer or some man they worked with would someday fall in love with them. She wasn't going to let herself fall into that trap.

"Even if I *don't* have a life of my own," she muttered to herself as she restocked the paper in the printer and began to plot out a schedule for Matt Temple's next week.

That was a bit of an exaggeration. She had friends and plenty of brothers and sisters nearby. Her life wasn't entirely empty. But there was no man in it, hadn't ever been.

"You're just too picky," her happily married sister said at least once a week.

"Yeah," her brother would chime in. "There comes a time, you know, when you have to settle for reality."

And they would look at her and she would be sure they were noticing a few new wrinkles around her eyes, a certain tiredness to the set of her mouth, and thinking, "Gee, she'd better jump at what she can get, poor thing. She's not getting any younger."

All done in love for her, she knew, but it was annoying as all get-out. She had to admit, she had once had a stray thought of what their faces would look like if she walked into Sunday dinner, just once, with Matt Temple on her arm.

All in all, he was quite a man and she knew it. But he certainly wasn't the type of man she would ever end up with. Even if he had been interested in her, she would have had to put a stop to it. Her goal was a big, happy family, just like the one she'd grown up in. It was that or nothing with her. And Matt wouldn't ever fit into a picture like that. He was the sort of man who was wedded to his work, and she was not about to end up with a husband who hardly remembered her name except on weekends. She'd seen the heartbreak that kind of union could inspire in the marriage of her best friend, as well as one of her sisters. He was not right for her. No, not her type at all.

And that was just fine because actually, when you came right down to it, there were a lot of things she didn't like about him.

"What I mean is," she told herself, overanalyzing as she always did. "My hormones have no trouble responding to him on a physical level. If we were still at the stage where we were running around in the jungle, I'd want his genes embedded in my children. But we're not running around in the jungle. We're living in modern America, and his type of gung-ho masculinity is just a little too much to bear.''

Besides, he'd never shown a spark of interest.

The elevator doors opened and there he was, striding down the hall toward her, glancing at his watch as he approached her desk.

"Listen, I'm running late," he said after a piercing look at her. "Miss Carbelli will be stopping by to pick me up any moment. We're going to that new play at Warren Theater.'' He looked into her face again and hesitated, as though something had thrown him just a bit off his stride. Then he frowned and went on. "Have Shirley make me a dinner reservation at the Station House out on the wharf, will you?" He glanced at her again, then headed for his office. "For six," he called back as he went. "That ought to give us time..." His voice faded as he disappeared in through the doorway.

Shayla nodded as though he could still see her and put in an intercom message to Shirley. But all the while, she was puzzling over the way he'd looked at her. "It was as though he'd actually seen me," she mused. "I guess he's never really noticed me before."

That had annoyed her earlier, but now that she thought about it, it was hardly surprising. What had she ever done to draw his attention, after all? He might as well have a robot working for him. She'd never shown him any other side than the industrious workaholic who did a little talking back, but not enough to ruffle any feathers.

"And do I really have another side?" she asked herself caustically. She certainly didn't do much with her time other than work.

But she didn't have much time to analyze her thoughts, as she heard the dulcet tones Pia Carbelli tended to emit come slicing through the late-afternoon hum of office work. The woman was a vision in mink and rhinestone, her red hair a flame that crackled around her pretty, pouty face.

"He's waiting for you, Miss Carbelli," Shayla said, smiling stiffly at the woman as she flounced into the area. "Go right in."

The door opened and the woman disappeared inside, trailing perfume like a wake in water, but before the door closed again, Matt Temple's voice exploded from his office.

"Conners!"

He'd seen the memo. Shayla smiled to herself as she rose and complied, obedient but unbowed.

He was standing at his desk, waving the paper in the air, his brow furled. "What is the meaning of this?" he demanded sternly.

She met his glare and shrugged. "As you can see, the..." She glanced quickly at Pia and realized she didn't want the woman to know about this. Maybe he'd told her, but then again, maybe not. "The, uh,

category you requested is in short supply these days."
She caught his gaze and waited.

He swore under his breath, obviously unhappy that
this was turning out to be such a problem. "I'm
afraid you're going to have to try a little harder to
find the source of that supply, Conners," he noted
coolly. "Or you're going to find yourself pitching in
to help me."

She blanched. What on earth did he mean? Would
he set up a day-care facility here in the office? And
assign her to it? Over her dead body he would!

"I'll see what I can do, sir," she told him quickly.

He nodded, somewhat mollified. "Good." He
glanced at his date for the evening. She was sitting in
a chair, humming to herself and checking out her
manicure, totally ignoring them both. He looked up
at Shayla again, then away, and Shayla blinked. Was
it her imagination, or did he look slightly uncomfortable? She gazed at him curiously. He was acting
in a way she'd never seen him behave before, and she
couldn't figure out why.

Pia seemed to sense something out of kilter as well,
and she tossed her flaming head, batting her enormous eyelashes at the man. "We better get going,
sweetie," she reminded him. "Time's a wastin'."

"Yes," he said quickly. "We're leaving," he told
Shayla, closing up his ledger and putting it away.

She nodded. "Shirley made your reservations," she told him, handing him a slip of paper with the information on it. "Have a nice evening."

She left the inner office quickly, but not quickly enough to avoid hearing Pia chirp and coo. What was that he'd said earlier? He wanted a woman who understood the issues of the day? That certainly wasn't the woman he was about to traipse off with. From what she'd gathered, the young lady's conversations consisted mainly of squeals and giggles, punctuated by the occasional low moan of pleasure.

"*Ooh*, Matt," she heard as the two of them prepared to leave the inner office. "Oh, you bad boy!"

That was followed with excessive giggling and the two of them emerged, arm in arm.

"I know what you're thinking," Pia was saying flirtingly to Matt, "and I'm going to have to make you pay for that, you little devil." She tugged on his arm, obviously planning to whisk him away as quickly as possible.

Shayla couldn't help it. She had to react. And she didn't think either of them would notice, they seemed so wrapped up in each other. So she made one little comment.

"Yech. Gag me with a spoon," she muttered, turning away from them in her swivel chair.

Matt came to a dead stop before her desk and suddenly the office seemed very, very quiet.

"What's that, Conners?" he demanded, glaring at her. "You said something?"

She looked up, surprised he'd noticed. "Uh... No sir, nothing at all."

His blue eyes held hers for a long moment, throwing daggers, and she held her breath, staring right back at him. Finally, his head went back and his eyes narrowed. Taking Pia's arm again, he turned toward the elevator. But he'd heard her, and her words and her look of disdain stayed with him as he left the building with his date. It had been a long time since he'd allowed another's criticism of his life or anything about it to cut him. And for some strange reason, this did. He couldn't imagine why.

Dinner tasted like dust and Pia's pouting was suddenly very boring. The play went on before his eyes, but he hardly saw it. His mind was a sea of seething images, from Remy's young face to memories of his father to the way Conners had looked as she glanced at him leaving with Pia on his arm. The pictures kept coming, he couldn't hold them off. The calm, even pace of his days was about to take a jolt of change, and he was going to come out of it a different person. That sudden insight hit him as he walked back to the car with Pia, and when she asked if he was coming up to her apartment, he stared at her as though he'd never seen her before, then made an excuse and left her to her own devices.

This was it. He was going to be a father.

My God, he thought, staring into the midnight sky studded with a million stars. *What am I getting myself into?*

Shayla's attitude still rankled in the morning. He respected her and usually, he respected her opinion. But he was seeing her a little differently now, noticing things about her he hadn't noticed before.

"Good morning, Conners," he said gruffly, eyeing her without smiling as he stopped before her desk at nine sharp. "I trust we'll get through this day without another critique of my behavior from you."

Shayla looked surprised. "Wh...what?" she stammered. The incident from the night before had completely slipped her mind.

He fixed her with a steady glare. "The comment concerning the insertion of a dining implement into your esophageal region was spectacularly ill timed. If you disapprove of the women in my life, or anything else for that matter, please keep it to yourself."

It took her a moment to digest exactly what he was talking about, but once she had it firmly in mind, her heart fell and she nodded quickly. "I'm sorry about that, sir," she told him sincerely. "I didn't mean for you to hear it. Really. I won't let it happen again."

Her remorse was genuine, and his resentment melted like spring snow. He liked the look of abject regret in her eyes. Suddenly he felt much better about it all.

"All right, then," he said, appeased. "Come into my office and we'll discuss what to do about this baby problem."

He turned and she took a deep breath and gazed after him in wonder. Their relationship had always been stormy, but it had been a superficial sort of tempest. Somehow things seemed to be going deeper all of a sudden. She wasn't sure if that was good or bad.

"I can always count on you, Conners," he added from the doorway to his inner office, and she shook herself, getting back on track immediately. "I want to hear what you've come up with."

The answer to that was not much, and she followed him into his office rather reluctantly. Sitting across the desk from him, she outlined the agencies she'd called already that morning, all of whom had given her the same answer she'd received the day before.

"This obviously isn't going to work, Mr. Temple," she told him as he frowned at her detailed report on the calls. He was going to have to admit defeat on this one. You can't hire a wife. So here went her own big idea. She sat forward. "You're going to have to hire a nanny. Maybe someone full-time who can live in and—"

"No."

She lifted her head and blinked at him from behind her owl-shaped glasses. "What do you mean, no?'' she asked, hoping he'd decided to find a better home for the baby.

But he wasn't about to give up on raising his brother's child. "The nanny business is okay," he began, leaning back in his chair and gazing at her from beneath half-lowered lids. "I realize I will need someone to care for the tyke in the daytime." He paused, then added in a measured tone that left no doubt about his intentions, "But I'm going to raise this kid, Conners, even if I can't find a wife. No matter what, I'm going to do it."

She stared at him and wondered if she really knew him at all. Insanity. That was what it seemed to her. But what could she do? "Help him all you can," her conscience told her. "And hope for the best." Aloud, she said very calmly, "I can see that you feel very strongly about this, Mr. Temple. And since that is the case, we had better approach the situation from another angle. We're going to have to find you someone who can teach you baby-raising skills."

She expected a frown for that, but he only looked at her quizzically. "Do you really think I need to be taught?"

"Of course. It doesn't come naturally, you know." And she couldn't resist adding, "Especially not to men."

His head went back, but he smiled. "There you go with the sexist comments again, Conners."

It occurred to her that he seemed to be in an awfully good mood for someone who was running into brick walls at every turn. "Sorry, sir," she said, studying him curiously. "Now there are agencies that hire out people to teach new mothers what they're doing. I'm sure we could get one of them to—"

"No."

He'd said it again. She frowned, searching his blithe face. "What now?" she asked.

He smiled at her, his widest, most seductive smile, the one he used when closing a business deal, the one he used when charming the most beautiful woman at the party, the one that came naturally to him when he really meant it, the one that made her heart beat just a little faster.

"We're not going to have to hire anyone at all. I want you to do it."

Her eyes widened and a shock ran through her. "Me?" she croaked.

"Yes, you." He leaned forward and held her gaze with his own. "Didn't you say you came from a large family? I'll bet you raised lots of little ones in your time."

He would have won that bet, but she wasn't ready to concede. Something inside her was shivering and she wanted to make it stop, very quickly. "They were sisters and one little brother. And that was years ago."

He smiled again. "There you are. You know all about it."

He had her cornered and she knew it, but she was going to go down fighting. "But I don't know the latest techniques, the latest theories," she said, feeling desperate. "I don't know if they're advising you to put your baby on a schedule or let it dictate the rhythm of the day. I don't know if you should begin cereals at twelve weeks or twelve months."

She would have gone on chronicling her deficiencies, but he shook his head and waved her to silence. "Give me a break, Conners. You and I were raised without all that claptrap. We survived. We can do this."

Her heart skipped a beat. She was a goner.

"*We* is hardly the issue here," she snapped, though most of the zing had gone out of her tone. "*You* are the one who is going to have to do this."

His smile was infuriatingly smug.

"Exactly. But *you* are the one who is going to teach me how."

"But..."

"Pack your sports togs, Conners. We'll have the whole weekend at my place out in Marin County. You can reorganize my house and teach me what to do. Do you think one weekend will be enough? I'm a pretty quick study."

Shayla didn't say anything at all. She was too stunned to speak.

Chapter Three

Matt Temple gazed around his sunken living room and tried to imagine a child playing on the thickly carpeted floor. The picture wouldn't come clear. What the hell did he know about babies, anyway? His life was in for a big change. Was he up to it?

He'd put on a face of confidence when talking to Shayla. She'd arrived a half hour ago, dressed as though she were spending the weekend in the office instead of here at his place in the country. Luckily she had brought other clothes, so he'd sent her up to the room he'd had the housekeeper prepare so that she could change. She ought to be down any minute, and then they would begin the lessons. Baby-raising lessons. For some strange reason, he was nervous.

He'd never thought about having children. It was one of those things that either happened or it didn't, as far as he was concerned. He hadn't avoided it, but he hadn't planned for it, either. Here he was, halfway through his thirties, and settling down had never been an issue for him.

He'd spent most of his adult life creating his business and driving it to the success that now seemed almost dizzying. Though he'd started out with a nice cushion of wealth in his inheritance, he'd definitely taken that nest egg and turned it into a thriving enterprise that had bought him respect and even awe in the marketplace. The next step should be to marry and pass on all this empire he'd built. But he'd never thought of things quite that way. Perhaps that was because he'd never known what it was to have a happy family when he was young. How was he supposed to replicate something he knew nothing about?

His parents had been very rich, but they'd also been very absent from his life. Proverbial jet-setters, they had been more at home in European nightclubs than in the nursery they'd left behind in San Francisco. His mother had died when he was nine. The headmaster of his boarding school had been the one to tell him about it. He'd been sent home to go to her funeral, but through some oversight, no one had come to pick him up at the airport. He'd finally taken a bus that had ended up in Santa Cruz and he'd missed the funeral entirely. But it hardly mattered. He hadn't really known her very well.

After that, his father had gone through a succession of wives, each younger than the last. Remy's mother had been about wife number three, if he recollected clearly. He remembered her as a shy, pretty woman, somewhat overwhelmed by his father's booming personality. She'd been very nice to him, even made a short-lived attempt to mother him in ways none of the other wives ever had. He'd been about twelve or thirteen and, as he remembered it, he hadn't been very nice to her, had shrugged aside her attempts to get closer. But memories of her kindness stuck with him, and even now, he often thought of her rather than his own mother, when the subject of mothers came up. His father had divorced her a few years later, and she'd died of cancer not long after, leaving behind a young son who'd had his own turn at boarding-school life. But Remy had inherited his mother's sweetness and had kept in touch with Matt over the years. Now he wished he'd made more of an effort to reciprocate.

"But I'm going to make it up to him," he told himself firmly. "I'm going to raise his baby. I'm going to do it right. No boarding schools for this little guy."

A sound on the stairs told him Shayla was coming down and he turned impatiently, ready to get on with the work he'd set out for them. But what he saw was a stranger, and he reared back, appalled.

"Conners?" he asked, staring at the woman coming down his stairway. "Is that you?"

Shayla wanted to laugh at his stunned expression, but she managed to hold back the impulse. "You're the one who insisted I dress down for this," she told him as she came up beside him, feeling like a teenager in her jeans, tennis shoes and soft sweater. "I was perfectly happy in heels and a suit."

He frowned. It wasn't the casual clothing that bothered him, he decided, although it did make her appear much younger and shorter than before. It was mainly her hair. He'd never realized that she had so much of it. She usually wore it pulled back tightly into a nice, professional bun, but for some reason, she'd taken out the pins and let it go wild. Gold with light blond highlights shimmering here and there, it cascaded around her shoulders in a very disturbing way, looking as if it belonged to a woman of free, impulsive habits, not the careful, controlled assistant he was used to. Somehow it brought up thoughts of passions and hot looks and other things he had never associated with her before. And yet when he looked into her eyes, they were still the cool, clear violet eyes he was used to. She hadn't really changed. Strange. Very strange. And he wasn't sure he liked it.

She could read his mind. Laughing softly, she reached into a pocket and pulled out a band, quickly pulling back her hair and making a casual ponytail. "There," she said, challenging him with the look in her eyes and the tilt of her head. "Is that better?"

He didn't answer. He really didn't want to get into it with her. And yet, it wasn't better at all. Now, wisps of hair curled around her face, making her look younger than ever, and very, very pretty, while the full, rich substance of her hair still swung from the back of her head. After studying her for a moment out of the corner of his eye, he turned as though ready for some purposeful enterprise.

"Let's get to work," he said gruffly. "Got a game plan here? Or are we playing it by ear?"

She looked up at him and took a deep breath. She hadn't wanted to come. She was very shaky on what was going to happen. But here she was, Matt Temple's guest for the weekend. And now he was looking at her as though *he* wished she hadn't come.

Paradoxically that rather cheered her. Maybe things weren't going to get as dangerous as she'd feared.

But it was best to be careful. "What we need, first of all, are guidelines," she told him, glancing around his extravagantly beautiful living room. "We have to maintain the employee-employer relationship. This is a working weekend. Not a vacation."

"Okay," he said, shoving his hands into his pockets and looking at her as though he were going to wait for her cues. "No problem."

She glanced at him quickly. He was being uncharacteristically agreeable. He looked very different, too. At work, he usually wore the most expensive suits, the whitest shirts and everything looked crisp and serious. Today he wore a soft, open polo shirt that clung to some nicely chiseled shapes and slacks that were casual and slightly snug. Something fluttered inside her chest and she frowned, not pleased. No, there was no reason he should look this good. No reason at all.

"Now tell me this," he said, unaware of her scrutiny. "How do I fix up this place so it's okay for baby raising?"

She turned slowly, biting her lip. "Number one," she said once she'd cased the joint, "we baby proof everything." Reaching into her pocket, she pulled out a sheet of brightly colored stickers and waved them at Matt. "I'll put a sticker on each object that has to go."

He raised an eyebrow. "You certainly came prepared," he muttered as he watched her go to work. But what had he expected? She was always prepared. Why would she change just because she'd suddenly revealed beautiful hair and become too short?

And she hadn't. She was a whirlwind, dashing through his house, putting stickers everywhere. He had only the foggiest notion of what she was doing at first. But as she continued her work, he began to frown.

"Wait a minute," he said as she slapped a sticker on his four-foot statue of an Etruscan love goddess that stood on the hearth of his massive fireplace. "What exactly is going to happen to these things?"

She looked up at him brightly. "They'll have to go," she said, seemingly quite cheerful about it. "Put them in storage, sell them off, whatever. But they can't be here when the baby arrives." And she popped a sticker on the marble coffee table without wasting an extra glance on it and went on to his dagger collection hanging on the wall.

He watched her, appalled, then turned and examined the statue thoughtfully, his hands shoved deep into the pockets of his slacks. "Uh, why is this, exactly?" he asked. "I mean, what does this piece of art have in common with the coffee table, since I notice you've pegged it for removal as well?" He turned to glare at her. "Are you making your judgments on the basis of taste or personal preference? I don't quite get it."

"Not at all," she assured him breezily, reaching back to refasten the band in her hair. "It's all a matter of safety. Look at this." She pointed out the square corners of the coffee table. "Sharp corners. Babies are always falling against sharp corners. And this." She nodded toward the statue. "Tall and heavy. A baby could easily pull it over and get bashed by it."

He looked pained. He loved that statue, and the coffee table had been one of his first selections when he'd decorated his own place.

"Next thing I know, you'll put a sticker on me," he grumbled. "How about if we just tell the little tyke, 'no'? Wouldn't that work?"

Her laughter came echoing back to him as she sped down the hall, slapping a sticker on his poisonous houseplant as she passed it.

"No matter how hard you try," she advised him, "you can never watch them every minute of the day. So you have to think ahead. The moment you turn your back is the moment they climb up and try rolling in the embers of the fireplace or diving off the kitchen counter into a fishbowl or eating the dogs' Crunchy Beef Nuggets.''

He frowned. Why would a baby do all these things? Something wasn't jibing here. ''Wait a minute. When I think of a baby, I think of a cuddly little thing wrapped in covers and sleeping in a basket.''

She looked back at him and grinned, shaking her head. The poor man was in for a rude awakening. ''No such luck. In retrospect, they're only like that for about five days, and then they're off and running and they never sit still again.''

The prospect was daunting and he lapsed into silence, watching worriedly as she littered the house with tiny iridescent signals of doom.

''Aw, not my baseball trophy,'' he complained as she made her way through his den.

''You can put it up on a high shelf where you can still see it,'' she told him, biting back a smile at his stricken look. ''Come on, take it like a man. Having a baby is serious business.''

''So I'm beginning to realize,'' he muttered, following her.

Once she was finished demolishing the artifacts of his life, he called the housekeeper rather grumpily and asked her to assemble a crew of workers to put everything Shayla had tagged into storage. ''Don't bury anything too deep,'' he said sadly, watching his Etruscan love goddess being carted away. ''I may want to visit these things from time to time.''

And then they climbed the stairs to the room that was to be the nursery. The floor was littered with books of wallpaper samples and paint swatches and fabric ideas.

"Boy or girl?" Shayla asked as she sank to the floor and began to flip the pages.

"You got me," he answered, sinking beside her.

Her head swung around, the ponytail bouncing, and she gaped at him. "You don't know the sex of your baby?"

He shook his head and patted his flat stomach. "Just like most people, I'll find out when it gets here," he quipped.

She shook her head in wonder and another thought came to her. "How about the age?"

"I don't know that, either."

Unbelievable. If she were awaiting the arrival of a baby and didn't know the sex or age, she would be going crazy, but he didn't seem to care. Shayla sat very still and watched him as he went through a book of wallpapering ideas. A feeling of dread was welling up in her. This was so crazy, him trying to take on the raising of a baby. It wasn't going to work. And it was going to hurt so much when it all fell apart—both for him and the child. But how was she going to convince him?

"Hey, what do you think of this?" he asked, showing her a sample that portrayed pirate ships and tiny cannons going off. "Isn't that great?"

She had to smile back at him. When he wanted to, she noted somewhat resentfully, he had one heck of a charming smile. "It's awfully cute," she agreed. "As long as the baby turns out to be a boy. If it's a girl..." She held up her own choice, tiny ballet slippers against a pink background.

Matt's face fell. "How about something in yellow?" he suggested, going back to the book. "Maybe cartoon characters."

They compromised on a darling pattern in both blue and pink, with teddy bears of both genders cavorting on clouds that transformed into spaceships and magic carpets.

"With drapes and a bedspread to match," she suggested, and they rose from the floor to take some measurements.

He held the measuring tape while she jotted down sizes, and he found his attention straying to her lush hair again. He frowned.

"I can't get over how short you are," he said as she stood next to him while he measured the window opening.

She glanced up at him and quickly moved away. "I'm just as tall as I've always been," she protested.

"No, you're not," he said, following her. "I mean, at the office, you seem taller. And it's more than just the heels."

She turned and looked into his eyes. Why did he seem to resent everything about her today? "At the office, I *am* taller," she said softly.

That wasn't exactly what she meant and she wasn't sure why she'd said it that way. Maybe because she felt taller at the office. Taller, more in control of things. Here, she was feeling very vulnerable—as though he could reach out and change her life with the flick of his wrist.

He was standing very still, caught by something in her gaze, caught and confounded again. She wasn't supposed to be able to get to him this way. *What way?* He didn't have a clue. All he knew was, she was making him nervous. She wasn't all business as she was at the office. And she wasn't a piece of whipped cream fluff as his girlfriends were. She was something else entirely and he didn't have the slightest idea how he was going to handle her.

"Why are your eyes that color?" he demanded suddenly, happy he'd found something else to complain about. "Is it contact lenses?"

No matter how prepared she thought she was, he always surprised her. "What?" she said, dropping her pencil and not even noticing as it skipped across the floor.

"It's not natural, that violet color you've got." He peered into her eyes as though they offended him, though the truth was, he was enchanted by their shade. Fringed with black lashes, her eyes had a sparkle that would do a diamond proud. He'd never seen anything quite like it, and to his chagrin, he found himself responding in definite physical ways. "How did you get that?"

"Witchcraft," she snapped, turning away in disgust. "My mother put a spell on me."

"You ought to wear your glasses," he muttered, feeling ridiculous, but bound and determined not to let her see how she affected him. "It's not as noticeable when your glasses are in the way."

Whirling, she confronted him, her hand on her hip, her chin in the air. "Listen, mister," she said as crisply as she was able, though she was shaking inside with anger at him by now. If he really hated everything about her, she might as well get out of his way.

"I arrived here dressed for the office. You're the one who made me go up and change. Now you don't like anything about me. You don't like my hair." She yanked the band out defiantly and let it fly around her face. "You don't like how short I am. You don't like my eyes." She pounded one small fist against her chest. "This is me. This is who I am. If you really can't take it, I'll just go and leave you to handle this thing all by yourself."

He'd tried to frown fiercely about halfway through her speech, but he found he couldn't really maintain the front. She was beautiful with her hair a golden mist around her face and her lovely eyes glistening with anger at him. He wanted nothing more than to sweep her up into his arms and take possession of all that effervescence.

"Listen, Conners," he began, trying to be stern, and then his armor crumbled. "No, dammit. I can't call you Conners." He shrugged, looking almost helpless, his eyes troubled, his mind fogged by this unexpected reaction he was having to her. "You're not Conners anymore. Maybe I should call you...what is your name again? Sheila or something like that?"

For just a moment, she was sure he had to be joking, teasing her, trying to get her goat. But then she caught his gaze and read the complete sincerity in his eyes and knew this was for real. He was just a jerk. A complete and utter jerk. What the heck was she doing here?

"Oh!" she cried, turning on her heel and starting for the door. "Let me out of here!"

She was escaping, and despite all his complaining, that was the last thing he wanted her to do.

"No, wait," he called out. "It's Shayla, I remember now."

His legs were longer, which made him faster and he reached the doorway before she did, grabbing her by the arm and pulling her back around to face him. "I'm sorry. I'm not very good at names." His smile was oddly endearing. "But you know that. You know me. All too well, it seems," he added softly, almost under his breath, as his gaze searched hers. "And I don't know you well at all."

"Good," she said, trying to pull away, avoiding a look into his face. She was angry and she wanted to stay that way. She knew one look at his smile would do her in. "Let's keep it that way, shall we?"

"It's too late for that," he said, and suddenly his free hand was touching her hair as though it were spun gold, something magical.

Her heart leaped into her throat, beating there like a wild thing, and she could hardly breathe. "No." She managed to grate out the words, and she reached up to push his hand away. "None of that," she warned, her eyes filled with wary apprehension.

She was right and he knew it, so he didn't push it. But he didn't move, either. Standing there, one hand on her arm, he looked down into her eyes and stared just a beat too long, as though he could read her mind if he looked long enough. She looked back, startled by the depth of something dark in his gaze, the strong pull of something she didn't recognize and couldn't identify.

"Okay," he said at last, and his hand slipped away from her arm. "Okay. We're all business. But you've got to stay. I need you."

She could have sworn her knees had melted. She wasn't going anywhere, and she hated herself for it. But she was here for the duration. If he needed her, she wouldn't let him down.

Silly, she chided herself silently as they moved on to choosing paint colors. *You're a fool if you think you mean a thing to this man. And an even bigger fool if you care.*

But she couldn't help it. Not only did she feel a duty as his assistant, but she felt a bond with him that she couldn't break at the moment.

"Like a woman in chains," she scoffed to herself melodramatically, but she followed him to the kitchen and began pointing out cupboards that would need protective latches.

He paid strict attention, but at the same time he was watching her, watching and wondering. Who was this woman he'd invited into his house? And how long could he get her to stay?

Chapter Four

The day passed more quickly than Shayla expected. She threw advice around as though she actually knew what she was talking about, and she had to admit, he took it all very well, jotting down notes, considering her opinions, compromising without his usual arrogance when they disagreed.

His house was amazing. She'd never been in such a gorgeous place before. The azaleas were blooming in the yard, white ones along one bank, pink along another. The swimming pool sparkled like a turquoise jewel in the sunlight, studded with rocks and small waterfalls so that it seemed to be a mountain pond, which Matt might have found on a hike and brought back as a souvenir. The house itself had an aging elegance, like a debutante from the twenties, all dressed up and still waiting for the right beau to come along.

Like Sleeping Beauty, Shayla thought to herself as she studied the rooms, breathing in the ambience. *Waiting for the prince to appear and awaken her.*

"Your house is so beautiful," she told Matt later when he joined her on a balcony overlooking the lawns and the swimming pool. "Have you had it long?"

"Since before I was born," he told her, leaning against the railing and looking more at her than at the view.

"Then it must be full of memories for you," she said, glancing at him and then back out at the azaleas.

He shook his head slowly, straightening and turning to look out as well. "Not really. I spent most of my time in boarding schools, so this was just a place I came on holiday. A place to sleep, somewhere to store things. No real emotional attachments here."

That sounded very sad. She looked at him sharply, wondering if he were pulling her leg. "But your parents... Surely you had good times together here."

He shrugged as though it hardly mattered. "I was hardly ever here. And neither were my parents for that matter. No one much was here but the caretakers."

She leaned on the railing, biting her lip. That explained the waiting atmosphere, as though the house had been built for great things but they hadn't happened yet. The place was almost like a museum. What was a baby going to do here? Matt had ordered a sandbox and swing set and monkey bars for the yard, but that was like putting a bonnet on a dachshund—it wouldn't change the essential character of the place at all.

Still, things would have to change with a youngster around.

"The baby might just bring this place to life," she murmured, more to herself than anything else.

"You're right," he told her. That was just what he'd been thinking. "And if it doesn't..." He shrugged and smiled at her. "I'll move to somewhere that's better for the kid."

His words astounded her and she wasn't sure she believed him. "You would do that for this new baby you haven't even seen yet?" she asked him, skepticism unmistakable in her voice.

But he didn't seem to notice. "Sure," he said. "When I go into a project, I go all the way."

She knew him well enough to know that was true. Still, he was Mr. Playboy, Mr. Don't-Tie-Me-Down. How could he possibly contemplate making a shift like this? He was dreaming. It just couldn't be done. "You may say that now," she began, her doubt in her eyes.

"You don't understand," he interjected before she could go on. "My life is going to change completely. I know that. And I'm ready for it."

She stared at him, searching for something that would convince her and not finding it. "But why?" she asked him softly.

He gazed into her eyes, his own clear and honest. "Because it has to be done," he said.

No. He couldn't go the distance. He just didn't realize the enormity of what he was getting into. He had no idea what it was going to be like, that this new being would demand his soul as well as his every waking moment from now until it left home. He was fooling himself. She had to find a way to make him see reality.

And yet—why? At first she wouldn't face that question. But finally, it nagged her down. Yes, why? Why did she care what happened to this man? Why didn't she just sit back and let nature take its course? He'd find out all these things soon enough. Why get involved?

"He's my boss," she told herself, tossing her head. "I . . . I care about him. I hate to see him make such a painful mistake if it can be avoided."

She thought about it for the rest of the afternoon, and when they finally sat down to dinner on the terrace and watched the sun set, she had some ammunition up her sleeve. But she waited, biding her time, hoping the wonderful meal of poached salmon, curried couscous and sautéed sugar peas would sweeten the way for her.

Little did she know, he might as well have been eating sawdust for all the attention he was paying to his food. There was no room for taste and texture—his mind was on Shayla. She'd changed for the evening meal and the changes were as disturbing as the previous metamorphosis had been. The white gown she wore was light, filmy and sort of Grecian, and his attention was on her luscious hair and her bare feet in the light sandals and the way her breasts filled the bodice of the dress. She was downright beautiful. Why hadn't he seen it before? What was he, blind?

But he didn't want her to be beautiful, dammit. She was supposed to be efficient and smart and loyal, a perfect administrative assistant. He knew she was all those things, but somehow being beautiful was beginning to obscure them. It was clouding his mind, and the last thing he needed at this point was a clouded mind.

She was clearing her throat. He glanced at her and saw that she was preparing to launch into a lecture of some sort. Silently he groaned. He didn't want any lectures right now. He was too busy lecturing himself to stay put for lectures from others.

"About this baby," she began.

"About *my* baby." He corrected her, smiling as the concept danced before his mind's eye. He was beginning to like the sound of that.

"About your baby," she amended. "I know you're excited about starting this new phase of your life." She hesitated, looking at him, and then launched. "You know, it's very odd, but you're very much like a teenage girl who's just found out she's pregnant. Her first reaction is shock, but once she's decided to go ahead and have it, she starts to dream about how it will be. She starts to imagine dressing the baby up and playing with her and showing her off to her friends." She paused. This part was harder.

"And...and she starts to believe that now, she'll have someone who...who loves her."

She glanced at Matt, wary and ready for fireworks. After all, she was implying that he was expecting, even needing, love from this baby. And yet, there was no evidence to support that, and she knew it. He got plenty of love. Half the women in San Francisco were ready and willing to give him all the love he needed. So she waited for his retort, but to her surprise, Matt seemed undaunted. He took another bite and chewed slowly, watching her as though he were truly interested. So, hesitantly, she went on.

"Then, when the baby gets a little older and starts to make all sorts of demands on her, she has regrets," she continued. "She begins to see what she's given up just to have this baby. And she begins to wonder why she gave up her life for this."

He nodded. He agreed with her. That sort of thing seemed to happen all the time to young girls. He could see that she was really concerned and it amused him somewhat. He wasn't a young girl, and he wasn't looking for love. He knew what he was doing. And anyway, what was the big deal? Didn't she know that he was usually successful at just about everything he tried? He had supreme confidence in this new adventure. After all, what could be so hard about raising a baby?

"Nice story, Shayla," he said, taking another bite of salad and making a face at her. "And I appreciate the spirit in which you told it. But that's not it at all."

She cocked her head to the side, looking at him. "Isn't it?" she asked softly, hoping he would think about her words, take them to heart and maybe glean a little understanding from them.

"No. I'm raising this baby because it's something I just have to do. For my brother. For... for my family." Odd, he'd never thought he had family feelings, but a strange emotion was welling in his chest. "And hey, for father's rights," he added with a grin, papering over the emotion he didn't know how to deal with. "That's it. Father's rights. Every man has a right to a kid, don't you think?"

She shook her head slowly. "What about baby's rights?" she said softly. "What about a baby's right to have a mother and a father? A real family?"

He avoided answering that one. Savoring the salmon for the first time all night, he glanced down at her plate. "You know, you haven't eaten a bite, and it's very good."

Shayla frowned, not hungry and unable to think about food right now. There was an edginess to the man at the moment, and she knew it wasn't the best time to push this, but she didn't have any choice. It was pretty much now or never.

"Mr. Temple," she began again.

Swinging around, he stopped her with a sharp look. "Mr. Temple is for the office," he told her. "If I'm going to call you Shayla, you'd better call me Matt."

That was precisely what she didn't want to do. She longed to get back to the more formal discourse between the two of them. Every time he said her name, his voice sort of rolling it in his mouth, she felt prickles down her spine, as though they were already too close, too intimate.

"All right," she said quickly, then avoided using it. "Please listen." Reaching into her pocketbook, she pulled out a handful of brochures. "I've got information here about a wonderful adoption agency. Just sit and listen for a minute, let me show you the details."

Glancing up, she could see a storm cloud gathering in his eyes, but she pushed ahead quickly, ignoring it as she spread the brochures out before him. "I want you to think about it, really think. There are thousands of couples out there who can't have babies of their own. There are waiting lists a mile long for any child under a year."

He was sitting very still and his knuckles were white, but he kept his voice steady and low. "Philosophically I agree with you. But I'm not going to do it."

Anything short of a shouting match was positive, she told herself. She was making progress and that spurred her on. "All those girls I was talking about want to raise a child without a father, which usually ends in disaster," she told him earnestly. "And now you want to raise this child without a mother. I have a feeling that will be even worse."

She held her breath, knowing she'd probably gone too far, waiting for him to explode. But that wasn't at all what she got. As she watched, he looked down at his plate and played with his fork in his food for a moment before answering.

"I haven't totally given up on the wife idea, you know," he said softly, looking at her.

"You haven't?" Her eyes widened in surprise.

"No. As a matter of fact, Pia actually volunteered." He smiled at her smugly. "And you thought I couldn't get anyone to take the job."

"No," she breathed, horrified. Pia Carbelli with a child? "Oh, no. Oh please, you wouldn't . . ."

His smile drooped, and the storm was back in his eyes. Pushing his plate away, he crumpled his napkin and threw it on the table.

"I'm kidding," he said shortly. "I didn't really tell her. I just wanted to see your reaction."

"Oh." Annoyance followed quickly on the heels of the relief she felt. "I'm so glad I can be here to provide you with entertainment," she said evenly, tossing back her hair.

"Shayla . . ." His large hand covered hers. "Don't try to talk me out of this. I have to do it. There's no choice."

She stared into his deep blue eyes and for just a moment, she got lost there. She had a strange sensation of walking through icy caverns, with stalactites hanging and a cool blast of wind tearing into her hair, and she pulled back, yanking her hand from his and blinking to avoid his gaze. "Don't," she protested, though she wasn't sure if she was talking about his hand on hers, or the mystery of his gaze.

"No problem," he said, but his tone made it clear that his words weren't sincere. Rising and turning away with barely a glance in her direction, he said, "I've got some papers I have to go over. See you later." He started to stride off, then turned back and added, "Meet me in the den at nine if you feel up to it, and we'll go over plans for tomorrow."

And with that he was gone. She sat where she was, sitting very still. She had a feeling she knew why he'd left so abruptly and it wasn't because he resented her trying to make him face reality. It was a lot more than that. They weren't comfortable with each other the way they'd always been before. And he didn't know what to do about it any more than she did.

She wasn't sure. Should she stay or should she go? If she left right now, things might get back to normal at the office on Monday. The house was awfully far out of town. He'd sent a limousine to her apartment to bring her here, but there must be buses, taxis, something she could take to get back to the city. She had a feeling it was going to be dangerous to stay.

There was a sense of electricity that simmered between them now, something that had never been there before, as though neither of them knew exactly where he stood with the other, and each was stepping very carefully so as not to break too far out of old patterns and find that there was nothing left to bind them together in any way.

She should go. That might be the only way to rescue her relationship with him, and her job. Lifting her face to the cool evening breeze, she let the power of the lovely estate wash over her, and thought again, drowsily, "Yes, I should go."

But she didn't move an inch.

Matt wandered down to the creek that ran through a small stand of aspen barely visible from the house. This was where he'd often come as a child, whenever Fate had left him here, usually alone. This was where he could get away from housekeepers and gardeners and people telling him to practice his tennis. No one ever thought to look for him here.

Funny how his childhood was coming back to him more clearly than it had for years—forever. He'd never been one to dwell on the past. But now, with the baby about to arrive, the past was a source he would mine to find a guideline. How was he going to be sure he was doing the right thing by this baby?

Shayla will know, a small voice inside his head tried to assert.

"No," he said aloud. He couldn't depend on her that way. Her help was only meant to be short-term. On Monday, he wanted her back in the office, back in her suit and sneer, back to work. She was his most valued employee. He couldn't risk losing her.

But as the reality of the baby became clearer, he was beginning to realize she was right about one thing: That kid was going to need a mother.

"And Shayla already has a job," he reminded himself, with a sad smile. The mother was going to have to be someone else.

He moved restlessly along the banks of the creek, throwing in a stick to watch it wash its way downstream. His mood seemed to be on a pendulum. One moment he was on top of the world and looking forward to his new direction, the next, he was wondering if he was losing his mind. He wasn't used to this sort of uncertainty. He was the guy who always had all the answers. He didn't know why he was wavering at the moment. He only knew it had something to do with Shayla.

"Maybe if I call her Conners again," he muttered, turning back toward the house. "Maybe that would put things back in proper perspective."

But it was too late for that. She was Shayla to him now. And he wasn't sure if he would ever be able to revert to the Conners relationship. Looking back toward the house, he sighed. Life hadn't been this complicated since he was a child.

"As soon as the baby comes, things will get back on an even keel," he told himself. But his confidence was finally beginning to show hairline cracks.

Chapter Five

In the end, of course, Shayla didn't leave.

She strolled through the garden, breathing in the scent of sweet peas, and browsed through the library, then went on and wandered through the exercise room, lifting a weight or two, and stopped by the kitchen before she realized the house seemed strangely empty. Earlier, there had been a gardener repotting plants in the gazebo and a housekeeper organizing the removal of the dangerous items and a cook who'd fixed that delicious dinner. Now there seemed to be no one. It was almost nine, and she went quickly to the den to meet Matt.

He was pacing the floor when she arrived, holding a glass filled with a rich brown liquid, and he saluted her with it as she entered the room.

"There's no one in the kitchen," she said before he had a chance to speak.

"That's right." He nodded, one eyebrow raised quizzically.

She shrugged. "Where are they all?"

"It's their night off. They usually leave on Saturday afternoon. They only stayed this long in order to serve you some dinner." His charming smile engulfed her. "Wasn't that nice of them?"

Alarms were going off all through her system. "When will they be back?" she asked warily.

"Monday morning."

Was it her imagination, or did his eyes seem to gleam in the shadows? "That means we're all alone in this house."

"That's right." He smiled again. "Hey, there's nothing to be afraid of. I'm here to protect you." He gestured toward the bar. "Would you like a drink?" he asked.

"No, thank you," she said automatically, glancing at the counter along the side of the room where an array of half-empty bottles sat cluttering the surface. Her eyes widened. Matt Temple had never been much of a drinker as far as she knew. She turned to him questioningly.

"I'm going to quit drinking," he announced.

"I see," she said, looking at him skeptically. "And you're swilling down every last drop as quickly as possible so that you can begin right away, is that it?"

"Right." He gazed at her with exaggerated wonder. "My God, you are perceptive, aren't you? That's exactly what I'm doing." He took a sip. "I don't want any liquor in the house while I'm raising the kid. So I'm getting rid of it."

He seemed awfully happy about it. She sank to the couch and watched him, her brows drawn together. "Do you have to finish the job tonight?" she asked him.

"Why not?" He stopped before her, considering her with his head to the side, his blue eyes veiled. "Why not wipe it out in one big blowout?"

Why not, indeed? She wasn't sure she had a good argument on that subject at the moment. Without waiting for her answer, he went to the bar and poured a glass of liquid that caught the light and glowed, returning to offer it to her.

"It will go much faster if you help me," he said. "Here. Have some wine."

She looked up at him from under lowered brows. "I don't want any wine, thank you. I don't drink." At least, not often and never much.

He regarded her with annoying good humor. "Any allergies? Medical problems? Religious considerations?"

"No, it's nothing like that. I just don't drink."

He set the glass before her on the coffee table. "You will drink tonight," he announced, as though he'd received a special message with that information enclosed.

She pulled her arms up, hugging herself and stared at the glass. "I don't like liquor."

He laughed and gestured with his glass. "Think of this as medicine. You need something to cure that terminal starched collar you're plagued with."

Her head jerked up and she would have laughed at that if she weren't so startled and appalled at being thought of that way.

"You took your hair down, you put on grungy clothes." He went on, as though he hadn't noticed her outraged reaction. "But somehow you missed the heart of the matter. We've got to do something to bend that concrete exterior you wear like a shield."

"Mr. Temple," she said icily. "I think you've had too much to drink yourself."

He sank into the couch beside her, shaking his head as though he were exasperated by her. "Okay, now this is serious," he said. "You've got to stop calling me that. My name's Matt. Use it."

"Mr. Temple . . ."

"Ah-ah." He held up his hand, warning her. "Say it."

She didn't make it on the first try, but finally she choked the name out. "M . . . Matt," she said.

He nodded happily. "See? That wasn't so hard." Sitting forward and reaching out, he took the wine-glass from the table. "One drink," he coaxed.

"No." She shook her head obstinately.

"Okay." He put the glass back down and put his hand up in the manner of one taking a solemn vow. "I swear to you, I won't take advantage of you or anything like that. You can feel perfectly safe if you get a little tipsy. Hell, you can get downright drunk if you want. Your bedroom is only steps away. You're not going to get hurt. And I promise, I will not do anything to tarnish your good name."

She was weakening. She wanted to laugh at his playacting, wanted to soften her stance. After all, she was tired and one glass of wine couldn't really hurt. "You promise?" she said softly, searching his eyes.

"On my honor as a scout. There will be no threatening behavior." He smiled as she took up the glass. "Kissing is all," he added as an afterthought.

"What?" She paused with the glass halfway to her lips, her violet eyes wide. "What did you say?"

His look was one of pure innocence. "Kissing." He shrugged. "I thought we might have a little innocent kissing. Why not?"

She put the glass back down on the table very carefully. "Mr. Temple!"

"Matt."

He was giving her that smile that melted ice on sight. She opened her mouth to protest again, but somehow her own lips were curving, and then she was shaking her head and laughing along with him.

"Matt," she said. "There will be no kissing."

He shrugged. "I didn't say there *had* to be kissing. I just didn't want to rule it out."

She stared at him for a moment, knowing she should be resisting his charm, his handsome face, his overwhelming masculinity, and knowing at the same time that she was enchanted by it and that there was very little hope her enchantment was going to dry up anytime soon.

Okay, she found her inner voice saying in her ear. *Go ahead. You can relax a little. Just as long as you never let him see that you...*

No, she told her inner voice silently. *Don't say it!*

But she found herself blushing, laughing and reaching for her glass of wine, all at the same time. "There will be no kissing," she announced, taking a sip. "But we could talk." She glanced at him. "Tell me about your brother and what you know about the baby."

"About the baby, I know very little," he said, sinking back beside her on the couch again. "And I must admit I don't know much more about Remy, either. His mother was my father's... let's see... second wife? Or was it the third? My mother was the first." His eyes sparkled as he went on, half teasing her. "I always felt like that made me the real crown prince. The others were more like pretenders to the throne. You know what I mean?"

He was joking, but there was just enough conviction behind what he was saying to make her wince. She rolled her eyes at him. "Oh, brother."

He grinned, glad she'd reacted. "You find that crass?"

"I find that pathetic."

"Hey. Nobody gave you permission to pass judgment on my private life."

"Then don't tell me about it."

"Well, I've got to tell you about it."

"Why?"

"Because I've got to tell somebody and you're here."

"Thank you so much." But she was feeling very warm and very happy. Maybe too warm and happy. Looking at the half-empty wineglass in her hand, she frowned distrustfully, and set it down as far away as she could reach. "Tell me about the younger ones," she suggested. "Your brothers."

He noted her interaction with the wineglass and suppressed a smile. "There are only two. There's Jared who's living it up on the French Riviera with a plethora of Continental starlets, and Michael, who's gone native in Bali and refuses to wear clothes or speak English any longer." He gave her a superior look. "You see, it's quite clear that I'm the only responsible one."

"Ah, yes."

His slow smile seemed to curl around her. "What do you mean by that sarcastic tone? You don't think I'm responsible?"

Her violet eyes sparkled. "I think you're responsible for a lot of things. Mostly bad."

"Ah, the lady jokes. But tell me this, Miss Comedian. Why haven't you married in all these years?"

Her smile grew more studied. She hadn't counted on the conversation turning to her quite this soon. "It hasn't been that many yet," she said evasively.

"You know what I mean. What are you, twenty-six, twenty-seven? Most women are married by that age, aren't they?"

Thirty was more like it. She hid a smile. Either he was being tactful, or he really thought she looked that young. Either way, she liked him for it, even though age didn't matter to her a bit. The only problem with age was the way a woman's window of opportunity began to close—the opportunity to have a family with lots of children. That had always been her goal, though it was beginning to seem a distant one.

"I'll tell you the truth," she said, turning to face him on the couch.

"Ah, the truth. You mean, rather than a wise-crack?"

She nodded. "Rather than a wisecrack," she echoed. A thrill ran through her. She didn't do this very often. Her fingers were tingling.

"The unadulterated truth."

"Exactly."

"And you think I can handle it?"

She gave him a baleful look and continued. "Okay, here it is. I've never married, because..." She risked looking directly into his eyes. "Because I've never been in love."

His teasing tone evaporated and his gaze grew serious, holding hers in thrall while he considered what she'd said. "Never been in love?" he said softly at last. "I thought women fell in love all the time."

She continued to stare at him, her wide, black-lashed eyes brilliant with candor. "Some do. I don't."

He frowned, looking her over. She was so unlike the women he usually dealt with. A Pia or a Faith or a Darlene would have made up a story rather than admit to having no real love life. Shayla was a beautiful woman—a warm, bright, intelligent woman. Why wouldn't she have a man in her life? It didn't seem to make sense. "But, you do date men, don't you?"

She nodded slowly and reached for her glass, taking another sip of wine. She was telling him things she'd never told anyone else, and she wasn't sure why she was doing it. The miracle was the way he was listening. Most men would be laughing or yawning or changing the subject. But he really seemed interested.

Still, she wasn't going to tell him everything. She wasn't going to explain that she wouldn't fall in love—couldn't fall in love—with a man who didn't want a big family. And these days, it seemed too many men were afraid of that sort of commitment.

"I did date for a while" was what she told him. "It got more and more depressing, though." For just a moment, she flashed back to all those years of hopeful dates made, and disappointing mornings after. "One broken man after another," she said softly, remembering. "I . . . I finally gave it up."

"Really? When did you do that?"

"Oh, about…" Suddenly she realized more truth. It had been about a year ago that she'd given up on men. Right after she'd started working for Matt. Before she could stop herself, she was blushing and she had to turn her face toward the fire to hide it. "A while ago," she said evasively, then turned back and gave him a bright smile. "I've told you a truth. Now it's your turn." She gazed at him speculatively, head to the side, debating what to ask him. "I know," she said. "Tell me about your childhood."

To her surprise, his face changed very quickly. The open, friendly expression was replaced by a mask of indifference, a look she immediately interpreted as a protective ruse.

"I don't like to talk about my childhood much," he said, pouring himself another drink.

She watched him as she asked, very softly, "Is it too close, too personal?"

He glanced at her, ready to deny it vigorously, but something in her face stopped him. "Something like that," he admitted reluctantly.

She smiled. "Then talk about it in the third person. Talk about that little kid named Matt as you remember him."

He laughed. "In the third person?"

"Try it."

He struck a pose and spoke out of the corner of his mouth. "It was a dark and stormy night…"

"You don't have to begin with the night you were born," she said, smiling. "Five would be a good age."

He looked at her and hesitated. Did he really have to do this? No, he didn't have to do it. He never did things like this. Spilling his guts was not his style. Better to stick with the jokes. And much safer.

"He was a lonely little boy with few friends and no one to love him," he tried in his best melodramatic voice, cocking an eyebrow for her reaction.

She knew he was still kidding around and she didn't believe it for a moment. She had every confidence he had been a charmer then, as now. "Maybe seven would be better," she suggested quickly.

"Seven." He tilted his head back and thought for a moment, and as she watched, his face changed, as though he were remembering something.

"Okay, here's a little story," he said, his voice normal at last. "Once when he was seven years old, little Matt Temple came back unexpectedly from boarding school." His eyes took on a distant look, as though he could see the past, see that little boy. "Whether his parents had mixed up schedules or there was a sudden outbreak of scarlet fever at the school, I don't know. But he was sent home to an empty house." Frowning, he settled back in the corner of the couch, retreating into his own history. "There was no one home but the servants, and to them, he was just in the way. Taking up a few of his toy cars, he went to play in the dirt along the side of the driveway, and as he played, a car rolled up with his father driving. His father stopped the car and leaned out, frowning furiously.''

His mouth twisted for a moment, but somehow it didn't look much like a smile. He stared at the fire for a moment, then seemed to remember where he was. Smiling quickly at Shayla, he went on.

''The boy was surprised that his father didn't seem at all glad to see him, surprised that he looked so angry. 'Hey, kid,' his father yelled, glaring at him. 'What are you doing here? Don't you know this is private property? Go back to the village where your kind belongs.'''

Shayla stared at him. ''Your father didn't recognize you?'' she asked in wonder.

He gave her a reproachful look. ''We're not talking about me, remember? We're talking about that weird little Temple kid.''

''Oh.'' She sat back, properly reprimanded. ''Sorry. Please go on.''

''If I must,'' he said, making a face at her. But finding no relenting there, he continued. ''The man looked down and did not recognize the little boy. You see...'' He winced as though the thought was not an easy one to face. ''You see, he didn't see the boy very often. To him, the boy was something of a nuisance. All boys were something of a nuisance. So when he saw the boy playing there, his instinct was to drive him away.''

She shook her head, appalled, and wished she could ring the neck of that callous man. Matt was trying to make this a lighthearted story, but the depth of his pain was clear. From the look on his face, she imagined it was surprising him, too.

''What did you do?'' she asked softly, tears threatening and choking her voice.

He sat still for a second, as though he were trying to remember, then turned and looked at her. ''Threw rocks at his car,'' he said with a sudden, happy grin.

''You didn't!''

''Yes, I did. I'd forgotten that.'' He laughed, giving his thigh a sharp slap. ''That got me grounded until the next day. Then they left to go skiing in Vail, so I got a reprieve.''

Shayla could hardly believe it. This was like no family she'd ever known. In the household where she grew up, there was always someone nearby who loved you, no matter how big a fight you might get into from one moment to the next.

''They left while you were still home from school?'' she asked.

''Sure. While *the boy* was home from school,'' he reminded her. ''We're talking impersonally here.''

''Matt...'' She wanted to reach for him. This was not the macho, disdainful man she thought she knew so well. This was someone else entirely. She blinked quickly, holding back emotion.

He smiled at her, wanting to dismiss it. "Hey, listen. I probably exaggerated a little. Don't go getting all weepy over my childhood. My parents weren't the greatest as parents, but I survived. And turned out pretty damn well, if I do say so." He shrugged it away. "It didn't hurt me that much."

Yes, it had. It had hurt him deep inside. There was no way for him to deny that. Even if the wounds didn't show, they still bled.

"But I do know one thing," he said, his resolve evident in his voice and in his eyes. "This baby isn't going to be raised that way. Remy, his father, was a good guy." His smile was rueful. "He even tried being nice to me. I'm afraid I didn't make it very easy for him." He looked at her, that pain she'd been sure he had showing plainly in his eyes for just a moment. "That's why I have to do this. I'm going to love this baby. I'm going to be the best father this baby could possibly have—other than Remy, anyway."

Shayla sat very still. She was touched, deeply touched, but also, deeply frightened. He was expecting so much, asking so much of himself and of the baby. What if things didn't turn out the way he thought they were going to? How would he accept still more pain? She ached with an agony of longing to help him somehow. And yet, she knew this wasn't something she was going to be allowed to do. This was his journey through life, not hers. She was a bystander, with no rights in the matter at all, and she couldn't even offer any meaningful advice.

But finally, she thought she understood. And she knew she wouldn't be trying to talk him out of taking the baby any longer.

They sat and talked for another half hour as the fire consumed itself and fell to embers. Shayla had another glass of wine, and Matt made her laugh. The room was warm and as the fire flickered out, the shadows grew around them, so that it almost seemed they were in a small circle of light that held them together, like ancient travelers around a campfire. The talk tapered off, and even the silence was companionable.

Like a dream, she thought as she luxuriated in the delicious sense of well-being. She stared into the coals in the fireplace, but all she saw was the man on the couch beside her, and she longed to slide slowly into his arms and...

"Uh, it's getting late," she said quickly, before the thought could fully form in her mind. Putting down the wineglass, she smiled at him. "I think I'd better get to bed."

He didn't say a word, but he rose as she did and went with her to the door of the den, holding it open for her. She hesitated in the doorway, smiling up at him.

"Good night," she said. "It's been very nice."

He smiled back and breathed in the scent from her hair and the next thing he knew, his hand was taking hold of the back of her head and his mouth was coming down on hers as though it were the most natural thing in the world.

She made a sound, but he didn't think it was a protest, so he went on, deepening his kiss, exploring the warm depths of her mouth and holding her closer to him so that he could feel the imprint of her breasts against his chest. It was all a part of a whole, the room, the fire, the wine, the sense of friendly attraction, the underlying desire that had smoldered in them both all day. She felt good against him, wonderful, all heat and flesh and sudden surrender. He was already glancing over at the couch and thinking of how he would carry her back there when she broke away from his embrace, surprising him with the sharp accusation in her eyes.

"This isn't part of our deal," she said, wiping her mouth with the back of her hand and glaring at him, shaken by how quickly and completely she'd responded to his embrace. It had been so long, after all, and she'd forgotten what a man felt like, how seductive human contact could be. "You can't do this."

"Shayla, I didn't do anything but..."

"Kissing, I know." She calmed as quickly as she'd come to anger, and almost smiled, despite herself. "But kissing leads to harder stuff, and we both know it." She'd noticed the glance toward the couch and she'd read his mind. "With you, it seems to happen almost instantaneously," she noted, a touch of light derision in her tone. "Haven't you ever heard of gentle wooing?"

His lopsided grin gave him a boy-next-door look, but there was more than casual friendship shining in his deep blue eyes. "Is that what it takes to win you, fair lady?" he teased.

She considered for a moment, challenging him with narrowed eyes. "No," she told him once she'd thought it over. "I just wondered if you'd heard of it." She was out the door and hurrying down the hall before he could react. "Good night," she called back. "See you in the morning."

He stood watching her disappear around a corner toward the stairway and he laughed softly to himself. It was probably just as well she'd stopped things. Losing his best assistant would have been a high price to pay for one night of passion. Shrugging, he returned to the den and poured himself a drink. He put another log on the fire, and settled into the big leather easy chair. He was tired, but there was tension in his shoulders and he knew he wouldn't be able to sleep if he went to bed right now. Better to use this time to think some things through. He had a lot of things to think about—starting with the baby who was set to arrive in one short week.

Chapter Six

Shayla woke with a start and stared into the darkness, listening hard. What was that noise she'd heard? Or had she dreamed it? Right now she could hardly hear anything but the wild thumping of her heart.

She'd only had a little sleep. The clock beside the bed said two. Lying back against the snowy white sheets, she stretched beneath the warm covers and waited for her pulse to slow. No sound. Nothing. But she was fully awake and she knew it was going to take a while to change that back into drowsiness. She let her mind drift for a moment, and the dream she was having when she awoke returned. What she remembered jerked her eyes wide open again. Matt. She'd been in his arms....

She groaned and beat her fists into her pillow. This was not supposed to happen. She was too smart to let this happen. She was not one of the women he dated for entertainment. She was hired for business, and the lines were firmly drawn between the two. She'd let the lines blur in the den in front of the fire. No wonder she was dreaming about him. The question was, did he realize how she felt? Could he tell she'd cared about him much too much for much too long?

She groaned again, knowing she'd let her guard down. It was this house. The place was seductive. She'd known from the moment she'd walked in the door that she couldn't stay too long. You couldn't let yourself linger in a place like this. That would be like taking drugs or eating too many rich foods. Such behavior might tempt you into changing your whole way of life, your whole way of thinking. And that wouldn't do.

Sliding out of bed, she began to pace her room, walking in and out of the silvery moonlight. No, that wouldn't do at all. And what was going to happen in the morning when they met over breakfast and he smiled at her and she went weak in the knees and... and...

She stopped dead and stared out the window into the night. Memory flooded back, memory of how she'd felt when he'd kissed her, how her defenses had melted away for a moment, how hard it had been to stop, to pull back and deny what they both wanted.

Could she do it again? Would she be strong enough? She had to be. She had no choice.

Turning, she knew she was in too much danger to ride on hope. No. This was not the right thing to do. She knew where she was going, where her life was headed. This would provide a very ugly detour if she let it happen. She had to leave. She had to get out while she could.

Breathlessly she changed out of her nightgown and back into the jeans and sweater and packed her things away in her bag. She thought of leaving him a note, but there wasn't any paper in the room, so she gave up on that. Making her way down the stairs, stepping as quietly as she could, she headed for the front entryway. But as she rounded the corner of the living room and turned into the hall, the light from the open door to the den fell across her path, and she stopped, paralyzed, holding her breath.

He was still up. Moving slowly, very slowly, she positioned herself to see into the room, and there he was, sitting in the enormous easy chair, staring into the embers of a fire that was still crackling. She drew back quickly and closed her eyes. She was going to have to pass by this doorway to get out of the house. That was, unless she wanted to try breaking a window to escape, and that didn't strike her as a particularly clever plan. Moving with glacial dispatch, she eased herself up to the doorway again and looked in.

He hadn't moved. There was a cup of coffee sitting next to him on the end table. His face was dark and brooding, his eyes troubled and filled with some cloudy torment, and with a jolt, she realized that what she was seeing was very likely the real Matt Temple—without the mask of control he usually wore. She saw naked heartache, naked longing that took her breath away.

Her first impulse was to go to him, to reach out and make it better, whatever it was. He was in obvious pain of some sort, and she ached to help him. He needed someone—or something—so badly. And yet, how could she be arrogant enough to think she could provide what he needed? No, there wasn't a chance of that.

She looked again, and the shadows from the fire danced across his face, making her wonder if what she'd thought she'd seen was real or an illusion of smoke and firelight. Because whatever it had been was gone, and he looked quite normal.

For all she knew, her own mind was playing tricks on her now. For a moment she felt as though the whole world was conspiring to force her into his arms. Her determination strengthened. She had to leave.

Holding her breath, she tiptoed quietly past the door, not letting herself breathe again until she was in the middle of the living room. She let herself out of the big front door, easing it shut. Starting down the path, she shifted her bag from one hand to the other and crunched quickly through the gravel. The long, winding driveway seemed to go on forever, but finally she'd reached the gates, and then she was out on the road. She knew it was going to be a mile or two into the little crossroads at the highway where she'd noticed an all-night coffee shop. Once she got there, she would find a phone and call a cab....

She felt the perfect fool, walking down the road with her suitcase in the middle of the night. Now that she'd left the house, she was beginning to wonder what had seemed so threatening, so dangerous, that she had to flee into the dark without saying goodbye. And what was she going to say to Matt on Monday morning? Regret welled up in her throat and she wished she'd stayed right where she was, safe and warm in the bed in Matt's house.

Suddenly there were headlights, coming up fast behind her. Her heart skipped a beat, halfway between relief and fear. Should she hide? Should she try to hitch a ride? What kind of person would be out here on this country road at three in the morning, anyway? And what sort of person would pick up some stray woman walking along the side of the road way out here? There was no time to do anything. The car was pulling up alongside her. The driver had seen her. Her heart was thumping wildly. She could pretend to live nearby, she planned a bit frantically. She could say she'd had a flat tire. She could—

"Shayla. What the hell are you doing?"

It was Matt. She hadn't recognized the car. It wasn't one he usually used.

She paused only a moment to bend down and look in at the driver. Once she saw his face, she remembered why she couldn't stay anywhere near him.

"I have to go," she told him firmly, pushing aside the hair she'd neglected to tie back. "It's way past time."

He didn't buy it. "Get in the car, Shayla."

"No, thank you. I'd rather walk." And she started off again, her bag bumping against her legs.

The car cruised along beside her.

"If you really feel you have to leave, I can take you. Get in."

"No."

"I'll take you anywhere you want to go. Honest."

She shook her head, staring straight ahead as she walked, not looking at him. *This is called resisting temptation,* she told herself silently. *Get used to it.* "You can't take me where I want to go," she told him aloud.

"Why not?"

She glanced at him and then away, still walking. "Because it's away from you," she admitted, feeling herself slipping to the edge of desperation. "That's where I have to go. Can't you tell?"

"Okay." He pulled the car to the side, slamming on the brakes and turning off the engine. In another moment, he was striding beside her. "If you want to walk, we'll walk."

Swinging around to face him, she felt all her energy draining away. "Matt, please," she said. "Don't do this. Let me go."

"But why?" His eyes looked black in the moonlight. "Shayla, tell me why."

She stared at him for a long moment, then dropped her suitcase and sank to sit on it. He went down on his haunches beside her, still waiting for his answer. He looked young and appealing in the big, open leather jacket he'd put on, and she longed to run her fingers through his unruly hair. Wincing, she turned away from him.

"I don't want to be here anymore," she said as firmly as she was able. "I . . . I don't want to be whatever it is that we're becoming."

"Shayla." He reached out to take her hand and then thought better of it. "We're not becoming anything. We don't have to, anyway."

She shook her head, not accepting his weak reassurances. "I want to go back to being Conners to you," she said, turning back to look into his face, her eyes filled with a smoky sense of regret. "I want to go back to calling you Mr. Temple. I want to be in my suit with my hair pulled back and my glasses on and you yelling out orders and me throwing back thinly veiled insults. And . . ." Her voice faltered. "And I'm just afraid we can't do that anymore. It's too late. Can't you see that? We've gone way beyond that."

He looked back at her silently for a long moment, then slowly rose, holding out his hands to help her up as well.

"I know what you're scared of," he told her softly.

She searched his eyes, but it was too dark to see into the shadows there. "What?"

He still held her hands in his and he pulled her closer. "It's the same thing I'm scared of."

Despite what she'd thought she'd seen in the den a little earlier, she didn't believe he could be scared of anything. She'd never seen any other evidence of it. She shook her head vigorously, wanting to deny what was undeniable. "No."

"Yes." He pulled her even closer and his arms brought her body against his. "You're scared of this," he murmured, and he kissed her again, kissed her gently, slowly, with all his desire leashed and barely showing.

She melted into his kiss as though she were sinking into a warm bath. There was no resistance in her. His touch set her pulse racing and his taste poured through her like hot, rich brandy. The kiss only lasted a moment and was gentle, unthreatening and sweet, but it proved her case. Proved it, and demolished all the defenses she'd built up against it.

"There now," he said as he drew back, sounding a bit breathless himself. "Was that so frightening?"

She looked up into his face and she told him the truth. "Yes."

"I know." He half laughed, half groaned, pulling her back into his arms. "Me, too."

She started to laugh and they laughed together, holding on, and when he turned and began to lead her back to the car, she didn't stop him.

He stowed her suitcase in the trunk and drove her back to the house. Taking her into the big, gleaming white kitchen, he brewed her a cup of tea and sat across the counter from her while she drank it. Her hair had frizzed up in the late-night dew and it flew around her head like a golden halo and her eyes shone violet in the bright kitchen light.

An angel, he thought. *That's what she looks like. And everybody knows you can't seduce an angel.*

"Feeling better?" he asked her aloud.

She nodded and smiled at him, and he groaned, because this untouchable angel was all too tempting.

"Think you can sleep now?" he asked.

She looked down into her teacup. "I don't think so," she admitted. "I'm just so wound up." She looked up quickly. "But you go ahead. Don't mind me. I can..."

"Come on." Rising, he stretched out a hand to her. "Come with me."

She seemed to have lost all will of her own. As she rose and let him take her hand, she made a feeble attempt to remember all those times she'd reacted to everything he said with a smart remark. But that spirit seemed to be dormant at the moment. She couldn't rouse it. She didn't want to, either.

He led her into the den. The fire was barely flickering, but he threw another log on and turned to her.

"Come here," he said, his eyes luminous in the shadowed light.

She came, trusting him beyond all reason.

He drew her close. "Don't worry," he told her softly. "I promised you no threats to your virtue, and I meant it."

She nodded. She knew he was telling her the truth. He always told the truth.

Taking her to the huge leather chair, he pulled her down into it with him, and she came, trusting him completely. He held her to him as if she were a child, her head cradled to his chest, her legs curled up in his lap. Stroking her hair, he told her gently, "Close your eyes. I'll watch over you tonight. You just relax."

She closed her eyes, squeezed them tightly, but two small tears rolled through nonetheless. She didn't know why she was crying. She only knew she had never felt so protected before, so completely safe. Every muscle let go, every nerve went dull, and she felt herself melt against him like butter on a hot plate.

How did he know to do this? How did this man who had never experienced the sort of love every child deserves know to hold her this way, to treat her so tenderly? It was a miracle, as far as she was concerned. A perfect miracle. And in no time at all, she was asleep.

* * *

He must have slept at some point, but it didn't feel like it. Dawn was painting the sky purple outside, and the fire had finally gone out in the fireplace when he became fully awake. She was still asleep in his arms and he shifted a little beneath her, restoring circulation to areas that had been cut off. Her hair was still a mop of spun gold, but it smelled like fresh flowers after a rain shower.

For a long moment, he enjoyed the feel of her against him and puzzled over the changes that had come between them in the past few days. He'd always liked her, respected her, found her completely necessary to the smooth running of his office. But on Wednesday, he'd begun noticing that she was more than the woman who kept him on his toes at work. He'd resisted it at first, but it wasn't long before he'd realized she was probably the most attractive woman he'd ever known. And now, here they were—at a crossroads. What came next would determine a lot of things for both of them.

He moved restlessly, annoyed with himself. After all, he had a baby coming to live with him. He really didn't have time to embark on a new romance now. He had enough complications in his life. He didn't need this one.

No, he was going to be strong and tough and responsible, for a change. He was going to do what was right for everyone involved. And just as soon as she woke up, he was going to tell her so.

"Matt?" She was stirring, stretching out her arms and smiling up at him.

"Hi," he said softly, looking down at her and forgetting all his good intentions. "You've been asleep for hours."

She smiled, nodding, loving the way his hair fell over his forehead, the way the morning light exposed the craggy nature of his handsome face. This man, this bear of a boss, this arrogant, conceited ladies' man, had held her while she slept, had watched over her protectively to make sure she wasn't afraid and wasn't harmed. She could hardly believe it had really happened. Was it a transformation, or had he always been this way and she just hadn't noticed?

Both. A little of both. She'd seen his tender side now, as well as the side that put shivers down spines all up and down the boardroom. And she knew two things: First, he might just make it raising this baby after all; and second . . . she loved him.

Reaching up, she cupped her palm to his cheek and looked at him. Her look said it all. His heart began to pump, though he was shaking his head, warning her.

"Shayla," he began, "I promised you . . ."

She stretched luxuriously and began to inch her way up to where she could reach him, wrap her arms around his neck, press a kiss against his cheek. "You can make all the promises you want,'' she murmured huskily. "I never promised a thing."

Looking at her, he laughed softly. After all, what could you do if the angel decided to seduce you?

And the angel turned seductress, indeed, with long, slow kisses that turned the heat up and a lazy, gliding hand that slipped beneath his shirt and quickly found how sensitive his skin was. He could only take so much coaxing before he'd turned from reluctant companion to a hard, aggressive male who was used to taking the lead in these matters. The kisses grew quicker and they slid down off the chair onto the thickly carpeted floor, rolling together and shrugging out of the constraints of clothing. Her breath was coming very fast and when he saw her naked body in the morning light, his stomach fell away as though he'd been slugged there, and he couldn't breathe at all.

She turned to him, reached for him, needing to feel like a woman in a way she never, ever had felt before. She'd never found what she was looking for and she didn't really expect to this time, but she had to hope. After all, no man had ever been like Matt, no man would ever be like this again.

She wrapped around him and reached for a fulfillment she could only dream of. He took her to him as though she could make him whole in some way, heal something deep inside him he hadn't realized was aching until he'd looked at her. She cried out as he thrust his way into the bond that would join them. She lifted to meet him, urging more from him, taking and giving at the same time, until they moved together, harder and faster, clinging as though they couldn't live without the touch of skin on skin, flesh to flesh. And finally, they fell, breath completely spent, into the shallows of an illusionary sea that lapped around them, calming the storm in their blood, the heat in their veins, the hunger in their bodies, and leaving them entangled in each other's arms, skin shiny with sweet sweat.

Chapter Seven

So now it was done. Shayla had taken that dangerous, irreversible step that drove their business relationship forever out of reach. And she didn't have a thing to show for it.

"Fool," she told herself as she showered in the plush bathroom off his bedroom. "You crazy, idiotic fool."

But her regret was only skin-deep. It barely scratched the surface. And down where it counted, she was a woman in love, a woman fulfilled as she'd never been before. She was happy.

They'd made love again, on his bed this time, and it had been even sweeter than before. They'd spent an hour tangled together, murmuring silly things and laughing. And then, reluctantly, she'd left him to take a shower. Now she was about to rejoin him on the terrace for a breakfast he'd fixed. What was she going to see in his eyes when she walked out into the sunshine? Slipping into slacks and a lacy top, she stopped to slash some quick pink color on her lips, fluff her hair, and then turned and went out to face the music.

He'd set the wrought-iron table with yellow china and put a handful of blue irises in a glass with some water and stuck them in the middle of the table. A pitcher of orange juice sat to the side, and a huge plate of crispy bacon joined some warmed muffins to fill out their meal. She stopped, mouth open, to stare at what he'd done.

"Wow," she said, gazing at him in wonder. Who would have guessed her demanding boss would have these hidden talents? "Where did you ever pick up these domestic skills?"

He shrugged, looking endearingly embarrassed. "Most summers and vacations when I was a kid, I hung out in the kitchen," he told her. "The cook was my best friend some years. I picked up a few things." He pulled out the chair for her. "Would you like some eggs? I'm great with omelets."

"Oh, no thanks, a muffin will be fine." She sat and turned her head to smile up at him. His gaze was open and amused, without a hint of regret or impatience, and her heart lightened. The scent of honeysuckle filled the morning air, and birds sang in the trees. It was going to be a wonderful day.

They didn't eat much and they spoke in fragments, but the feeling between them was warm and happy. She laughed at his jokes and made a few herself, but all the while, her left hand lay in her lap with her fingers crossed. It was wonderful, but it couldn't last. It never did, did it?

"A week from today, the baby will be here," Matt said as they began to clear away their dishes and carry them to the kitchen. "I guess I'll be taking a few days off work while the baby gets settled in," he mused.

Shayla suppressed a smile. He would be taking off more than a few days unless he found himself a good nanny by then.

"I can hardly wait to hold the little guy in my arms," he said, his hands full of dishes but his eyes on the future. "To see those tiny feet. To see those little eyes gazing up at me, that little tiny mouth making baby bubbles, the little hand grabbing my finger..."

His voice broke and Shayla swung around to look at him, stunned. "You really are looking forward to this," she said softly, searching his face and finding only candor.

He nodded, looking slightly abashed. "Yes. Yes, I am. I've always wanted a child."

She looked away from him as they entered the kitchen and began to load the dishes into the sink. "You just didn't want to lay the groundwork and marry someone to get there," she suggested rather caustically.

His wide mouth twisted. "Always looking for ulterior motives, aren't you, Conners?" he challenged. "The fact is, I never really thought about it. But ever since that lawyer called, I've realized how much I want a son or daughter. It's only natural. I'm at that age. It's time."

She stared at him. For almost a year she'd been studying him, watching every move he made, and she'd thought she knew him so well. But she'd never dreamed of these things that lay at the depths of him. He was much more than she'd ever thought.

They shared doing the dishes, then sat down at the breakfast nook and began to talk over other things that had to be done to prepare for this baby.

"You're going to need to fence in the pool," she told him, making a mark on her checklist with a big black marker. "You'll need gates on all the stair-cases, top and bottom. The gardening tools need to be stored away in a locked shed. The cleaners and other chemicals in the kitchen should be stored up higher, out of reach of little climbers."

He leaned back in his chair and groaned. "My God. It would be easier to start from scratch and build a childproof home."

She grinned at him. "Millions of people have babies every year. They manage. You will, too."

His eyes darkened. "I hope so," he murmured.

She set down the list and looked at him. There was a lot to do and little time to do it. She wanted to help him all she could. And at the same time, she felt a restless need to get away from him for a bit, to put things into perspective. "We don't have much time. Maybe we should each go our own way today, so we can get twice as much done," she suggested.

"Okay." He nodded. "I'll get a hold of the con-tractor and get plans going on the pool fence and some other things."

"And I'll go looking for baby furniture and order the wallpaper and drapes." She jumped up. Things had moved awfully quickly in the last day or so. She needed some space, to stand back and see what was really going on here. "I'll go to the mall. Where are the keys to your car?"

He watched her drive off and waved until she was out of sight. "Don't be gone too long," he muttered, then turned back into the house and listened to the silence. Just twenty-four hours and he'd already grown used to having her around.

But that wouldn't last. It never did. He had a lot more faith in his ability to give lasting love to a baby he'd never seen before than to a woman he had every respect and affection for. It had been his experience that these things just didn't last.

He called the contractor and made an appointment, and he was searching for the number of a good iron worker when the front bell rang. He frowned, realizing he'd left the gate open, but it was with no trepidation at all that he sauntered to the front door and opened it. There on his doorstep stood a harried-looking woman. A limousine was parked behind her with the engine still running. She seemed to have a large basket at her feet. It looked like the sort of basket some people put dogs in when traveling, and he had already begun to form the words of refusal— "I can't keep a dog, I just don't have the time"—

when the woman cried out, "Señor Temple? Is you, no?"

"Uh, yes, I'm Matt Temple. What can I do for you?"

"I am sick, Señor Temple," the woman screeched, clutching at her throat. "Baby's here, but I am sick. Please, please, you have a room for me?"

"The baby?" He stared at the basket and every nerve in his body was suddenly tingling with anticipation. "Remy's baby?"

"Si, Señor, but I must have a room. I am very sick."

The woman's tone of desperation finally penetrated his consciousness and he looked up, noting her extremely green pallor. The woman was definitely sick. There was no doubt.

"Are you the nurse?" he asked.

She nodded. "Please, please," she moaned, swaying and turning a chalkier shade of green.

The nurse. The baby. He could hardly believe it. They weren't supposed to arrive until the next weekend, but here they were.

"Hey, mister." It was the limo driver who called out. He was taking baggage out of the car. "Better get her to a bathroom. She's been like this since I picked her up at the airport."

"Bathroom." He glanced at the basket curiously, hesitating. But then again, this woman looked very sick. First things first. "Sure. Of course."

He had ordered the housekeeper to set up a room for the nurse he'd been expecting to accompany the baby, and she'd done so, at the back of the house. The room had its own bathroom and even a little office on the side. He led the poor nurse to it now.

"Here you go. Let me know if you need anything," he said as he escorted her into the room and shut the door. But his mind was still on the doorstep with that basket, and he hurried back.

The basket hadn't moved. He looked down at it and his mouth went dry. There was something inside, something making a noise. This was it. His baby was here. He was a daddy.

Carefully he pushed back the visor. A little round face stared up at him with gray eyes as big as saucers, and his heart nearly stopped. This was the most beautiful baby he'd ever seen. Devon said the name on his little bib.

"Devon," Matt whispered, staring down and hardly daring to breathe. "Hi, Devon," he said, his gaze taking in every detail, from the wispy golden hair to the feet in little yellow socks that were kicking away a blanket. Two fists began to wave at him and a determined look came over the round face. He let out a sound that was somewhere between a coo and a grunt, and Matt blinked, surprised at such a big voice coming out of a baby.

"Hey, you're a big boy, aren't you?" he noted, beginning to frown. This baby was bigger than he'd imagined they were, bigger and—

"Say, mister," called the limo driver, interrupting his thoughts. "Better get this one, too."

Matt rose to his feet and looked out at where the driver had piled the luggage. There was another basket, identical to the one at his feet. For just a moment, his mind refused to assimilate that information, and he stared at the second basket as though he were seeing things.

"Wait a minute," he said slowly at last, frowning suspiciously. "What is that?"

The limo driver grinned, unwrapping a stick of gum as he watched Matt's face. "What do you think it is? Can't you hear him fussing?"

Matt lost all power of speech for a moment, and his voice was as rough as ground glass when he finally did speak. "No. That can't be. There are two babies?"

The limo driver nodded, unwrapping a stick of gum. "You got that right. The nurse said they're twins."

"Twins?" he echoed stupidly. "Twins? Two babies?"

The limo driver looked concerned at his tone as he popped the gum into his mouth. "Hey, mister, are you okay? Listen, that nurse knows what she's doing. Once she gets better, she'll help you, don't worry. There were two of them, you know."

"Two?" The word was echoing in his brain and he wasn't sure if the limo driver had actually said it again, or he'd just heard his own brain repeating it.

"Yeah. Two nurses, I mean. Two got off the plane. But the other one hated everything she saw and she turned right around and got a ticket on the next plane back to Argentina. They had a big long argument right there in the airport. And Lola—that's your sick nurse there—she came on out with the babies, even though she's sick as a dog. The other one's going back."

Matt couldn't quite get all this information straight in his head. "Two?" It had almost become a mantra with him now.

The limo driver frowned. "Listen, you go on and carry that one in, I'll get this one. Where you going to put them?"

Matt watched the driver lift the second basket and then he bent down and picked up Devon. The little fist waved again, hitting him square in the eye as he took hold of the basket, but he hardly noticed. The word "two" kept reverberating through his head. He was numb.

They stowed the two baskets in the living room, and Matt gave a lingering look at Devon before turning to take a look at the other one. The driver pushed back the visor and there was a carbon copy of the first baby, fists waving, feet kicking, face turning red as though he were making some major effort at something. David said the name on the bib. Matt stared at him, still stunned. "Two," he repeated softly.

The driver gave him a baleful look. "You got some woman around here who can help you?" he asked doubtfully.

That brought Matt back to life. He swung around and glared at the man. "What do I need a woman for? I can handle this," he insisted stoutly.

"Sure you can," the driver said, backing toward the door. "Listen, I didn't mean anything by it. Uh…you'll do great with the kids. I guess you've had a lot of experience, huh? You know what you're doing. I'll just be going, then."

Matt handed him a large bill as a tip and ushered him out the door with hardly a thought. His mind was consumed with his two arrivals.

"Two," he repeated as he turned back to them. "What am I going to do with two?"

Two pairs of gray eyes stared up at him. Two little mouths were open, one forming a perfect circle, the other stretching wide in a yawn. They were awfully cute. Matt started to smile, first at Devon, then at David. Twins. Twin boys. They were his now. Pride tried to shoulder out terror in his heart, but it wasn't strong enough yet and his smile faltered. He still wasn't sure what he was going to do with them.

As he watched, Devon's face started to crumple. The fat lower lip began to quiver. The eyes squinted almost shut. A whimper came out of the tiny mouth.

"Oh, no. Don't cry." Terror was definitely going to win this round if that happened. Matt looked at the baby, then looked at his own hands. He was going to have to hold it, wasn't he?

The whimper had become a wail. Matt worked fast, undoing the seat belt that held Devon in the basket, pulling away the blankets that were stuffed all around him, and pulling him up by his shoulders. The wail became a howl. Matt held him out the way he might hold a soaking wet towel and stared at him. He was crying hard and waving his arms. This kid was mad. What now?

The nurse. She would know. Grabbing the child to his chest, he raced through the house to the room where he'd led the nurse.

"Excuse me," he called, knocking on the door and raising his voice so that she could hear above the din Devon was making. "What do I do when they cry?"

"You must hold him, Señor. Or feed him. The bottle is in the blue bag." Her voice disappeared into a fit of coughing.

Matt's heart sank. He'd been hoping she would be well enough to come out and help him. She sounded worse than before.

I'd better call a doctor for her, he thought as he turned away, the child still screaming in his arms. A doctor. Yes. They knew what to do with babies, too, didn't they? It was a professional duty of theirs.

He went back into the living room. Devon was not only screaming, but he was now wriggling as though he wanted to break free and make a run for it.

"Hey, you're awfully strong for a baby," Matt muttered, putting him down on his back on the floor near the basket where his brother was still staring out at the world with big eyes. "You stay right there. I've got to go call the doctor."

He made his way quickly to the den and found the doctor's number, dialed it and got his service.

"Please give me your name and number. The doctor will call you as soon as he can."

"Make that semi-immediately," Matt ordered, a note of hysteria in his voice. "We've got an emergency here."

"Would you like me to call 911 for you, sir?"

Matt considered for a moment, but decided this wasn't quite that much of an emergency. "No, thanks. Just get the doc to call me back."

"I'll do what I can, sir."

Matt hurried back to the living room, following the sound of the wailing child. The crying was going strong, but when he reached the room, there was a very empty spot where he thought he'd left the baby. He stared at it for a moment, as though the baby had turned invisible and would reappear if he just looked hard enough. Then he glanced around the room. No baby. The crying was coming from David now. He was waving his arms and legs and turning a bright red as he screamed out his annoyance at still being strapped into the basket while his brother was off having all the fun.

"Wait a minute," Matt muttered, tearing his hair distractedly. "How can this happen? Where the heck is he?"

The answer came in the sound of a crash coming from the dining room. Matt raced to find Devon sitting in a pool of water and broken daffodils, the hem of the tablecloth in his hands.

"Oh my God. Are you okay?"

The happy smile and bubbling gurgle that came from the baby answered that question. Matt scooped him up, ignoring the mess, and carried him back to the living room. David was roaring like a young, angry lion, and Matt hesitated. Devon was happily kicking his heels against Matt's stomach. At least he wasn't crying. But if he put him down while he picked up David, would Devon head out for more disaster? He looked down into the happy face and met eyes brimming with adventure. There was no doubt about it.

Did babies follow orders like dogs? That was probably too much to hope for. But he had to try. What else could he do? He set Devon down in a sitting position on the floor and held out the flat of his hand as though he were a terrier. "Stay!" he said firmly. "Stay!" Devon looked up at him with eyes full of wonder.

Turning quickly, he began to unbuckle David from his basket seat. Out of the corner of his eye, he saw movement. Devon was scooting along the floor, heading for the doorway.

"Stop!" Leaving David half unbuckled, he raced after the fleeing tyke. Grabbing him around the waist, he lifted him and brought him back. "Stay!" he said again, though he didn't think his message was really getting through.

He tugged at the strap on David's basket, freeing him, but Devon was off again, gurgling happily as he went. Matt crossed the room in three strides and scooped him up again, turning just in time to see David scrambling out of the basket and heading for the opposite door on all fours.

"Hey!" he called out, dashing back and scooping up that baby, too. Now he had them both, two wriggling, fussing babies, one for each arm. What now?

The nurse had said something about bottles in a blue bag. The luggage was still sitting outside, but there was the blue bag, stashed in the entryway. He maneuvered himself into position to reach down and grab the strap and pull it back into the living room. Both babies were struggling harder, each determined to get away and explore the house. He contemplated putting them back into the baskets, but he knew they'd scream if he did, and besides, while he was buckling in one, the other would head for the hills.

But there were bottles inside the bag. Maybe if they got a look at those bottles, they'd calm down. He carefully put down the babies on the couch and pulled the zipper open on the bag. Bottles and other supplies were neatly stowed inside. He pulled two bottles out and waved them at the wiggling boys.

"Look, guys. Food!"

They both stopped, stared for just a moment, as if they didn't really trust him to fork over the real thing, and then two pairs of arms reached eagerly for sustenance. They each took a bottle and lay back, drinking greedily, their eyes half closed.

For the first time in half an hour, Matt felt as though he could catch his breath. He sank onto a chair and leaned back, exhausted. This baby stuff was rough going. He just needed a minute to relax, to regroup. The babies drank, and every muscle in his body went limp, and in a moment, his own eyes were drooping. He just needed a minute...

He didn't know what woke him, but something did, and for a moment, he didn't remember why he was here, sitting in a chair in the living room in the middle of the morning. Then he heard something that sounded almost like a giggle, and his head snapped around in time to see two little toddlers disappear down the hallway toward the kitchen. For three seconds he sat still, paralyzed. The figures he'd seen had been upright, wobbling, arms in the air for balance, but moving fast on chubby, sturdy legs.

His mouth dropped open and he groaned, his head in his hands. ''No. They're walking!'' he cried.

And then he was up and after them again, reaching them just as they reached the swinging kitchen double doors, grabbing each around the waist and holding them to his chest, as they let their outrage be known and kicked and wrestled as hard as they could. They'd seen the promised land of pots and pans and cupboards and they wanted to go on in. He'd caught them just in time.

That was when he began looking at the clock rather desperately and wondering where Shayla was. She should have been back by now. But that meant she should be back any moment. If he could just hold out until she returned, maybe he could survive this.

But it wasn't easy. He spent the next hour in a state of constant motion, chasing one while holding the other, quieting one while the other got into mischief behind his back, learning that Devon had a wicked laugh that usually meant he was about to dive off the couch onto his head or climb the drapes, and David didn't smile much, but he watched every move Matt made, moving his eyes without moving his head, until he saw his chance and he made another run for the kitchen every time. Matt stopped by the nurse's room twice to make sure she was okay, and he tried calling the doctor again, but Devon pulled the cord out of the wall in the middle of the call. He felt like a man on a hamster wheel, running like mad and getting nowhere.

Finally he had an idea. Taking the two of them into his arms, he went into the den and flopped down on the big leather chair, sinking down with the two of them held closely. And then he rocked. At first, they both struggled, whimpering to be let go. But the rocking seemed to soothe them very quickly. First Devon began to relax, then David, and soon two little blond heads were resting against his chest. They were asleep.

Matt sighed with relief, and then went stiff with the realization that he'd only sealed his own fate. They were quiet, but one false move and they would be wide-awake again. He was a prisoner of his own cleverness.

Well, this was what he'd wanted. Only, this was a bit too much of a good thing, wasn't it? He closed his eyes. Maybe he was dreaming. Maybe if he fell asleep again, he would wake up and it would all have been a dream.

Shayla returned, her car filled with wallpaper and drapery fabric. She drove up the driveway and looked curiously at the pile of luggage near the front door. Guests? He hadn't said anything about guests. And then she had to smile at the vague feeing of disappointment she felt. She'd wanted to be alone with him again and she might as well admit it.

"Ah, yes, ain't love grand?" she muttered to herself as she parked the car, turned off the engine and went into the house.

The place was as quiet as a library. She frowned, looking up and down the hallways from the entryway. There was an eerie silence.

"Matt?" she said, but not too loudly.

There was no answer. She walked through the parlor and peeked into the kitchen before heading for the living room. The two baskets and the blue bag spilling out its contents from the couch brought her to a halt. Frowning, she turned slowly, wondering where to search next. Something drew her to the den. She could see the top of Matt's head over the back of the chair, but instead of calling out a greeting, she approached slowly, instinctively careful.

What she saw stopped her heart in her throat. Matt was sound asleep, and so were the two babies he held.

"Two?" she gasped softly, realizing this must be Remy's child—or Remy's twins, at any rate.

Matt twitched, but he didn't wake, and she stood there filling her soul with the sight of them. His handsome face was relaxed, and the babies were gorgeous beyond belief. He looked like a father, looked like a man who could build a family, and she almost wished that she could freeze this moment in time. If he could be like this, if he could commit to the babies and...

But she didn't want to think that way. She was here temporarily and they both knew it. Reaching out gently, she ran her fingers through his thick hair, pushing back a stray lock that had fallen over his forehead. When his eyes opened, she smiled into them.

"Who are these?" she whispered.

He groaned, throwing his head back. "Thank God you're here," he said. "It's been a nightmare."

An icy shiver shook her heart, and disappointment filled her. "It can't be that bad," she said softly. "They're the most beautiful babies I've ever seen."

He stared at her dully. "The lawyer lied. About everything. Not only are there two instead of one. These aren't even real babies. They walk."

"Oh." She held back a short laugh. "Yes, they look about ten months or so. Some do walk by then."

He looked mortally offended. "I never bargained for walking. I expected a nice little baby in a pram. Something that wouldn't move."

But now the two of them had begun to stir, yawning and frowning and stretching their pudgy little bodies.

"Look out," Matt warned, tightening his hold on them. "They take off like rockets." He frowned down at them. "And to top it all off, they hate me."

She couldn't hold back the laughter any longer. It bubbled up and spilled out like champagne, and it continued, even while Matt protested, even while she picked up David and propped him against her shoulder, rocking him and holding him tightly. She laughed while she taught Matt how to change diapers and she laughed while she prepared the bottles and found where their toys were packed and she laughed while she showed him how to hold a baby—even a big, walking baby—on his hip while doing other things.

And then she tried to hold back the laughter while she checked on the nurse and got through to the doctor and pulled together a quick lunch for the two of them. But it came back every time she remembered the look on Matt's face.

"You seem to take it all so personally," she explained when he complained about her sense of humor.

"It *is* personal," he grumped. "These babies are now a part of my life. I feel like I've been invaded."

She could have said "I told you so," but she held it back. Instead she stopped laughing, and she asked him, "What are you going to do?"

"Do?" He looked at her blankly. "I'm going to raise two babies instead of one, that's what I'm going to do. What else can I do?"

She'd made her suggestions and she wasn't going to make them again. Right now, she only wished he looked happier about his decision.

The doctor came and checked over the twins after he'd seen Lola, the nurse.

"It's my opinion that the nurse's illness was provoked by traveling more than anything else, and that being the case, the babies shouldn't be harmed in any way. Keep an eye on them. If they begin to exhibit any symptoms, give me a call and I'll come out again."

"A doctor who makes housecalls." Shayla marveled as he left them. "I thought they'd gone the way of the dinosaurs."

"My father and he were close friends," Matt told her. "I don't think he does this for just anyone."

But he'd pronounced the twins hale and hearty and as healthy as young horses, and when Shayla looked at them, something seemed to bubble in her heart. They were so adorable! And so full of mischief.

"Grab him!" was a phrase heard often that afternoon, as the two of them chased down the little ones. A desperate plea from Shayla brought an express delivery of two cribs from the furniture store. The nurse's supply of diapers and baby food was enough to hold out for the night. Matt and Shayla fed them, gave them bottles and walked them, until the babies' eyelashes dropped reluctantly to brush against their rosy cheeks, and their little round heads drooped against the adult shoulders, and they were laid carefully in the cribs. Matt and Shayla lingered just a moment to smile at how lovable they looked while they slept, and then the two of them tiptoed out of the room.

Once in the hallway, Matt stretched, twisting his back and grimacing. "My God. The first day of boot camp must feel a lot like this," he grumbled.

"Tomorrow will be better," she promised, then glanced at him curiously. Under the original plan for the weekend, she would have been home by now. Nothing had been said, but she'd assumed he would want her to stay. But just to be sure, she probed him. "Think you can handle them by yourself now?" she asked lightly, smiling at him.

A look of pure panic crossed his face. "You can't go," he told her firmly. "You can't leave me alone with them."

She shrugged and pretended to be considering. He grabbed her by the shoulders. "Don't forsake me now, woman," he demanded. "What do you want from me? An admission that I, an ignorant and incompetent male, can't do it alone? You've got it. It's true. I need you as badly here as I've ever needed you at the office."

She laughed and pushed back his disheveled hair. "With these two, I would have a hard time myself. And you've been doing a wonderful job." Her hand brushed his cheek. "I'll stay until the nurse feels better," she offered.

He pulled her close and kissed her soundly. "Thank you," he said, his voice husky. "Let's go to bed."

She laughed again, feeling warm and toasty but very much aware he might just be pleading exhaustion rather than passion.

He disproved that theory soon enough, seducing her quickly with words and kisses. They tangled together as though they'd been kept apart too long, reaching for an ecstasy that stayed just tantalizingly out of reach, and then swooped down to engulf them in a wild ride that left them gasping for breath and laughing in each other's arms. It took a few minutes to recover, and to lose the laughter. Finally they lay side by side, breathing easily and enjoying the feel of companionship they shared.

Lying back against the pillow, Matt stared at the ceiling and thought about the day to come with trepidation.

"We'd better get hold of a nanny right away," he said.

Shayla propped up on one elbow and looked at him. "No," she said gently, stroking his chest.

He turned and glared at her. "What do you mean, no?"

She shook her head firmly. "It's not right, Matt. You have to get to know them first, before you hire someone to take care of them. They're your babies. If you want to farm them out to someone else, you still have to be the prime parent to them, and they need to know you first. And you have to know them."

She was right and he knew it, but that didn't stop him from uttering a harsh curse under his breath.

"All right then, I'll take a week off," he said, compromising.

"At least," she murmured, smiling.

But he paid no attention. Instead he reached for her and began dropping sizzling kisses along her collarbone. "But you have to promise to stay," he muttered between nibbles.

"You won't need me," she teased. "You'll have the nurse."

"The babies will have the nurse," he said, running his hands down her naked back and settling at the base of her spine. "I'll have you."

She sighed happily, sinking into the tempting heat of his embrace. No man had ever made her feel the way he did so effortlessly. His touch was magic. She knew this wasn't meant to last, but while it was there for her, she was going to grab it with both hands.

Over the next few days, their lives were saturated with child care. At first, Matt made some effort to stay in touch with the office, but he abandoned all that soon enough. There just wasn't time. There just wasn't the mental space to think about work. Babies filled their thoughts and dictated their every action.

The nurse was fine in the morning and she took over some of the more mundane routines, but Matt and Shayla were involved in every aspect of the babies' daily existence. Matt learned very quickly how to play patty cake and "Itsy Bitsy Spider" and "Monkeys on the Bed" but diapering came hard to him. In no time at all, he had bandages on all his fingers from where the diaper pins had struck home.

"We'll go to disposable diapers," Shayla told him soothingly when he showed her his wounds. "They're easy. No problem."

A man with a degree in engineering and a knack for woodworking should have been able to get the hang of disposables, but Matt seemed to have a blind spot there, too. He put them on backward and sideways and inside out, until Shayla began to suspect him of doing a bad job on purpose.

"You just don't want to do it, so you're making sure you're incompetent at it," she accused him, laughing.

He looked at her, shamefaced. "That's not true," he said dejectedly. "I'm really trying. It's just that there's so much else going on every time I try to put on a diaper."

It was true, they didn't sit still for it. They had to be held down with one hand and cooed and coaxed and sometimes ordered to quiet down in a stern voice, but Shayla and the nurse could manage it. Why Matt couldn't do it was a mystery.

He was good at the game playing, and when he swung them into the air, they each came back and begged for more, raising their arms to him and crowing with delight. He played hide-and-seek until they were rolling with baby laughter, and he carried them around easily, showing them the stream and the fields and the deer in the woods.

Shayla watched him and her love grew, until she was almost sick with it. She loved him and there was no hope for her. She was also growing to love the babies, and that was going to turn around and hurt her as well. She knew all that. But she didn't shy away from it. It was all a part of life and she would handle it. Somehow.

The nurse was a godsend. She'd worked for Remy and his wife and, devoted as she was to Devon and David, she would be the link to their past. She'd brought along with her a huge scrapbook full of pictures and anecdotes about the twins' past and about what their parents were like, a resource that was going to be invaluable as the boys grew up.

"Nina Castillo—she was the best friend of Remy and Marta—she got all their friends together and they wrote these little stories about what they knew," Lola told Shayla when she showed her the scrapbook. "Nina put them into this book for the babies, so that they could know what their parents were like."

"That's wonderful," Shayla said, tears springing to her eyes as she thought of Marta and all that she was missing. The boys were settling in beautifully and didn't seem to realize that something very important had been ripped from their lives, but she knew that deep down, they felt the loss, and that their pain would come back to the surface at some time in their future. And when it did, this book would help sustain them.

In the meantime, she was worried about Matt and how he was adjusting to his new life-style. He was trying very hard. He played with the twins, talked to them, fed them, cared about them. But there was an edginess to him that wouldn't go away. When the two of them were alone, he lost it, and he was a lover any woman would dream of. Lover, boss and friend. It was an odd combination and she wasn't sure it could work for long. But for now, it was heaven.

He loved the babies—she thought. He liked them, anyway. He enjoyed the playfulness. Now and then he made gestures of affection, such as dropping a kiss on a fat cheek or patting a blond head. But there was something missing. Something was not quite there yet.

"It's just not the way I pictured it," he admitted when she finally got up the nerve to confront him about it. "One would have been easier to get used to. The two of them seem . . . almost like they're a closed front against me sometimes."

"They love you!" she protested.

"Do they?" His gaze was hard and unrelenting. "How do you know that?"

Her heart sank. It wasn't working. Chiding herself, she realized she'd been dreaming. In the dream, Matt would turn into an instant family man, Father of the Year, and that maybe, just maybe, he might want her to join their little family. But it wasn't working out that way. She could see it in his eyes, hear it in his voice. If it didn't come together for him soon, he might start asking to see those brochures she'd brought about adoption.

Well, wasn't that what she'd wanted all along?

No. Oh God, no. Not anymore.

He was so wonderful with them. Why couldn't he see that? What was making him so uneasy?

At one point, she wondered if she ought to go and leave him with them—that maybe she was part of the problem. Used to babies as she was, she'd fallen for these two right away, had picked them up and held them and bonded as naturally as if she'd been their mother. They turned to her when they were hungry and they turned to her when they were sleepy. They clung to her when strangers came around. And she'd opened up her heart and taken them in from the beginning. There was no question about it.

But Matt was another story. Something in him resisted, and the babies seemed to sense it. He often got bogged down in the mechanics of things, such as why the baby carriage didn't run smoothly and why the crib creaked and why the baby food processor liquefied peas instead of mashing them. The twins were still objects to him, challenges to be overcome, things to adjust to. He hadn't fallen in love.

And it was hard to figure out why, because he acted very loving to her. His touch, his **casual** glances that met hers, his smiles, all told her that the feeling between them was growing all the time. Still, something wasn't quite right.

One day, after the babies had been there for almost two weeks, she prepared a picnic lunch and they took the babies and hiked out into the hills behind the house, sitting in the sun and watching the little ones play. When clouds began to gather, a rolling round of thunder came crashing into their little scene, and the two boys ran screaming for Matt, throwing their pudgy bodies against him, hiding their faces into his wide shoulders, hanging on for dear life as he comforted them. For just a moment, he looked pleased, and Shayla held her breath. She watched the way he dealt with them and hope was rekindled in her breast. Tomorrow. Surely each day would bring him closer to them. Tomorrow would be better.

But it wasn't.

Things seemed to go pretty well in the morning, but in the afternoon, she realized the cupboards were bare and she would have to run in to the market to do some grocery shopping, and the nurse was taking the afternoon off.

"I'm going to leave you alone with them," she told him. "Do you think you'll be okay?"

"Oh, sure," he said, all confidence. "I've learned how to handle these guys by now."

She left a bit doubtfully. But after all, what could happen in one short hour?

Not much. Just disaster.

Things started out quietly enough. Matt played with the boys, having them sit opposite him and rolling a ball to each in turn. David laughed uproariously and Devon quickly learned to throw the ball, though it didn't go anywhere near his target, if he actually had one. When they tired of that, he placed them in the mesh playpen that had been set up in the living room, but they weren't in the mood for that sort of confinement, and they fussed until he took them back out again and set them down to play with cups on the floor of the den while he went through some bills. Somehow his attention drifted away from them as he puzzled over some sums that weren't coming out right. Their play was background noise, and he didn't notice when it faded from two voices to one. He didn't know what made him glance up and look out the window, but when he did, he saw Devon running far out across the grass as though demons were behind him, his fat little legs churning. David was still absorbed in stacking cups, but Devon was out of control and racing down the hill toward the stream, his blond hair shining in the sun.

Matt swore and ran out through the living room and out the French doors to the garden. A stiff wind was blowing and it caught his hair as he ran. He reached the top of the hill and Devon was nowhere in sight. He'd already made it to the trees and any second, he would reach the stream. Matt ran faster, pounding the ground, his breath ragged in his throat. Visions of a little blond head floating in the swirling water loomed like doom in front of him.

His eyes, used to the bright light, were blinded when he went into the gloom in among the trees. "Devon?" he called. There was the stream, but where was the baby? Had he already fallen in? Was he being swept down toward the river? "Devon!" he called again, running alongside the water.

Suddenly there was a giggle and he stopped dead, turning around on a dime. There was a flash of blond hair as the tyke scrambled in among the rocks. Matt closed his eyes, holding his heart. Devon was okay and it was all right to breathe again.

Erasing the distance between them in a few long strides, he grabbed the little devil around the waist and swung him up into his arms, holding him tightly and kissing one fat baby cheek. Then he held him away and looked at him sternly. "Don't run away like that, Devon," he ordered. "Don't you ever do that again!"

The lower lip began to tremble and the little eyes filled with tears and he groaned, holding him close again, feeling manipulated. Why couldn't he get this right? Maybe... he hated to let the thought surface, but it had been lurking in his mind for a long time now. Maybe he wasn't cut out to be a father. He loved these little guys, but he just didn't feel as though this was working.

He carried Devon back up to the house and into the den. The cups had been abandoned. David was gone.

Before he had a chance to get excited, a high-pitched screech of joy told him what direction David had gone in. Still carrying Devon, he headed for the kitchen. The double doors swung open and there was David. He'd found the flour bin and pulled it over on himself, and now he sat on and under a huge pile of flour, taking handfuls of the white powder and throwing it into the air, creating his own flour mist. He was flour from head to toe, and his eyes were mere slits in the flour mask he wore. Matt stopped, stunned, and Devon slipped from his arms, crowing with delight as he tumbled head over heels into the flour to join his brother.

For a long moment, Matt stood and stared at them, hardly breathing. It was just too much. There was always something. He really wasn't sure he could handle it any longer.

"I've go to get back to work," he told Shayla when she'd returned and the boys had been cleaned up and put down for naps. "I'm going crazy here."

She nodded. The way things had been going, she'd been expecting this. "What about the babies?" she asked softly, not looking at him.

He hesitated, and she turned and confronted him. "There are plenty of wonderful couples who are waiting for babies like these," she said, though it broke her heart.

A look of pain shot through his gaze and he winced. "No," he said quickly. "No, I'm not ready to do that." He tried to read her face and failed. He hated this. "It's time to go ahead and hire a nanny, though," he said. "You'll help do that, won't you?"

She nodded. "Of course. And I'll stay with them until they get used to her."

He frowned. "Oh. Sure. But I'm going to need you at the office, too." He ran a hand through his hair, grimacing. Hell, he needed her everywhere. And he wasn't too happy about that, either.

But she smiled sadly and shook her head. "I won't be going back to the office," she told him firmly. "We can't go back to that. Not now."

She was right and he knew it, but anger rose in him and he wanted to smash something. Turning from her, he made his way out and down to the stream, and he stayed there a long time, but he didn't make much progress in finding solutions, no matter how hard he stared into the water.

Monday morning, he drove off to work and she watched him go. It wasn't that he was going back to the office that filled her with such melancholy. After all, most fathers did that, didn't they? It was what it meant, what it symbolized—and the fact that he'd done it as a way to get away from the babies. The dream was fading away, and she might as well admit it.

Matt spent a week getting back into the swing of things at work. He felt himself drifting farther and farther away from what was going on at his house. He returned from the city late and left early, and his relationship with Shayla was falling apart. He felt like a man in a maze—no matter which way he turned, he was only getting himself farther and farther from where he wanted to be.

Despite all that, Shayla put off interviewing nannies. The babies weren't ready yet. She couldn't bear to think of leaving them. And yet she knew she was going to have to.

"Are you sure you won't come back to the office?" he asked her one night. "The place is going to hell without you." He stroked her cheek with his thumb. "I'll call you Conners again. You can pin up your hair and throw around the old insults."

She twisted in his arms and kissed him. "No," she told him bluntly. "It wouldn't work and you know it." Besides, though she didn't know how to tell him, her interests had changed. She was reading everything she could about babies, about food, about exercise for toddlers, about teaching methods. She was into raising kids right now, and it felt right. *This is my time,* she told herself. It was just a shame it couldn't last.

Two weeks after Matt went back to work, she forced herself to do the right thing, and she called an agency to arrange for prospective nannies to start coming by for interviews.

"There are three of them coming today," she told Matt the next morning as he arranged things in his briefcase and prepared to leave for the city. "Do you have any preferences I should know about?"

He looked up and saw the shadows in her eyes. Frowning, he looked away again. "No. You make the decision. You know more about these things than I do."

His admitting it depressed her more than ever, and as she waved him off, she felt a cloud developing, a bit of gloom that was going to stick around for quite some time.

Matt was in a surly mood as he drove across the Golden Gate Bridge. He wasn't looking forward to his day. Meetings and more meetings, a call to the East Coast, lunch with his accounts lawyer. Work just didn't seem to have the same spark to it these days. When you came right down to it, things were downright boring.

Part of that was because Shayla wasn't with him. He'd never become so dependent on an employee before and it puzzled him that her absence could make such a big dent in things. He knew he was crazy about her. But it was more than that.

He pulled into the parking garage below his building and waited for another car to pull out of a space so he could pass.

It was a warm morning and he hadn't put on the air conditioner, and now he was sweating. Reaching into his pocket, he pulled out his handkerchief and began to wipe his brow, but it felt funny, rough and strangely shaped, and there were little straps flopping on his nose. He drew it down to take a look. He did a double take. He hadn't pulled out a handkerchief at all. Instead he'd wiped his forehead with a bib that had a small blue teddy bear embroidered on it.

"How the heck did that get in there?" he muttered, laughing to himself. What if he'd pulled it out in the middle of a board meeting? That would have turned some heads.

He looked at it again, then put it to his face and drew in the fresh, baby smell of it. Was it Devon's or David's? He couldn't tell, and for just a moment, a picture of them both swam before his eyes and he smiled. They were his babies, a part of his life. His. Something twisted in his heart, something broke open and left him gasping. His. The emotion that word conjured up took his breath away. He loved them.

Shayla's beautiful face swam into the picture as well. He loved her, too. What was the matter with him? Why was he risking losing everything that he loved this way? What was he doing here?

Someone was honking for him to get out of the way, but he didn't hear a thing. The people he loved were all still at home. And here he was, pursuing—what? He'd made his fortune. He had a smooth-running company that didn't really need him any longer. And yet he was here instead of at home where certain people did need him. Was he crazy?

Yes. He was crazy. And it was time to put a stop to it.

Ignoring the honker, he put his car into reverse. As if he were a man in a dream, he backed out of the garage and turned his car toward home. That was where he really wanted to be. So why didn't he go there? There were a thousand things he could do there. He could start a new company, work on improving baby products, do something related to this grand new adventure he'd begun—and then almost turned his back on. Why had it taken him so long to wake up to the truth? The babies were his. He wanted them. And he wanted Shayla. And he was going to get what he wanted. Didn't he always, in the end?

Shayla was taking the babies outside to run in the grass when his car rolled up. She shaded her eyes as he got out, smiling at him.

"Did you forget something?" she called.

"Yes, I did," he called back, striding quickly toward her. "I forgot you," he said, taking her up and whirling her around so that her yellow sundress sailed out around her.

She laughed and when he dropped a hot kiss on her mouth, she kissed him back.

''I was just sitting in my car,'' he told her, still holding her, enjoying the look of her outdoor freshness against his impeccable suit, ''when it occurred to me that I would rather be with you. So I came back.''

Before she had a chance to respond, the twins caught sight of him and they both came streaking back across the lawn, crying out.

''Hey, guys,'' he said as each grabbed a leg and held on, little faces turned up toward his.

''Da-da,'' Devon said softly, looking eager. ''Da-da.''

Matt's jaw dropped and he looked up into Shayla's face. ''Did he just say...?''

She nodded happily. Something told her this was the key. ''Yes, he did,'' she told him. She grinned. ''They're very precocious you know.''

That seemed to strike him as a very wise thing to say. ''Of course they are. They're my babies.''

Her heart swelled at his words, and something choked in her throat. Was she imagining things, or was something happening here?

He looked at her slyly as the twins ran off again. ''You want them, too, don't you?'' he noted softly. Turning, he took her in his arms again. ''Admit it.''

She looked up at him, not sure where he was going with this. "What?"

"You want them. You've wanted them from the beginning." He kissed her hard, then drew back and said firmly, pinning her with his hard gaze, "Well, there's only one way you're going to get them."

She stared up into his eyes, confused. "What are you talking about?" she murmured.

"How you can have them, too." He went on, talking as though it were all quite sensible. "You can marry me."

The world was spinning now, the sky where the grass should be, and she was giddy with it. Leaning back in his arms, she shook her head slowly, staring at him. "What, so you can have a nanny without having to hire one?" she teased.

"No," he said, dropping a kiss on her neck, and then another behind her ear. "So I can have the woman I love at my side," he growled huskily. He looked into her face for a moment, then threw out an arm grandiosely. "So we can raise these babies together. So they can have the best mother they could possibly have, and I can have the best lover who—"

"Don't you dare!" she warned, putting a finger over his lips to stop him.

"Why not?" he said, his words muffled. Reaching up, he took her wrist in his hand and pulled her fingers away. "It's true. Lovemaking is important to a good marriage.'' He smiled at her. "That's why we have to practice it a lot."

She laughed. "So it will be perfect?"

His eyes darkened. "It's already perfect," he said, stroking back her hair. "Everything is perfect. As long as you say yes."

"Yes."

"Yes, you'll marry me?"

"Yes, I'll marry you."

His kiss was tender, sealing their bargain, but the sound of galloping babies drew them back to reality. Turning, they saw David and Devon coming toward them, blond hair bouncing as they ran on their stout little bowed legs.

"Da-da!" Devon shouted as they came.

"Da-da," David called out as well.

"Da-da, Da-da," they cried in unison.

Matt looked at her, his face full of a special light. "They really are saying Daddy," he told her, incredulous. "I didn't believe it at first. But I think they really are."

She nodded, her eyes sparkling with tears. "Of course they are." She smiled. "I've been training them for days," she whispered to herself.

She watched as he leaned down and took both babies into his arms and began to swing them, talking to them as they shrieked with pleasure. And then she closed her eyes as happiness began to crest in her like a wave, and she let herself sink back into the dream. It was coming true after all. In the final analysis, the baby invasion was a complete success.

* * * * *

If you liked this story by Raye Morgan, then don't miss BABY DREAMS, Book #1 of her THE BABY SHOWER series, available now in Silhouette Desire!

Dear Reader,

Motherhood is a strange career. "They" don't pay you the big bucks, but nothing else gives you so much pride, so much fear, so much joy. The only thing I resent about it is the lack of sleep. They tell you how you won't get any sleep that first year, when the baby wakes up, every hour, all night long. But they don't warn you that it's déjà vu once your child has his driver's license, as you lie awake until dawn, praying for the sound of a car in the driveway. I've already been through that stage with three boys, and my fourth is fifteen.

Still, being a mother is usually my favorite part of being alive. It's the most wonderful thing in the world, and from the very first, "What do you mean, gas? I *know* that's a smile!" to, "Look, he's pulling himself up! I think he's going to walk, I think he's going to... Oops!" right on into, "You'll get the keys back when those grades come up, young man, and not before!" until you hit, "Darling if you really love her, we love her, too," time goes so quickly. Too quickly.

Motherhood—catch it while you can!

Raye Morgan

A Funny Thing Happened on the Way to the Baby Shower...

When four college friends reunite to celebrate the arrival of one bouncing baby, they find four would-be grooms on the way!

Don't miss a single, sexy tale in

RAYE MORGAN'S

Only in

BABY DREAMS
in May '96 (SD #997)

A GIFT FOR BABY
in July '96 (SD #1010)

BABIES BY THE BUSLOAD
in September '96 (SD #1022)

And look for

INSTANT DAD, WILL TRAIN
in November '96

Only from

Silhouette®

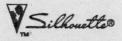

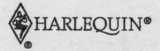

This July, watch for the delivery of...

An exciting new miniseries that appears in a different Silhouette series each month. It's about love, marriage—and Daddy's unexpected need for a baby carriage!

Daddy Knows Last unites five of your favorite authors as they weave five connected stories about baby fever in New Hope, Texas.

- **THE BABY NOTION** by Dixie Browning
  (SD#1011, 7/96)

- **BABY IN A BASKET** by Helen R. Myers
  (SR#1169, 8/96)

- **MARRIED...WITH TWINS!**
  by Jennifer Mikels
  (SSE#1054, 9/96)

- **HOW TO HOOK A HUSBAND (AND A BABY)**
  by Carolyn Zane
  (YT#29, 10/96)

- **DISCOVERED: DADDY** by Marilyn Pappano
  (IM#746, 11/96)

Daddy Knows Last arrives in July...only from

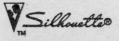

DKLT